Callie was a puzzle...

Her intentio... ...irable,
but Jack didr... ...she
was up agains... ...uld
have a hard t... ...like
this.

Had her life back in Ohio been so terrible that even with what happened to his brother, she—

Jack gave his head a shake. He'd let her get under his skin. He had to remember that her personal problems were no concern of his. She wanted to challenge his claim to his nieces and nephew, and that made her his opponent.

Family mattered. That was something only he could offer his nieces and nephew.

But still…he'd never met a woman like her. Callie was…he hadn't quite figured out what she was, besides being a thorn in his side. And just plain wrong about her rights in regard to Annabeth and Simon and Emma.

On the other hand, could he really say the kids would be better off with a wandering bachelor than with his brother's widow?

Books by Winnie Griggs

Love Inspired Historical

The Hand-Me-Down Family

WINNIE GRIGGS

is a city girl born and raised in southeast Louisiana's Cajun Country who grew up to marry a country boy from the hills of northwest Louisiana. Though her Prince Charming is more comfortable riding a tractor than a white steed, the two of them have been living their own happily-ever-after for thirty-plus years. During that time they raised four children and an assortment of dogs, cats, fish, hamsters, turtles and 4-H sheep.

In addition to her day job at a utility company and her writing career, Winnie serves on committees within her church and several writing organizations, and is active in local civic organizations—she truly believes the adage that you reap in proportion to what you sow.

In addition to writing and reading, Winnie enjoys spending time with her family, cooking and exploring flea markets. Readers can contact Winnie at P.O. Box 398, Plain Dealing, LA 71064, or e-mail her at winnie@winniegriggs.com.

WINNIE GRIGGS

The
Hand-Me-Down
Family

Steeple
Hill®

Published by Steeple Hill Books™

STEEPLE HILL BOOKS

Steeple
Hill®

Recycling programs
for this product may
not exist in your area.

ISBN-13: 978-0-373-82808-1
ISBN-10: 0-373-82808-X

THE HAND-ME-DOWN FAMILY

Copyright © 2009 by Winnie Griggs

www.SteepleHill.com

Printed in U.S.A.

Chapter One

California, May 1888

"Hey, Jack!"

Jack bit back an oath at the hail, then turned in a slow, controlled movement. He pinned the foreman's errand boy with a cold stare, holding his peace for three long heartbeats, just enough time to set the unthinking messenger to fidgeting in his saddle.

Finally, Jack pulled the sliver of twig from his mouth. "You got a death wish, Dobbins? Or didn't you see those yellow flags marking off this area?"

The young man's expression faltered. "Yes, but you're still—"

Jack snapped the twig and tossed it away. "I'm inside the perimeter because I'm setting charges. Which means I'm working with enough explosives right now to blow you, me and most of this pile of rock to smithereens."

Dobbins's Adam's apple bobbed, but he stuck out his chin and pulled a paper from his pocket. "A telegram came for you. Mr. Gordon wanted—"

Jack's jaw muscle twitched. Fool kid. "I don't care if it's a set of executive orders from President Grover Cleveland himself. When I'm in the middle of a job, you don't cross the perimeter unless it's life or death." He narrowed his eyes. "Because it just might turn into that."

A quick nod signaled understanding.

Jack wiped his brow with his sleeve, already regretting his harsh tone. The heat and the hours were starting to wear on him. He waved the intruder forward. "Well, now that you're here, you might as well give me the thing."

Dobbins nudged his horse forward and handed the folded paper to Jack. His eyes rounded when he saw Jack slide it into his pocket without so much as a glance. "Aren't you gonna read it?"

"Not 'til I'm done here. I don't need any more distractions right now." He raised a brow. "Anything else?"

Dobbins got the message. "Guess not." With another nod, he jerked on the reins, turned his horse, and headed back in the direction of the base camp.

Jack frowned as he watched the messenger gallop off.

A telegram. Now who would—

He was doing it already, he realized.

He shoved the telegram out of his mind. Right now he needed to focus on the work at hand. Like he'd just told Dobbins, he couldn't afford distractions while he was on the job.

Twenty minutes later Jack stood and tilted his hat up. He stepped back far enough to take in the remainder of what just a week ago had been a steep, rocky hillside. He drew his elbows back behind him, stretching the kinks out of cramped muscles.

Then he mentally reviewed the placement of all four charges one more time. You just couldn't be too careful.

Satisfied everything was in order, he headed back toward the stand of scrub he'd designated as the meeting spot for his two-man team. Hopefully they were already waiting for him. He was more than ready to wrap up this job.

As he crossed the uneven ground, Jack fingered the folded sheet of paper tucked in his pocket. The only people who'd be likely to send him a telegram would be his sister or brother.

He'd just gotten a letter from Nell a few weeks ago. She hadn't had anything new to say—just updates on what was going on back home and sisterly admonitions to visit soon, coupled with a bribe to bake up one of his favorite apple pecan pies.

No, he couldn't picture either Nell or Lanny sending a telegram. At least not to deliver good news.

The back of his neck prickled and his step slowed.

Putting off reading the thing was becoming more of a distraction than whatever news the telegram contained could possibly be.

Jack jerked the crumpled paper out of his pocket and read the four stark lines written there.

And as surely as if someone had detonated the charges prematurely, he felt the world rock under his feet.

Chapter Two

Texas, four days later

Callie studied the man seated across from her as the stage-coach swayed and bounced, bringing her ever closer to her new life.

She placed a finger to her chin. No, he wasn't a sea captain. The hat was all wrong and he had an air about him that seemed more akin to earthiness than saltwater.

She scrunched her lips to one side as she examined his features more closely. He was actually quite handsome, in a dangerous, rugged sort of way. Rather than detracting from his looks, that faded scar on the left side of his chin served to lend him an adventurous air. She refused to believe a man who looked as he did was anything so mundane as a farmer or shopkeeper.

He could be a Texas Ranger. Yes, that would fit. He had that lean, grim-purpose look about him.

She settled into her mental tale-spinning. So, if he *was* a ranger, what was his story? Perhaps he was returning home for a well-earned rest after grueling weeks of tracking down desperate outlaws. Or maybe he was traveling to Sweetgum on official business in search of—

Callie straightened in her seat. Was it her imagination, or had they slowed down a bit? A quick glance out the window confirmed that the tree-lined countryside had given way to scattered farms. And if she wasn't mistaken, the edge of a small town was just up ahead.

This was it. Her new home—Sweetgum, Texas.

She adjusted her poke bonnet with hands that weren't quite steady, then laced her fingers tightly together and closed her eyes.

Heavenly Father, I'm truly grateful to You for getting me all the way here from Ohio without a hitch. But we both know that was the easy part compared to what comes next. And since this whole undertaking was actually Your idea, I know You're going to help me figure out what to say and do when I step outside and come face-to-face with my new husband for the first time.

Bolstered by that thought, Callie began gathering her belongings. Then she paused and slanted a glance toward the object of her former musings.

Her unsociable traveling companion seemed completely unaware of their arrival.

Should she say something to him?

He'd climbed aboard at their last stop and, after the briefest of greetings, settled into the opposite corner, closed his eyes and hadn't moved since. Not that she resented his lack of attention.

After all, being this close to such a man was a new experience for her, and his closed-off demeanor had given her an opportunity to study him unobserved. Besides which, trying to concoct a history for him from only the hints provided by the rough and calloused look of his hands, his weathered complexion and his firm, wiry build had been an interesting way to pass the time.

One thing she'd decided about thirty minutes into her story-weaving was that, whatever his profession, he was not someone at peace with his world. There was something about his very stillness, about the hint of tension in his stubble-covered jaw, that pointed to a weary or troubled spirit.

Before she could make up her mind whether or not to disturb him, his eyes opened and their gazes collided. The lack of any residual drowsiness in those startling blue eyes made her wonder whether or not he'd truly been asleep.

The heat rose in Callie's cheeks. How mortifying to have been caught staring so rudely! She tugged on the edge of her bonnet again. Thank goodness it already hid most of her face.

"We're here," she blurted, then mentally cringed. Why did she always feel compelled to rush in and fill the silences?

He straightened. "So I see."

The hint of dryness in his tone warmed her cheeks even further. But the driver opened the door, rescuing Callie from more embarrassment.

As she rose to leave the coach, the glimpse of the dusty street and plank-lined sidewalk forcibly reminded her that she had left her familiar world behind. A bubble of panic rose in her throat.

What if Mr. Tyler was disappointed when he met her?

What if she couldn't learn how to adjust to life in this rural community?

What if—

Callie took a deep, steadying breath. *Forgive me, Lord. I know we already wrestled with my doubts before the wedding. This is the ministry You gave me. Mr. Tyler and his daughter need me, and I need them. I—*

"Ma'am? Are you all right?"

Her companion studied her with a worried frown, no doubt wondering why she wasn't moving. After her earlier actions, he must think her completely addled.

Callie offered an apologetic smile. "Yes, I'm fine, thank you. Just making certain I have all my things." She adjusted her bonnet once more, squared her shoulders and stepped down from the stagecoach onto the sidewalk's dusty boards.

Pasting on what she hoped was a confident smile, Callie waited for her husband to step forward and introduce himself. But, while she received curious glances from some of the passersby, no one greeted her.

Her smile faltered. Where was he?

She continued scanning the sidewalk even as she moved aside to allow her fellow passenger to exit the stage.

Why wasn't Mr. Tyler here? Surely he wouldn't keep her standing alone in foreign surroundings where she didn't know anyone…

I will never leave thee, nor forsake thee.

The remembered verse calmed her. She wasn't alone. God was with her.

Mr. Tyler had undoubtedly been delayed. Poor man. He was likely as nervous about this meeting as she was. And he had little Annabeth to tend to as well. It must be difficult for him to care for a child and a farm all on his own.

Well, he wouldn't have to any longer.

Trying to ignore the stubborn prickling of anxiety that wouldn't quite go away, Callie turned to study the community that she would now call home. These people would be her neighbors and, hopefully, her friends.

The town itself was just as Julia had described in her letters. The stage had stopped in front of the Sweetgum Hotel and Post Office. To her left she could see an apothecary shop and the mercantile with a long wooden bench out front. On the other side of the hotel stood a bank, and past that the doctor's office.

Callie glanced across the street and frowned in dismay. About a block down the road, one of the buildings had been reduced to charred timbers. She immediately offered up a prayer that strength and healing be afforded to the lives that had been touched by that calamity.

What business had it housed? It was next to the barber shop, so—

The sight of a gentleman hurrying toward the stage jerked Callie's attention away from the puzzle.

Her heart stuttered a few beats.

Was this him?

She stood straighter and adjusted her bonnet. But instead of approaching her, he absently tipped his hat in her direction and stopped in front of her fellow passenger.

"Jack, welcome back," he said as the two men shook hands. "I just wish it were under happier circumstances."

Callie turned away, deflated. It wasn't Mr. Tyler.

Well, at least now she had a name for her traveling companion. Jack. A good, solid name. And, if the greeting he'd received was any indication, she'd apparently guessed right as to his troubled spirit.

The two men spoke in low tones and Callie immediately focused on other sounds, avoiding the temptation to eavesdrop.

A buckboard clattered down the street accompanied by the muffled clop-clop of horses' hooves. A shop bell jingled as a woman emerged from the mercantile with a loaded basket. Two boys raced down the sidewalk, a yipping dog at their heels.

Such bustling normalcy all around her. Yet she felt isolated, apart from it all, like a stranger peeking in through a window at a family gathering.

The minutes drew out as the driver unloaded luggage and parcels from the back of the stagecoach. It was hotter here in Texas than it had been in Ohio. Callie longed to loosen her tight-fitting bonnet, or better yet, take it off altogether, but she dared not. Not until she was away from prying eyes and safely inside her new home.

A number of townsfolk stopped to speak to Jack, but though she received a few friendly nods in addition to more curious glances, no one stepped forward to greet her.

Finally, the last of the baggage and cargo was unloaded and the driver stepped inside the hotel with a mail sack. The man, Jack, lifted two of the bags, easily hefting the larger one up to his shoulder.

Callie couldn't help but wonder—would Mr. Tyler be as fine and strong a figure of a man as this Jack?

As if feeling her eyes on him, the man paused and met her gaze. His expression was gruff and a muscle twitched at the corner of his mouth. "Is someone meeting you?"

She smiled, grateful for his show of concern, reluctant though it might be. "Yes, thank you. I'm certain my husband will be along soon."

Something akin to surprise flashed across his features but it was gone in an instant.

"Good." He nodded and allowed his friend to take one of his bags. "If you're sure you don't need any help…" He tipped his hat and turned.

As she watched him walk away, it was as if the last link to her old life were being severed. A foolish notion, since she really didn't know this man at all. But before she could stop herself, Callie took a small step forward. "Excuse me."

Both men turned, facing her with questioning glances.

"Ma'am?" Jack prompted.

"I was wondering if perhaps either of you know a Mr.

Leland Tyler? He was supposed to…" Her voice tapered off as she saw their startled reactions.

Jack's jaw tightened visibly. "Why would you be looking for Lan— Leland?"

Callie noticed his familiar use of her husband's name. "So you *do* know him."

That tic near the corner of his mouth made another appearance. "Yes." He didn't expand on his one-word answer, and his expression remained closed, unreadable. "But you didn't answer my question. How do you know Leland?"

Callie offered up a quick prayer that Mr. Tyler would arrive soon. He should be the one making the introductions to his neighbors and friends. "I'm Callista Johnson Tyler, his wife."

"Wife!" Jack set his bag down with a loud thump and sent a sharp look his companion's way. "You know what she's talking about, Virgil?"

The other man shook his head. "Lanny never said anything about a new wife."

They certainly were reacting strongly to her news. She knew Julia had only been gone about four months, but it wasn't unusual for a widower to remarry so soon, especially when he had a young child to care for.

For that matter, why didn't they already know about her? Surely Leland wouldn't have kept such momentous news from his friends and neighbors? Unless he'd worried she wouldn't show up.

Or was there another, more disturbing reason? Her heart beat faster as possibilities whirled through her mind.

Realizing the men were watching her, Callie tried to hide her confusion behind a confident air. "I'm not certain why Mr. Tyler chose to keep this a secret. Perhaps he was planning to surprise everyone. But be that as it may, I assure you, I am indeed Mrs. Leland Tyler. If you'll be so good as to tell me where my husband can be found, I'm certain he'll verify my identity."

Jack took another step forward. "Perhaps we should introduce ourselves first." He swept an arm toward his companion. "This is Virgil Wilson."

She smiled and nodded acknowledgment. "Mr. Wilson." The name was familiar. Oh, yes, he and his wife owned the farm that adjoined Leland's. Perhaps he could transport her there if Leland didn't show up soon.

The farmer touched the brim of his hat, ducking his head respectfully. "Ma'am."

When she turned back to Jack, he was studying her intently, as if trying to read something from her countenance. Holding her gaze, he extended his hand. "And I'm Lanny's brother, Jack."

Brother! Of course—Jack Tyler. Julia had mentioned Leland's brother in many of her letters. It had grieved her friend deeply when the breach had grown up between the brothers, and even more so when Jack had left Sweetgum and all but cut himself off from his family and friends.

No wonder he was startled by her news. If he was just now returning to Sweetgum after all these years, of course he wouldn't know about Leland's second marriage.

Feeling her anxiety ebb, she grasped his outstretched hand eagerly. "Then you are my brother-in-law. I'm so very pleased to meet you."

She smiled, relieved and happy. Jack Tyler. Perhaps he was part of her mission here—maybe she could help heal whatever rift existed between the two brothers. Julia would have wanted that.

When her newfound relation released her hand, Callie adjusted her bonnet again. "If I'd realized who you were, I would have waited before I said anything. I'm certain your brother wanted to tell you himself."

"No harm done." His expression, however, hinted that all was not well. Did he resent hearing about the marriage from a stranger?

"Well, it's a wonderful circumstance that we should arrive together." She was more certain than ever that the Lord's hand was in this. "Since your brother is delayed, perhaps you would be so kind as to escort me to his home." Surely he couldn't refuse her request, no matter what rift existed between himself and Leland.

But Mr. Wilson intervened, clearing his throat. "I'm afraid that—"

Without taking his eyes from Callie, Mr. Tyler interrupted whatever his friend was about to say. "Leland isn't at home right now."

The hairs at the nape of Callie's neck prickled.

There was something strangely intense about the look he was giving her.

And how would he know Leland wasn't at home when he'd only just arrived in town himself?

Chapter Three

"I don't understand."

Jack saw the uneasy flicker in the woman's expression. Fair enough. He wasn't sure he knew what to make of her, either.

How was he supposed to believe her claim that Lanny had married again, had replaced his first wife with someone so unlike the vibrant, delicate and pretty-as-a-spring-meadow woman Julia had been?

Not that this woman was unattractive. He couldn't see much of her face, but she had a nice enough smile and a trim figure.

But she wasn't Julia.

In Nell's last letter she'd mentioned how hard a time Lanny was having dealing with Julia's passing. It was one of the reasons Jack had been thinking about making a visit home.

This remarriage thing just didn't make sense.

"Excuse me, ma'am." He tried to keep his voice even. No point fanning her distrust. "I know you have questions. To be honest, I have a few for you as well. But it's a mite hot out here on the sidewalk."

He nodded toward the open door to the hotel. "Why don't we step inside and find a more comfortable place to talk." Not to mention less public.

He saw her hesitation and spoke up again before she could object. "I'm sure Virgil won't mind watching our bags while we figure this out."

"Uh, yes, ma'am." Virgil gamely followed his lead. "I mean, no, I don't mind at all. You two just go right ahead. And take your time. I mean, you have a lot—"

"There, that's settled." Jack used his best take-charge tone to cut off Virgil's rambling. He wanted to give her the news his way, in his time.

He pointed to the trunk and carpetbag still sitting on the sidewalk. "So, are these yours? We'll just set them with mine over here out of the way."

Once he got her inside they could sort through her story without the whole town looking on. It was a pretty sure bet that once he told her why Lanny wasn't here to meet her there was going to be a scene of some sort.

Which was another good reason to get her inside—it would be right handy to have her already seated in case she decided to swoon. He just hoped she wasn't one of those melodramatic females who were prone to hysterics.

But her lips compressed in a stubborn line. "Just a minute, Mr. Tyler. I'm not going anywhere until you tell me where my husband is." She tugged on that bonnet again. "And what exactly did you mean by 'figure this out?'"

Just his luck—she was going to be muleheaded. "Ma'am, trust me, you really don't want to have this conversation out here in the middle of town." He crossed his arms and raised a brow, trying a bit of intimidation. Couldn't she see that he just wanted to make this easier on her?

Rather than backing down, though, the obstinate woman

tilted her chin even higher. "It's a simple question, sir, requiring a simple answer. Where is my husband?"

Jack dropped his arms and narrowed his eyes. At another time he might have admired her spirit, her stubborn resolve. But not today. He was too tired from four days of travel and frustrating delays—four days of trying to absorb the impact of what had happened—to continue this argument.

She wanted to know where Lanny was, then so be it. "Have it your way. I'll take you right to him."

"Huh?" Virgil almost dropped the bag he held. "Jack, what are—"

Jack raised a hand. "No, no, it's okay." He gave his friend a tight smile. "I planned to pay a visit when I got here anyway. No point putting it off, and this lady might as well come along."

Virgil shot a look toward the far end of town, then shifted his gaze uncertainly from the woman back to Jack.

Jack clapped him on the shoulder before he could protest again, or worse yet, blurt out something that would set off a scene. "You don't mind seeing to our luggage while the lady and I take a little walk, do you?"

"No, of course not. But—"

"Good." With a short nod, Jack turned back to Lanny's self-proclaimed bride and swept his hand out in a gesture that was more challenge than good manners. "Shall we?"

She didn't answer immediately. Instead, she drew her lower lip between her teeth and gave that odd-looking bonnet another tug forward.

Jack's flash of irritation turned inward. There he went, taking his frustrations out on someone else.

Again.

He rubbed the back of his neck, feeling wearier than he ever had in his twenty-nine years. He hadn't had more than the odd thirty-minute nap here or there since he'd gotten that telegram.

And he still hadn't figured out what he was going to do now that he was here. Just the thought of—

He shook his head, trying to focus on the current issue. That other business was his problem, not this woman's. Given the circumstances, she deserved better treatment. "Look, ma'am, I—"

"Very well." She spoke over his attempted apology as if he hadn't opened his mouth. Her spine was rail-spike stiff, all signs of hesitation and uncertainty replaced by an air of determination. "Lead the way."

It was Jack's turn to hesitate. He could tell she was still a bit uneasy and admired her pluck, but maybe this wasn't such a good idea after all. Yes, taking her along would give them a bit of privacy, but it would also put him alone with her when he broke the news. He wasn't good at dealing with emotional women. And he certainly wasn't in any shape to deal with one today.

Then he shrugged. She had to be told, and his gut said she wouldn't get all hysterical on him.

"This way."

They started down the sidewalk, Jack matching his pace to her shorter stride.

They walked in silence. Jack kept his eyes focused straight ahead and refused to slow his step, halting any would-be greetings from the folks they passed with a short nod. He wasn't ready to talk to his former friends and neighbors right now.

He had to get this over with first.

He carefully avoided looking at whatever was left of Nell and Jed's café, but as they drew even with it he could smell the acrid odor of scorched wood and ashes that still lingered in the air, threatening to suffocate him.

Jack shot a quick glance at the blackened remains in spite of himself.

A definite mistake.

Loss and guilt slammed into him again, harder this time, like a fist in the gut. It was as if he'd tossed a stick of explosives into the building himself, leaving this grotesque skeleton of charred timbers and debris.

He scrubbed a hand along the right side of his face. Perhaps if he'd made plans to come home before now, to make amends. If he had been here when—

"Pardon me."

His companion's breathless words interrupted his thoughts. A quick glance her way revealed she was struggling to keep up.

He slowed immediately. "Sorry, ma'am. My mind was on something else."

She glanced over her shoulder at the charred rubble, then back at him with dawning dismay. "That building, it was the café, wasn't it?"

He felt that betraying muscle in his jaw twitch. "Yes." And just how did she know that?

Unspoken questions tumbled across her face, a growing dread clouding her eyes. Apparently she knew of the café's significance to him.

And to her as well, if she was who she said she was.

How did she know enough to read the situation from a burned-out building she'd never seen before? Had Lanny *really* married this woman, this apparent stranger to Sweetgum and everyone here?

Twice her mouth opened then closed again. For a change she seemed to have nothing to say. Instead, she gave him an assessing look, nodded and increased her pace.

He spared a moment to ponder over the puzzle this woman

presented. In the short time he'd been in her company she'd proven herself to be more stubborn, outspoken and full of spit and vinegar than might be seemly for a female. Yet just now she'd seen no-telling-what in his expression and held back her questions. Not at all the reaction he'd expected.

The walk through town seemed endless. The closer they got to their destination, the tighter the tension inside him coiled. Everyday sounds like dogs barking and harnesses jangling seemed both magnified and distant. He felt eyes focused on them from every angle. It was as if the two of them were the main characters in some sort of stage play, only he'd forgotten all his lines and even which role he was assigned.

"Watch your step." He automatically took her elbow as the sidewalk ended. As soon as they stepped down onto the well-packed dirt path, she withdrew her arm. But not before he felt the slight trembling of her muscles.

So, the lady wasn't as composed as she wanted him to think. Was it because she'd already figured out what had happened?

Or because she still didn't trust him?

The main section of town gave way almost immediately to greener expanses. Up ahead was Sweetgum's schoolhouse. The church was just beyond, close enough that it was difficult to tell where the schoolyard ended and the churchyard began.

Both of these places had been a central part of his world, his life, at one time. But no more.

He'd outgrown the schoolroom at sixteen.

He'd outgrown the church a few years later, when he'd decided it was finally time to get away from Sweetgum and strike out on his own.

Jack shook off those memories as he led his companion across the schoolyard, past the church building and up to the white picket fence that marked the boundaries of the cemetery.

He paused and turned to her, removing his hat and raking a hand through his hair.

She stood there, rooted to the spot, her eyes wide, her gaze fixed on the neat rows of grassy mounds.

"Ma'am?"

She started, and her gaze flew to his.

Her pallor roused a protective response in him. She looked nearly as white as the ribbon on her bonnet. Jack could see the shock, the inner battle she was fighting between denial and a sickly acceptance.

Was he going to have to deal with a swooner after all?

"Steady now." He took her elbow. "I'm sorry to break it to you like this. But I thought it was better to have a bit of privacy. I—"

She raised a hand. "No, I understand." Her gaze slid back to the somberly peaceful green, and she swallowed audibly. "Was it the fire?"

He nodded.

"And your sister?"

Ah, Nell. His sweet, peacemaker of a sister. To die like that…

Not trusting himself to speak, he pulled the crumbled telegram from his pocket and handed it to her. He didn't have to look at it again to know exactly what it said.

The words were burned into his memory.

Café fire. Nell, Jed, Lanny killed. Please return to Sweetgum earliest possible. Children need you.

Callie tasted the bile rising in her throat as she read the terse missive. These people were her newly acquired family, the people she had so eagerly looked forward to meeting and befriending. To learn that they had died under such horrific circumstances…

Everything seemed to go silent, to pull back from her. A heartbeat later her vision clouded over and the earth swayed under her feet.

"Whoa, there."

Mr. Tyler's hand was under her elbow, steadying her, lending her a measure of strength.

Sounds and objects came rushing back into focus, racing to keep pace with the emotions that careened through her like water rushing over a fall. Horror at the thought of their deaths, confusion over what this meant for her future, and a guilty relief that her husband had not deliberately shunned her after all.

She attempted to smile at her concerned brother-in-law. "Thank you. I'm okay now."

He raised a brow. Probably worried she'd faint on him.

"Look, there's a bench over yonder under that cotton-wood." He nodded his head in the direction of a tall leafy tree. Then he cleared his throat. "Why don't we sit for a spell? It'll be cooler in the shade and you can tell me the story of how you came to be married to my bother."

Callie glanced toward the cemetery, then nodded. She could pay her respects to Leland after she and his brother had their talk.

Then she realized how selfish she was being. These people were his family, his siblings and the people he'd grown up with. "I'm sorry to have made this more difficult for you, Mr. Tyler," she said softly. "And my condolences on your loss."

He nodded silently, leading her across the grounds.

"When did it happen?" Callie was still trying to take it all in. "The fire, I mean."

He released her arm as they reached the bench. "Four days ago." Both his face and voice were controlled, giving no hint of whatever emotion he might be feeling.

Then it hit her. She plopped down onto the bench. Could it be?

She clasped her hands tightly and stared up at him. "Do you know what time?"

His brow wrinkled in confusion. "Pardon?"

"At what time did your brother die?" She heard the shrillness of her tone, saw his brow go up. No doubt he thought her hysterical. But right now she didn't care.

He lifted a hand, palm up. "I don't know. I wasn't here. I only—"

"Do you have any idea?" she pressed. "Morning? Afternoon? Please, this is important." Her heart beat with a dull thumping as she waited for his response. A few hours one way or the other could make all the difference in the world.

The thing was, she didn't really know what answer she wanted to hear.

He scratched his chin. "Virgil did mention the café was nearly empty because it was after lunch…"

"I see." She sagged back in her seat, not sure whether she was relieved or disappointed.

Help me to see Your will in this, Father. Because right now, all I feel is confused and adrift.

"And just why does the time matter so much?" Jack asked, interrupting her silent prayer.

Callie dug in her handbag and pulled out a packet of papers. She stared at them for a moment, then held them out to him. "Because, as you'll see if you look through these documents, your brother and I were married by proxy four days ago. At exactly ten o'clock in the morning."

She gave him a humorless smile. "Which means, since the ceremony occurred before the fire, I am indeed a widow without ever having met my husband."

Chapter Four

As he took the papers from her, Callie closed her eyes, trying to absorb the fact that she had become a widow without ever knowing what it meant to be a wife. Yes, it was true that Leland had meant this to be a marriage in name only, but she had secretly hoped that, given time…

Stop it! Callie gave herself a mental shake. She should be mourning the man, not the end of some foolish daydream.

More to the point was the fact that she no longer had a reason to be here.

Had she come all this way for nothing?

Heavenly Father, I thought this was Your answer to my prayers. But was I too impulsive yet again? Was this mere wishful thinking on my part rather than Your intent for me? Please, help me understand what it is You want me to do now.

The sound of rustling papers drew her attention back to her companion.

He leaned forward, pinning her with that intense gaze again.

Her skin prickled. Even though they were out in the open rather than closed up in a stagecoach, being alone with him suddenly felt much more dangerous than it had earlier.

"So tell me," he asked, "how did this proxy marriage of yours come about?"

She bristled at his suspicious tone, forgetting her previous discomfort. Then she softened as guilt washed over her.

How could she sit here feeling sorry for herself while he dealt with such pain? He might seem gruff and overbearing, but how could she blame him? He'd lost his family less than a week ago, and now he was confronted with a sister-in-law he hadn't realized existed until just a few moments ago.

At the very least he deserved an explanation, something to help him make sense of the situation.

No matter how humbling it might be for her to tell him the story.

"Your brother was in need of someone to help raise his daughter," she said evenly. "And I wished to find a husband and household of my own. It was a mutually beneficial arrangement.

"As for why we did it by proxy..." She shrugged. "My family wouldn't hear of my leaving Ohio without ironclad assurances that the wedding would actually take place, and this seemed the best solution."

His eyes flashed with an emotion she couldn't identify. "Forgive my bluntness, ma'am, but why you? I mean, you just admitted the two of you never met. And, unless things around here have changed more than I realized, I'm sure Lanny could have found a local girl more than willing to marry him and help raise Annabeth."

She gave the edge of her bonnet a little tug. He was treading on uncomfortable territory. "Your brother is—was— a good-hearted, God-fearing man. He was very open about the fact that he wasn't looking for, nor could he offer, a love match." She brushed at an imaginary speck on her skirt. "He loved Julia very much and was certain he would never feel the same about another woman. I understood and accepted that."

Callie titled her chin up as she met her inquisitor's gaze. "I think he found it easier to say those things in a letter, and to someone he hadn't grown up with."

At his raised brow, she looked down at her clasped hands. "Besides which, as I said, your brother was a very kind-hearted man. He knew I would receive his offer in the same spirit in which it was given, and as the possible answer to a long-standing prayer of my own."

He handed the papers back to her. "Ma'am, you just raised a whole wagonload more questions than you answered with that statement."

His tone had lost some of its belligerent edge. He seemed to be leaving it up to her as to whether she continued her story or not.

And his consideration lifted some of her reluctance to explain. "So ask your questions."

"It sounds like, in spite of what you said a moment ago, you and my brother knew each other."

"Knew *of* each other would be more accurate." She tucked her marriage papers back in her purse. "Through Julia."

He made a small movement of surprise. "You knew Julia?"

Callie nodded. "Yes. Her family lived next door to mine when we were children. We were best friends, closer than sisters, and almost inseparable. It was one of the saddest days of my life when I learned they were packing up and moving to Texas. She and I kept in touch after that through letters." She smiled. "Julia wrote the most wonderful letters. I feel like I already know the people and the town here."

He sat up straighter. "Wait a minute. You said your name was Callista. You're Callie."

Her brow furrowed at his abrupt statement. "Yes."

"Julia talked about you all the time when she first moved here. Really looked forward to getting them letters from you, too."

Her smile softened. "As I said, we were close. Even after she moved here, I always felt I could confide anything to her. Julia was that kind of friend."

He rubbed his chin. "So that's how my brother knew so much about you."

She nodded. "Once Julia was married, she shared some of the things from my letters with her husband. She asked first, of course, and I didn't mind. And naturally her letters to me were sprinkled with references to him."

"Naturally."

She wondered at his dry tone, but continued with her story. "Julia assured me she and Leland often included me in their prayers, a consideration I cherished. It also let me know that Leland was familiar with both my dreams and my situation."

"Situation?"

Callie took a deep breath and loosened the strings to her bonnet.

This was it.

Time to get it all out in the open. How would he react? Would he be as understanding as his brother? "Yes, my situation. The reason why I'm nearly twenty-six years old and unmarried. The reason why I always wear this stuffy bonnet when I'm in public. The reason why I would probably have remained a spinster the rest of my days if your brother hadn't made his generous offer."

Slowly she pushed the confining bonnet back until it hung loose behind her neck. She'd thought she was past feeling self-conscious. She shouldn't care what this man thought of her appearance, but somehow she did.

She lifted her head and waited for his inevitable reaction.

* * *

Jack watched her remove her bonnet and got his first good look at her face. He wasn't sure what he'd expected after her dramatic lead-in, but it wasn't this.

While not beautiful, she was passably fair, pretty even, at least in profile. Her hair was sandstone brown and her green eyes were brighter now that they could more fully reflect the sunlight. She had a small crook in her nose, but that added interest to her appearance rather than detracted from it.

So what was this "situation" she'd mentioned? "I'm sorry, ma'am, but I don't—"

Then she turned to him and he stopped cold. He winced before he could stop himself.

Along the left side of her face, from mid-cheek to hairline, her skin was stained by a palm-sized blotchy patch of a deep red color. It was difficult to see past such disfigurement to the pleasant picture she'd presented a few seconds ago.

Her gaze drilled into his, allowing him to look his fill, waiting for him to say something.

But he had no idea what to say.

She finally turned away, presenting him with her unblemished profile again. Her shoulders drooped slightly, but she gave no other sign that she'd noted his reaction.

"So now you know." Her voice was steady and surprisingly unemotional as she reached back and pulled her close-fitting bonnet up once more. "Your brother understood what he was taking on by marrying me. And he also understood why I would see his offer as a welcome opportunity to finally have a family of my own."

Her acceptance of his unguarded reaction made him feel like a complete oaf, like the worst kind of mannerless fool. "I—"

She raised a hand, palm out. "There's no need to say

anything, Mr. Tyler." She faced him fully again, her smile perhaps a little too bright. "I assure you I'm quite accustomed to such first-time reactions."

It was good of her to give him an out, but his momma raised him better than that. "Look, ma'am, I'm sorry I was so rude. You caught me by surprise, is all. And, well, I don't believe in fancy speeches or anything, but I want you to know I admire you for agreeing to my brother's scheme and coming out here on your own the way you did. I'm sure it wasn't an easy decision."

At least the whole situation made more sense now. It was exactly the kind of grand gesture Lanny would make.

Her smile warmed a bit. "You'd be surprised." Then she brushed at her skirt. "Now, if you don't mind, I think I'm ready to pay my respects to my—our—family."

Jack recognized her desire to change the subject. "Agreed." He helped her rise, then offered his arm as they made their way across the churchyard.

Once through the cemetery entrance, he led her around the inside perimeter, past the graves of his parents, to three freshly turned mounds with markers. Nell and Jed rested side by side, and Lanny was buried a few yards away, next to Julia's grave.

Jack stopped in front of Nell's grave while his companion trudged the last few steps to Lanny and Julia's resting places.

Somewhere nearby a blue jay squawked his displeasure. A heartbeat later Jack caught a flash of movement as a squirrel raced down the trunk of a nearby pecan tree.

Other than that, everything was hushed, still.

He frowned at the half dozen or so pink roses someone had placed on his sister's grave. That wasn't right. Daisies were Nell's favorite flower.

The memories pelted him, one after the other, piercing

him with their clarity, battering his attempts to hold them at bay.

He could see his little sister, skipping along the fence row, pigtails bouncing, picking armloads of the yellow blooms. Then she'd sit under the oak tree in their yard and make braids and crowns and other little girl treasures for hours on end.

Ah, Nell, I'm so sorry I didn't come home sooner like you kept after me to. You always warned me I'd be sorry I waited so long, and as usual, you were right.

He twisted his hat brim in his hands.

I'll find you some daisies tomorrow, I promise. Bunches of them.

A leaf drifted on the breeze and landed on the grassless mound. Jack stared at it as if memorizing the nuances of color and the tracery of its veins were vital.

About those young'uns of yours. You know I don't know anything about being a father. And they sure deserve a lot better than me. But I swear to you, whatever happens, I'll do my level best to see that they're taken care of proper.

He wasn't sure if mere seconds or several minutes passed before he finally looked up and took his bearings again.

The woman, Callie—easier to think of her as Julia's friend than Leland's wife—stood between the markers that served as Lanny and Julia's headstones with her head bowed and her eyes closed.

Was she feeling faint?

Or praying?

As if she felt his gaze, she looked up and drew in a deep breath, then let it go on a sigh. Jack joined her and stared silently at his brother's grave.

Lanny, the big brother who was good at just about everything he attempted, who could be bossier than the day was long, but who bent over backwards to lend a hand where it was needed.

Regret threaded itself through Jack's feeling of loss. Why hadn't he come here sooner, made peace with Lanny, offered him the apology he deserved?

Now he would never have that chance....

Movement drew his gaze to Julia's grave. He watched as a butterfly, its wings the same deep blue that Julia's eyes had been, landed briefly on her marker, then fluttered toward them. It rested momentarily on Callie's bonnet before drifting away on the breeze.

When he looked back, he found her watching him. He straightened and shoved his hat back on his head. "Ready?"

She nodded and took the arm he offered. Their silence was companionable this time, all of the tension that had been there when they marched through town earlier having evaporated.

He was surprised to realize how glad he was that she'd been here these past few minutes. Somehow it felt right to have her share this graveside visit, to mourn alongside him for a few moments over their mutual loss.

"Those poor little ones," she said softly. "They must be so confused and frightened by what's happened."

The mention of the children brought back his earlier worries. Was he up to the job of playing nursemaid to three confused and frightened young'uns?

"Who's been looking out for them since the accident?" she asked.

"Mrs. Mayweather." At her questioning look, he elaborated. "Sweetgum's schoolteacher. She offered to take them in until I could get here."

"How kind of her. Does she have children of her own?"

Jack smiled at the thought of the major general of a woman that was Alberta Mayweather having a husband to "take care of her." "The 'Mrs.' is more of a courtesy title," he explained. "She never married. But Mrs. Mayweather's been school-teacher here since before I was born, and she knows what she's doing when it comes to watching over young'uns."

Unlike me.

Jack's gut tightened. He had quite a tangle to deal with, and it kept growing. He still hadn't figured out what he was going to do about the three kids, and now he had to add Lanny's widow to the mix.

Of course, he probably wouldn't have that added worry for long. Now that Lanny was gone, she'd likely head back to Ohio where she'd be amongst people she knew.

"Then they're lucky to have someone like her looking out for them." Her steps quickened slightly. "But the sooner they can settle into a permanent home again with family around them, the better it'll be."

Hah! Easy enough for her to say. She didn't have the re-sponsibility of making it happen.

Her sigh interrupted his thoughts. "I just pray that, with God's help, I can be a good mother to Annabeth."

Mother? Jack stopped in his tracks.

"Wait just a minute. You can't honestly believe you're going to take charge of my niece."

He might not know how to be a father, but he'd just made a solemn promise to Nell and Lanny to give it his best shot. And there was no way he'd break a promise like that. No sir, he wasn't about to hand any of those kids over to a stranger.

No matter who she'd been married to.

Her eyes widened, but she didn't back down. "In case you've forgotten, helping to raise Annabeth was the reason Leland asked me to come here. I'm still Annabeth's step-mother. Of course I'm going to take care of her," she said as if it was the most logical thing in the world.

"Stepmother!" He rubbed the back of his neck, more to keep himself from reaching out to shake some sense into the woman than anything else. "You were married to my brother for less than half a day. Why, I'll wager you've never even laid eyes on Annabeth, have you?"

She crossed her arms and he saw a flash of temper in her eyes. "Have you?"

He didn't much care for the ring of challenge in her tone. "I'm her blood kin," he argued, sidestepping the question. "It's my responsibility to—"

She yanked the marriage papers from her handbag and held them in front of his face. "Not according to these documents."

The woman was downright maddening. If she thought for one minute he was going to let her lay claim to Annabeth, she was going to be mighty disappointed.

He was maddening! Why couldn't he see that this was something she needed to do, was meant to do? It *had* to be why God had led her here.

That reminder drew Callie up short.

There she went, making assumptions again.

"I'm sorry." She offered a conciliatory smile. "I don't believe either of us is thinking clearly right now. I'm certain we both have Annabeth's best interests at heart, and that's what counts. We just need to make certain we understand what those are."

His expression didn't soften a bit. "The best thing for her right now is to be with her family. And that's me and her cousins."

Callie took a deep breath and tried again. "Mr. Tyler, why don't we call a truce for the moment. At least long enough to pray about it. I'm sure God will help us resolve this if we just look to Him for guidance."

Her oh-so-stubborn brother-in-law didn't answer right away. Instead, he gave her a peculiar look.

A prickly unease stole over her, engulfing her like a scratchy woolen cloak.

No. She must have misinterpreted his expression.

Leland and Julia had been such steadfast Christians. Surely Leland's brother…

She forced her lips to form the question.

"You *do* believe in God, Mr. Tyler, don't you?"

Chapter Five

Callie watched as Jack paused, rubbing the back of his neck. Then he gestured back the way they'd come. "My dad helped build that church and my mother was the organist there for years."

She frowned. What his parents did or didn't do had nothing to do with—

"It's just, well, I'm not really the praying sort."

The words shocked her. "I don't understand."

He shifted his weight. "Look, I don't have anything against folks praying if they've a mind to. It's just that I don't believe in asking for handouts myself. I cotton more to the 'God helps those who help themselves' way of thinking."

Callie blinked. Surely she'd misunderstood. "Mr. Tyler, asking for guidance and direction from our Heavenly Father is *not* the same as asking for a handout." She saw the skepticism in his eyes and tried again. "Besides which, there is absolutely nothing wrong with humbling ourselves before the Almighty."

He waved his hand as if to brush her words aside. "Ma'am, you just go right ahead and pray for guidance if that makes you feel better." Then he folded his arms across his chest and his eyes turned flinty. "But I'm telling you right now, there's nothing on earth—or in heaven, for that matter—that's going to convince me to turn any member of my family over to a stranger, no matter how strong that stranger might think her claim is."

Callie pursed her lips, not trusting herself to respond immediately. It wasn't about just Annabeth now. All three youngsters deserved to have a proper Christian influence in their lives. It was what their parents would have wanted for them, and it was the right thing to do. Actually, it was the most important thing.

She might not be the best person to fill that role, but God could use even the most flawed vessel to do His work. She was more determined than ever to have a hand in raising these children.

She focused again on Leland's brother. He seemed to have nothing in common at the moment with the compassionate, generous man she'd come to know through years of correspondence.

Not the praying kind indeed!

Time to try another tack. "Mr. Tyler, I find myself quite weary from the day's events, and would prefer not to stand here arguing with you. I'd like to meet Annabeth and then find a place to refresh myself, if you don't mind."

His eyes narrowed and she wondered for a minute if he would continue to argue despite her request. But he gave a quick nod. "Of course. This way."

As he offered his arm he gave her a warning look. "Just don't think this means I've changed my thinking. You're welcome to stick around if you've a mind to. But the care of the children—*all* of the children—is my responsibility."

We'll just see about that. After the briefest of hesitations, she placed her hand on his arm, giving him her sweetest smile. "I must admit, your concern for the well-being of the children does do you credit, Mr. Tyler."

Jack escorted his suspiciously compliant sister-in-law to Mrs. Mayweather's home. The woman wasn't fooling him with that winsome smile and those sugar-coated words of hers. He knew good and well she hadn't given up the battle yet.

Well, she could scheme and plot all she wanted. It didn't change his mind one jot about his duty to Annabeth, Simon and Emma.

But as they drew closer to Mrs. Mayweather's home, his thoughts turned from Lanny's widow to the three children.

What was he going to say to them? He was their closest living kin, but he'd never laid eyes on them before—not since Nell's oldest was an infant, anyway—and they certainly didn't know him.

How much had their parents told them about him? Or had the subject of their absent Uncle Jack ever even come up?

How would they react when they met him? How would he deal with their grief when he was still trying to absorb the loss himself?

His free hand clenched and unclenched. How could this woman walking beside him talk about looking to God for guidance when that same God allowed such a thing to happen in the first place? If the Almighty had wanted to take another Tyler, it should have been him. His passing, unlike that of his brother and sister, wouldn't have left a hole in anyone's life.

His face must have betrayed some of what he was thinking because Callie cast a questioning glance his way. Luckily, they had finally reached Mrs. Mayweather's front gate.

"Here we are," he said, cutting off any comment she might

have made. He opened the gate without meeting her gaze and gestured for her to precede him up the flagstone walkway.

Before they'd made it halfway to the porch, a tall, spare woman stepped out to greet them.

Age had definitely not interfered with Mrs. Mayweather's commanding presence. From the top of her tightly wound, steel gray bun to the hem of her no-frills, severely cut skirt, she still had that force-to-be-reckoned-with schoolmarm look that could quiet a classroom full of rowdy children with just a raised brow.

"Hello, Jackson. It's good to see you back in Sweetgum again. My condolences for your loss."

Facing her, Jack felt like a ten-year-old schoolboy again. "Thank you, ma'am." He quickly turned to Callie. "This is—" He paused for the merest fraction of a second and she immediately stepped forward.

"Callista Tyler, ma'am. I am—was—married to Leland Tyler."

Mrs. Mayweather nodded. "Yes. Virgil stopped by to explain the situation. Most astounding." She paused a minute. "I must say, you seem to be holding up remarkably well under what must have been a terrible shock."

"It's kind of you to say so, ma'am." She gave her bonnet a tug. "I'm afraid the full impact of the situation hasn't entirely sunk in yet."

"Understandable." Mrs. Mayweather tilted her head thoughtfully. "Callista. Unusual name, that. You wouldn't by any chance be Julia's friend Callie."

"Why, yes." Her smile warmed and some of the tension eased from her stance. "It seems my fame precedes me."

"Well then, that explains quite a bit." The schoolteacher nodded in satisfaction as if she'd solved a puzzle of some sort. "Julia always spoke of you in such glowing terms. It's no wonder Leland turned to you for this special kind of help after she passed on."

She waved toward the far end of the porch. "By the way, since we weren't certain how things would sort themselves out, I instructed Virgil to deposit your baggage here for the time being."

"Why, thank you, I—" The widow seemed a bit overwhelmed by their hostess.

Jack knew the feeling. He stepped forward. "Where are the children?"

"They're upstairs, digging through an old trunk of mine. I'll call them down shortly, but I thought it would be best if we had a chat first."

"Of course." Jack felt a guilty surge of relief at being able to put off the moment of truth a little longer.

Mrs. Mayweather stepped aside. "Now come on in to the parlor. You both look as if you could do with a cool glass of lemonade, and we have matters to discuss."

Callie nodded. "Thank you. That sounds lovely."

Jack removed his hat and followed the ladies inside.

"You may set your hat on the hall table there, Jackson." She turned to Callie. "Feel free to set your bonnet and handbag there as well."

He tensed in sympathy. What would Callie do? How would she handle this?

Once again, she surprised him. Though she moved with a sort of deliberate slowness, her initial hesitation was so brief he doubted Mrs. Mayweather noted it.

With steady hands, she loosened the strings to her bonnet and let it fall behind her head.

Mrs. Mayweather studied her for a minute. "A birthmark, I presume?" At Callie's nod, she pursed her lips thoughtfully. "Yes, indeed. I'm beginning to understand why Julia had such respect and admiration for you."

* * *

Callie was startled by the woman's words and didn't know how to respond, so she said nothing. She pulled her bonnet back up, wondering exactly how much Julia had said about her and to whom.

Mrs. Mayweather raised a hand to stop her. "No need to do that on my account."

Callie smiled, but firmly tied her ribbons. "Thank you, but I'd rather that not be the first view the children have of me."

"As you wish." A slight nod accompanied the words. "But I think you would be surprised by how accepting children can be."

A few moments later, they were seated in the parlor and Mrs. Mayweather was pouring glasses of lemonade.

"I know a man of the world such as yourself would probably prefer something stronger," she said as Jack reached for his, "but I'm afraid you will have to make do with this for now."

"This will do just fine, thank you." He took a long drink, then set the glass down. "So how are the young'uns doing?"

Mrs. Mayweather's face softened in concern and Callie saw a whole new side of her.

"About as one would expect. They went through such a horrid experience. At least they didn't have to witness the fire firsthand."

Callie sent up a silent prayer of thanksgiving. She'd worried…

"As it happens, Simon had taken Emma and Annabeth down to the livery," Mrs. Mayweather continued briskly. "He wanted to show them a new foal that had been born the day before. When they heard the alarm, they headed back to the café. Luckily, the O'Connor sisters spotted them and had sense enough to keep them from going anywhere near the fire."

Callie saw past the woman's businesslike tone. "And so you took them in."

Mrs. Mayweather nodded. "I had the room and the time to see to them, since school had let out for summer the week before."

Jack stood and moved to one of the windows. "Still, I'm very beholden," he said without turning around.

"I just thank the Lord I had the means to step in." She refilled Callie's glass. "But back to your question. The tragedy has affected each of them differently. Simon has turned from an active, outgoing boy to one who is belligerent and aloof."

She waved a hand. "Emma has always been a quiet child, but now she clings to Simon like bark to a tree. She can barely stand to have him out of her sight for more than a few minutes. Simon is taking his role of big brother seriously—too seriously, if you ask me. He insisted I set his cot in the room with the girls when Emma balked at separating from him even in sleep."

"And Annabeth?"

Mrs. Mayweather sighed. "I'm not certain. Bless her, she was just beginning to move on from the loss of her mother, then this happened. She misses her father terribly, of course. But the child, who's normally quite the little chatterbox, has barely said a word since the accident, except in answer to a direct question."

Callie twisted her hands nervously in her skirts. "Do you think she knows? About me, I mean."

Mrs. Mayweather gave her a sympathetic smile. "If so, she hasn't given any sign. But, as I mentioned, she hasn't said more than a handful of words since her father passed. Besides, even if Leland did say something to her, she may not have understood. She's only four, after all."

Jack turned to face them and crossed his arms. "It doesn't

matter whether she knows or not. Like I said, Annabeth is my concern now."

Callie carefully set her glass down, resisting the urge to retort in kind. *Lord, give me patience. Please!*

She caught a measuring look Mrs. Mayweather gave the two of them.

The woman stood. "Well, I can tell the children certainly won't want for family willing to take them in. You two help yourselves to more lemonade while I let them know you're here."

Jack's expression gave nothing away, but she saw him rub the back of his neck. Was he as nervous about facing the children for the first time as she was?

Moments later, Callie's entire being focused on the sound of footsteps tromping down the stairs.

Simon entered first, looking both ready to take on the world and achingly vulnerable at the same time. His sister, Emma, was close by his side, her arm wound tightly with his, her eyes wide and uncertain.

But it was the third and youngest of the children that captured Callie's attention. The little girl hung back a bit while still holding on to Emma's other hand.

Callie would have been able to pick Annabeth out of a ballroom full of little girls. She looked so much like Julia it made her heart ache. The same bouncy blond curls, the same bright blue eyes, the same pink bow of a mouth.

Mrs. Mayweather spoke up first. "Children, remember I told you that your Uncle Jack would be coming?" She made a flourishing movement with her hand. "Well, here he is."

Then she gestured toward Callie. "And we also have a surprise visitor."

Annabeth stared at Callie with wide, questioning eyes. Was it possible the child was expecting her after all?

Simon, however, seemed to be the designated spokesman for the trio. He completely ignored Callie as he gave Jack an assessing look. "So you're our Uncle Jack."

Jack strode to the middle of the room. "That's right. And I've come to take care of you." He smiled at the two girls. "All of you."

None of the three returned Jack's smile.

"Momma talked about you some." Simon's tone hadn't softened. "And she read your letters to us when they came." His eyes narrowed. "It made her sad that you never came around."

To Callie's surprise, Jack didn't attempt to make excuses.

Instead he nodded and walked right up to his nephew. "I'm sorry about that—more sorry than you can rightly know. I should have been a better brother to both her and your Uncle Lanny." He laid a hand on Simon's shoulder. "But I'm here now."

Simon didn't seem appeased. "She said you had to move around a lot 'cause you work for the railroad." The boy put a protective arm around his sister's shoulder. "Does that mean we have to travel around the country with you?"

Callie found herself as interested as Simon was to hear Jack's answer.

Jack took a minute, stepping back and crossing his arms again. "Well, now, I plan to stay right here in Sweetgum for the time being. We're going to stick together, just like families are supposed to."

Emma sidled closer to her brother's side, drawing Annabeth with her. "But where are we going to live? Our house is all gone now." Her voice was so soft Callie had to lean forward to hear her.

Jack nodded solemnly. "I know, and I've been giving that some thought. Your house may be gone but Annabeth's house is still sound. And I'll just bet she'd be glad to let us all live there with her."

Annabeth, who hadn't yet taken her eyes off Callie, turned to Emma. "Oh, yes," she said, nodding her head emphatically. "There's lots and lots of room there. You could even bring Cookie and nobody would care how much he barked out there."

"There now." Jack gave Emma an encouraging smile. "You've been to Annabeth's house before, haven't you? It's the same house your momma lived in when she was your age."

Emma nodded, tentatively responding to Jack's smile.

But Simon was far from won over. "Annabeth's house is on a farm way out in the country. All of our friends live here in town."

Annabeth's face crumpled into a hurt expression. "But Simon, it's a very nice house. Don't you want to come live with me?"

Emma gave her young cousin's hand a squeeze. "Simon didn't mean anything by that. Of course he likes your house." She gave her brother a little nudge. "Don't you?"

Simon gave a grudging nod.

Appeased, Annabeth turned her attention back to Callie. She let go of Emma's hand and took a tentative step forward, her head cocked at a questioning angle. "Are you going to come live with us, too?"

Callie clasped her hands together tightly, fighting the urge to reach out for the child. She didn't want to frighten her. "Would you like for me to?"

Annabeth crossed the room and stopped directly in front of her. With pudgy fingers that weren't quite clean, she reached up and started to push aside Callie's bonnet.

Callie's first instinct was to pull back, to stop the child from revealing the hidden ugliness. But something about the hope in the little girl's expression changed her mind.

Forcing herself to sit completely still, Callie held her breath and waited for Annabeth's reaction.

Chapter Six

As soon as the bonnet fell back, Callie heard a startled gasp from Emma and peripherally noted the way Simon's eyes widened.

But Annabeth's response was entirely unexpected.

A large smile blossomed on her face and she touched the discolored skin almost reverently. "It's you," she said, her voice tinged with delight. "You finally came."

Callie's heart hitched painfully as she expelled the breath she'd been holding. "Annabeth, do you know who I am?"

The child nodded emphatically. "Oh, yes. You're the lady Daddy said was going to come live with us, to be my new mommy." Her face took on a more somber expression. "I was so scared you wouldn't come since Daddy wasn't here anymore."

"Oh, sweetheart, there wasn't any reason to worry." Callie smoothed the child's hair. "I came here as much to be with you as with your daddy."

Callie's heart lightened at this further evidence that Leland had never wavered in his commitment to keep his promise. "So, your daddy told you about me?"

"Yes, ma'am." Annabeth smiled. "He said we were lucky you were coming to stay with us, that you were a friend of Momma's ever since she was my age. But it was supposed to be a secret so he could tell Aunt Nell and Uncle Jed first." She gave Callie an anxious look. "I didn't tell anyone, I promise."

Callie touched the child's cheek. "I know you didn't, sweetie. Your daddy would be very proud of you. But how did you know I was the one?"

"Because of what daddy said about you. He told me you were very special because you have angel kisses on the side of your face."

A lump formed in Callie's throat. That's what Julia used to say when they were little girls. It had always made her feel so special.

Annabeth stared deep into her eyes. "Do you think my daddy is up in heaven getting angel kisses, too?"

Callie pulled the child onto her lap. "Of course I do. And your mommy is right there with him. I imagine both of them are watching you and smiling at how brave you are."

Annabeth gave a satisfied nod and then threw her arms around Callie in a tight embrace.

Callie buried her face in the child's curls, feeling an immediate bond with her. The fierceness of her desire to cherish and protect Julia's child was almost frightening.

Dear God, please don't put this sweet child into my life just to separate us again. If it be Your will, help me make Lanny's brother understand that I need to be here.

She glanced up to find Jack staring at her, frowning uncertainly. Surely he could see how right it was that she have some hand in the child's upbringing, couldn't he?

But Annabeth wasn't the only child who needed reassurances here. Callie gave Julia's daughter one last squeeze. Then she put her down and stood, looking at the other two children.

"You must be Simon and Emma Carson. I'm a very good friend of your Aunt Julia, and I came here to live with Annabeth."

Neither child said anything, but their gazes remained locked on the red splotch that marred Callie's face.

Callie drifted closer, casually pulling her bonnet back in place and tying the ribbons as she did so. "Your Aunt Julia and I used to write to each other. Her letters were quite long and wonderful. She shared all kinds of things about this town and her favorite people here. And that included you two, of course."

"It did?" Emma seemed more at ease now that Callie's bonnet was back in place.

"What kind of things did she say about us?" Simon's voice held a note of challenge.

"Well, I know you're eleven years old, that you're a good student, and that you're also good at building things."

Simon seemed surprised by her words, but she noticed his chest puffed out with pride a bit.

Callie turned to Emma. "And as for you, young lady, you are eight years old and your Aunt Julia thought you were a very fine artist. She said you were always drawing her the prettiest pictures. Her favorites were the ones with flowers and rainbows."

"I like to draw," Emma acknowledged. She finally met Callie's gaze. "Why do you call it angel kisses?"

Callie was relieved the girl was comfortable enough to talk about it. As Mrs. Mayweather had said earlier, children were usually much more forthright in confronting the subject than adults.

"I was born with this mark," she explained. "Sometimes, when your Aunt Julia and I were little girls, she would tell me that she thought it was there because just before God sent me down to be with my parents, one of his angels bent over and kissed me on the cheek."

Emma studied Callie's face, as if trying to see past the bonnet. "Does it hurt?"

"Not at all. It's always been just a part of who I am." Callie gently touched a spot near the corner of Emma's mouth. "Just like this little mole right here is a part of you."

"Oh." Emma's hand reached for the spot Callie had touched. "And like my friend Molly's freckles?"

"That's right. But I tell you what. I know it's a little scary right at first. So why don't I just keep this bonnet on for the time being, at least until we get to know each other better."

Emma nodded. Then her brow furrowed. "What are we supposed to call you?"

Caught off guard, Callie glanced up at Jack. She had no real claim on Simon and Emma. But, then again, she *had* been married to their uncle. She turned back to Emma. "Why don't you just call me Aunt Callie?"

"Aunt Callie." Emma tried out the name, then nodded approval. "That's nice."

"That's settled then."

"So you *will* be living at the farm with us." Annabeth made the pronouncement with all the confidence of a self-assured four-year-old.

Jack cleared his throat and Simon started to voice another protest.

But Mrs. Mayweather stepped in before either of them got very far. "Children." With that one word, she claimed everyone's attention. "Why don't the three of you go outside and check on Cookie. Simon, there is a bone left over from yesterday's supper on the kitchen counter that you may take to him."

Once the children left the room, Jack turned to Mrs. Mayweather. "I want to thank you again for taking them in until I could get here." He rubbed the back of his neck again. "I suppose I should ask them to pack up their things so we can head on over to the farm."

Callie sat up straighter. No! He was *not* going to sidestep her claim that easily. Those children needed her. "I don't believe that is your decision to make, Mr. Tyler."

He frowned. "We've already—"

She cut off his attempt to play the kin card again. "As your brother's widow, I believe I should have some say as to who will be staying at the farm."

"Are you saying you want to go out there yourself?"

"I don't—"

Mrs. Mayweather held up a hand to halt their discussion. "It appears to me that the two of you have some things to work out in respect to the children's future. After all, you only learned the full extent of the situation a few hours ago."

"It seems pretty cut and dried to me," Jack groused.

Mrs. Mayweather drew herself up. "Jackson Garret Tyler, I will thank you to mind your tone when you are in my home."

Apparently it didn't matter how old Jack was—he would always be a recalcitrant schoolboy to Mrs. Mayweather. Callie carefully swallowed a grin.

Jack mumbled an apology, chafing under Mrs. Mayweather's obvious censure.

He wasn't sure what was wrong with him today. One minute he was breaking out in a cold sweat at the thought of taking sole responsibility for the three kids, and the next he was ready to fight to the death against anyone who'd dare try to take that privilege from him.

Mrs. Mayweather smoothed her skirts and gave them both equally stern looks. "Now, you've had a long day, both physically and emotionally. This is probably not the best time for you to make any major decisions."

Callie nodded. "I agree. It would be best if we spent a little more time seeking guidance in this matter."

Jack bit back a retort. There she went with that "seeking guidance" talk again. Didn't the woman know how to make a decision on her own? Or did she think her delaying tactics would give her some sort of advantage in their tug-of-war?

Mrs. Mayweather, however, didn't give him an opportunity to voice his objections. "Quite sensible. I insist the children stay here with me another night or two, while you two get everything worked out. It would be criminal to uproot them again before there is some certainty as to where they will live and with whom." She looked from Callie to Jack. "Are we agreed?"

"Yes, ma'am." Callie's response was quick and confident.

No surprise there. It was exactly what she wanted—time to build her case. But he couldn't come up with an argument that didn't sound petty, so, under Mrs. Mayweather's stern gaze, he had no choice but to follow suit. "Yes, ma'am."

"Very well. Jackson, you are welcome to stay for supper. The more time you and Callista spend in the children's company, the better for everyone. Afterward, I suggest you spend the night at the farm. It will relieve Virgil of the responsibility of taking care of the chores in the morning. You may use my horse and buggy to get there."

She rose as if the matter were settled. Which he supposed it was.

His brother's widow stood uncertainly. "I suppose I should get a room at the hotel."

Mrs. Mayweather frowned. "Nonsense. You'll stay here with me and the children."

She held up a hand, halting any protest Callie might make.

"This is no time to stand on ceremony. Your presence has already made such a difference to Annabeth. She's spoken more in these past few minutes than she has the last four days."

Jack frowned at this point in Callie's favor in their battle for guardianship of the children.

"Besides," Mrs. Mayweather continued, "you can help me with some of the extra chores that have resulted from the presence of the children."

That seemed to seal the deal for Callie. "Of course. Thank you."

There was a feeling of feminine conspiracy to this. Not that the arrangement didn't make sense from a strictly logistical standpoint. The only problem was, it let his sister-in-law have free rein with the kids while he was exiled to the farm. Which gave her a leg up in winning the children's favor.

He'd have to find a way to level the field.

Callie had mixed emotions that evening as she watched Jack walk out Mrs. Mayweather's kitchen door.

Just as when he'd started to walk away from her beside the stagecoach this afternoon, she felt as if a lifeline was slipping away from her, leaving her stranded in unfamiliar territory.

Strange. As stubborn as the man was, she felt they'd formed a connection of sorts. After all, when he wasn't being so pig-headedly combative over the matter of the children, he was actually nice. And even in that matter, one had to admire a man who was willing to take his perceived responsibilities so much to heart.

Callie turned away from the door with a tired sigh.

So much had happened today. It had begun with her looking forward to starting life as a wife and a mother, and ended with the discovery that she was a widow who would have to fight to maintain her claim on her stepchild. What a welcome to Texas. Her father would—

Oh, no! She raised a hand to her mouth and spun around to face her hostess.

"My goodness, dear, you look as if you just burned Sunday dinner and the preacher's at the door. Whatever is it?"

"I promised my family I'd send a telegraph when I arrived so they would know I was safe. It slipped my mind until just now." She grimaced. "I hate to impose, but would you have a piece of paper and a pen I could use?" Silly of her to feel this sense of urgency since she wouldn't be able to send the telegram until tomorrow. But doing this would provide a small bit of normalcy to a day that had spun out of control.

A few minutes later, Callie sat at a small desk tucked in the parlor. She dipped the pen in the inkwell, then paused.

What would she say? How much *should* she say?

Her family worried about her so. No good would be served by adding to their concerns. After all, she had confidence that God would see her through this.

But she couldn't lie to them.

Best to keep it short and non-committal for the moment. Nodding to herself, she quickly jotted down three sentences.

Have arrived safely in Sweetgum. Already made new friends who have welcomed me warmly. Will send a letter with further news soon.

As she set the pen down, Callie's thoughts turned to resuming her battle of wits with Jackson Garret Tyler in the morning.

Surprisingly, her feeling about this was not dread—but anticipation.

Chapter Seven

Jack clicked his tongue, encouraging the horse to pick up the pace as the sun edged lower on the horizon. Not that he needed daylight to find his way. Even after eleven years, the road was as familiar to him as his own face.

He'd already made a quick stop at Virgil's place to let him know he wouldn't need to worry about handling the chores at the Tyler farm any longer. Luckily he'd caught Virgil out in the barn so he hadn't had to spend time on pleasantries with his friend's family. There'd be time enough for neighborly visits in the days to come.

Jack didn't really consider himself a sentimental man, so the little kick of expectation that hit him when he turned the buggy onto the familiar drive surprised him.

As soon as the house came into full view, he tugged on the reins, halting the horse and buggy. The sight that greeted him was at once soul-deep familiar and strangely foreign.

The same two-story gabled structure sat on the lawn like a fat hen guarding her nest.

The same large oak tree spread its made-for-climbing branches over the left side of the lawn.

The same red barn pointed its cupola to the sky.

But Lanny and Julia, not to mention Father Time, had made noticeable changes. There was now a roomy swing on one end of the wraparound front porch. The oak tree was several feet taller and its branches shaded a much larger patch of ground than Jack remembered. And the gray-and-black speckled dog that came bounding from behind the barn was nothing like ole Clem.

With another flick of the reins, Jack directed the horse around the house and into the barn.

There were several changes in here as well. The old buggy had been replaced with a roomier one and it seemed Lanny had invested in some interesting-looking tools and equipment. It might be worth his while to do a little exploring in here when he had some time.

But for now he had to take care of bedding down the animals while there was still light enough to see by. He gave the energetic dog a bit of attention, then unhitched the horse and patted the animal as it moved past him toward the water trough.

As he worked at the chores that had once been second nature, his mind wondered over the day's happenings.

Callie was a puzzle to him. Her intentions and determination were admirable, but he didn't believe she understood what she was up against. Such an obviously sheltered city girl would have a hard time adjusting to life in a place like this. Especially now that she didn't have a husband to smooth the way for her.

Still, there was something about the woman, something about the way she faced a fracas head-on rather than shying away that he found intriguing.

Had her life back in Ohio been so terrible that even with what had happened, she—

Jack gave his head a shake. He'd let her get under his skin. He had to remember that her personal problems were no concern of his. She wanted to challenge his claim to Annabeth, and that made her his opponent.

He gave the carriage horse one last brush with the currycomb then patted her again, sending her into an empty stall.

Once he'd fed and watered the other animals and taken care of the evening milking, Jack headed for the house. As he climbed the porch steps he ran a hand over the familiar support post. The etched image of a rearing horse his father had carved into the wood one rainy summer afternoon was still discernable, even under the layer of new paint.

Family mattered. Shared history mattered. That was something only he could offer those kids.

Jack stepped inside, noting the addition of a new screen door as he passed. He wandered through the first floor, feeling strangely disoriented by the mix of the familiar and the new. Everywhere he looked he could see where Julia and Lanny's lives together had left a lasting imprint on the Tyler family home. New curtains here, a new chair there. A tin type picture of Julia's parents now shared space on the mantle with those of the Tyler family. There was also a tintype of Lanny and Julia. Julia held an infant on her lap.

He soon discovered a room had been tacked on to the back of the house. Inside sat a shiny porcelain bathtub and some new-fangled laundry equipment. A hand pump stood against the far wall, sprouting from the back lip of a large metal sink. Next to the sink, a small iron fire box supported a large kettle, ready to heat the water when needed. Large windows set high on three of the four walls would provide ventilation without sacrificing privacy. Someone had even strung a cord below the rafters, no doubt to be used for hanging wet laundry when the weather made it uncomfortable to do so outside.

Not for the first time Jack admired his brother's ingenuity. He could see how this setup would have been a great convenience for Julia. And it would make his life here with the kids that much easier, too.

Jack climbed the stairs, curious to see the bedchambers.

The first room he stepped into was the one he and Lanny had shared as children. Gone were the rock collections, pouches of marbles and patched overalls that had once marked it as the room of two active boys.

Now, everything was clean and neatly arranged. A number of subtle feminine touches had been added, too, no doubt thanks to Julia.

Still, if one looked close enough, the memories were there, lurking in the shadows. Memories of horseplay and fights, of discussions in the dark long after they were supposed to be asleep, of the big brother he'd adored and resented by turns.

Jack stepped farther into the room, looking for the wooden chests his father had built for them. He and Lanny had used them to store their few personal possessions.

Lanny's was nowhere in sight but Jack found his tucked below the window sill with a lace doily and a needlework picture of some flowers on top.

Inside were the things he'd treasured growing up, the few items that had been his alone, that had never belonged to Lanny. He lifted out a leather pouch with a grin. It contained exactly twelve marbles—two nice sized aggies and ten immies. Lanny had given him two of these and taught him how to use them, but the rest Jack had won for himself from schoolyard games.

Of course, he'd never beaten Lanny. Lanny had been good at just about everything he tried. Much as Jack loved his brother, growing up in his shadow hadn't been easy.

Which was one of the reasons he'd left Sweetgum. Only he'd never intended to stay away so long.

Jack shut the lid on the chest and left the room. Too bad he couldn't shut out his feelings of guilt so easily.

He walked across the hall and opened the door to Nell's old room. It still had the stamp of a little girl occupant—lace and frills and brightly colored hair ribbons everywhere. This had to be Annabeth's domain now.

A rag doll lay on the bed. He should bring it to her in the morning, to give her back a little bit of her home.

Jack reached for it, but his fingers curled back into his palm. There was no similar memento he could bring to Nell's kids. How would they feel as they watched Annabeth enjoy her piece of home?

He turned and left the room empty-handed.

Jack skipped the room next to Annabeth's and moved instead to the one across from it. This used to be his mother's domain. Its main function had been as a sewing room, but it had served a multitude of other purposes, too. A pull-down bed had turned it into a guest room when the rare overnight visitor came calling. Spare odds and ends had been stored on shelves that lined two of the walls. And his mother had also hung dried flowers and herbs in bunches from the rafters.

As soon as Jack pushed the door open, he was assaulted by the familiar smells of his childhood. Floral scents mingled with dill, mustard and mint. He could almost imagine his mother working in here, humming in that off-key way she had.

As he looked at the room, he noticed a nearly finished lap quilt attached to the quilting frame, patiently waiting for the seamstress who would never return.

A moment later it hit him that it wasn't a lap quilt but one made for a baby's bed.

He turned abruptly and left the room, closing the door firmly behind him.

The only room left to visit was the one that his parents had slept in. Except it would now be Lanny's room, the one he and Julia had shared when she was alive. The one he had, no doubt, been prepared to share with Callie.

Jack decided he'd faced enough ghosts from his past for one night. He took the stairs two at a time and headed straight for the front door. Stepping out on the porch, he took a deep, soul-cleansing breath. Leaning his elbows on the rail, he listened to the night sounds and stared out at the shadowy forms of the landscape.

So many reminders, so many pieces of his family's history—and dreams for the future—encompassed in this building, this place.

Did it all really belong to Lanny's widow now? Just because of some quirk of timing that had her married to his older brother for a few short hours before his death?

If a person really decided to press the matter, he could argue that you couldn't even call it married.

But it seemed mean-spirited to challenge her claim. After all, she'd come out here in good faith, pursuing her own dreams, and none of what had happened had been her fault.

It might be better for all concerned if he offered to buy out her claim on the farm. That way she could either purchase herself a place in town or head on back to where she came from with a nice little nest egg in hand.

As for the guardianship of Annabeth, Callie would come around on that once he talked to her again. Sure, he didn't know exactly how he was going to handle raising the youngsters on his own, but he'd find a way. After all, there was no arguing that it was his responsibility to take care of Simon and Emma, so it just made sense for him to take Annabeth as well.

How much extra work could one little girl be?

The crux of the matter kept coming down to the fact that he and the kids were blood kin. Even a woman as stubborn as Lanny's widow was proving herself to be couldn't deny that they belonged together.

Yes, that was the best way to go.

And hang it all, he still believed someone like her just didn't fit in here in Sweetgum, especially not all on her own. She'd be as out of place as a canary in a hen house.

Not that the woman lacked spirit. It had taken a lot of gumption for her to make it this far. And she certainly didn't let the thought of what others might think of that birthmark stand in her way. Yes, all in all, quite a spirited woman.

Too bad she was so all-fired muleheaded.

Jack pushed away from the porch rail and jammed his hands in his pockets.

He'd never met a woman like her. True, it had been a while since he'd spent much time in what his mother used to call "polite company," but he figured things hadn't changed all that much. Callie was…well…hang it all, he hadn't quite figured out what she was, besides being a thorn in his side. And just plain wrong about her rights in regard to Annabeth.

On the other hand, could he really say the kids would be better off with him than with her?

Rather than pursue that thought, he decided to turn in for the night.

Callie gently eased her armload of dirty breakfast dishes down on the counter next to the sink. She started rolling up her sleeves, then paused at the sound of a knock on the back door.

Mrs. Mayweather, who'd just placed a large kettle on the stove, glanced over her shoulder. "Callista, would you see who that is, please?"

Callie had a pretty good idea who was on the other side of

nabeth giggled. "They don't live in the pantry, silly."

"hey don't?"

Allie smiled at the teasing tone in Jack's voice. Perhaps
been wrong about his ability to relate to the children.
be she should just step back and let him—

The memory of his declaration that he wasn't "the praying
d" interrupted her move toward retreat and stiffened her
olve. It just plain didn't matter how charming he could be,
se children needed her in their lives, too.

But for now, she'd give him his share of time to create a
nnection with his nieces and nephew.

"They're animals, not food," Annabeth explained with ex-
ggerated patience. She began to tick them off on her fingers.
Cinnamon is my pony and Taffy is the big yellow cat who
ives in the barn and Pepper is our dog."

"Oh!" Jack did a good job of sounding surprised. "Well,
in that case, yes, I saw all three of them."

The child twirled a curl with one pudgy finger. "Do you
think they miss me?"

"I'm certain they do."

Emma set her elbows on the table next to Simon. "I have
a dog, too."

Jack turned his attention to his other niece. "Do you?"

She nodded her head. "He's a beagle and his name is
Cookie."

"Now, would he by any chance be that fine looking animal
I saw outside next to Mrs. Mayweather's carriage house?"

Emma beamed at the compliment. "Uh-huh. And I had a
bird, too. Mr. Peepers. But he…" Her lower lip began to
tremble.

Callie caught the panicked look on Jack's face and quickly
stepped in. "Emma, would you please bring me the empty
platter from the stove?"

the door, and she was certain Mrs. Mayweathe⟋ she dutifully wiped her hands on her borrow⟋ course."

As expected, she opened the door to find J⟋ there. He had a pail in one hand and a basket in⟋

"Ah, Jackson, there you are." Mrs. Maywea⟋ him in from behind Callie. "We saved you a bit of⟋

"Thanks. It sure does smell good." He lifted his⟋ "I brought some eggs and fresh milk for your larde⟋

Studying his easy smile and friendly manner,⟋ decided the man could be something of a charmer w⟋ set his mind to it.

Mrs. Mayweather obviously agreed. She beamed ap⟋ ingly as she held out her hands. "Wonderful. I'll take t⟋ and put them away. You go on to the sink and wash up."

She nodded to Callie as she passed. "Would you hand h⟋ a plate, please?"

Callie nodded and stepped past Jack, reaching into th⟋ cupboard. "Mrs. Mayweather brewed a pot of coffee. Would you like a cup?"

"Yes, thank you."

There was a formality about their interactions today, a sort of stiff truce. But at least it *was* a truce.

She watched him heap a pile of eggs and two biscuits onto his plate, then he took a seat at the long kitchen table. Simon was still picking at his own breakfast but the girls had finished theirs.

Annabeth immediately moved to Jack's side. "Did you see Cinnamon and Taffy and Pepper last night?" she asked before he'd even settled in.

"Cinnamon, Taffy and Pepper." Jack drawled the words as he smeared jam on his biscuit. "Some of my favorite flavors. But I'm afraid I didn't look in the pantry."

"Yes, ma'am."

Jack gave her a small nod and she felt a warm glow at this ever-so-slight sign of gratitude. Maybe he was finally beginning to see how she could help with the children. Perhaps they could work this whole matter out amicably after all.

A few moments later he carried his dishes to the sink. Then, without so much as a glance her way, he turned back to the children. "I plan to head back out to the farm to take care of some chores. Why don't you all come with me? Annabeth, you can visit with your animals. And Emma and Simon, you can take Cookie along and let him run as far and as long as he wants to."

Callie stiffened, the glow quickly evaporating. Was he actually planning to take the children and not her?

Annabeth clapped her hands in excitement. "Oh, yes! Do you think Mrs. Mayweather will let me bring some of her sugar cubes for Cinnamon?"

"We'll ask her," Jack answered. "But I'm sure it'll be all right."

"And Aunt Callie can come, too, can't she?"

Bless Annabeth's innocent little heart.

Jack cut her a quick glance, that stiff formality firmly back in place. "Yes, of course. That is, if she wants to?"

Was it her imagination, or did it sound as if he'd rather she declined the invitation?

She lifted her chin and smiled sweetly. "I need to make a stop at the telegraph office first, but I can't think of any place I'd rather be."

Chapter Eight

"Here we are."

Callie breathed a small sigh of relief, glad that she would finally be able to escape the confines of the buggy. The only men she'd been in such close proximity to before were her father and her sisters' husbands. Jack was a different sort of man altogether, and she wasn't exactly certain how to talk to him.

Not that he'd seemed to want to talk. The only conversation during the entire carriage ride had been among and with the children. The two adults had barely said three words to each other.

She certainly hoped the children hadn't picked up on the tension between her and Jack. They had enough to deal with at the moment without this added burden.

She leaned forward as Jack brought the carriage to a stop, forgetting her discomfort in her eagerness to view the homeplace Julia had written about in such loving detail over the years. The house, fronted by rosebushes and shaded on the left by a venerable oak, was as charming as she'd imagined it to be. An oversized swing hung from one end of the roomy front porch, and Callie could picture Julia sitting there with Annabeth beside her, reading stories or doing a bit of needlework.

And surrounding the place were acres and acres of open farmland, God's handiwork, uncluttered by people or crowded buildings. Callie wanted to hug herself for the pure joy and sense of freedom it gave her.

The carriage had barely stopped before Annabeth scrambled down. A gray dog, his coat sprinkled with black spots, bounded up to meet them. Tail-waggingly ecstatic to see a familiar face, he nearly knocked Annabeth over in his eagerness to lavish her with dog kisses.

Annabeth giggled as she knelt down and hugged the dog. "That tickles."

Cookie barked at the duo from the safety of the buggy.

"Stop that," Emma chided, scratching the animal's ears. "You know Pepper is just playing with Annabeth."

Annabeth stood up. "Aunt Callie, this is Pepper. Don't be afraid, he won't hurt you."

"My, but he certainly is an exuberant animal."

The girl wrinkled her brow. "Zu-ber-ent?"

"Ex-u-ber-ent. It means joyful, active in a playful sort of way."

Annabeth grinned proudly as she stood up. "Yes, Pepper is *very* zuberent. If you come to the barn I'll show you my pony Cinnamon. He's not as zuberent as Pepper, but you'll like him."

Callie hid a grin. Annabeth had obviously found a new favorite word. "You go on. I'll be along in a minute."

By this time Simon and Emma had climbed down as well. Pepper and Cookie took a moment to check each other out, then started vying for the youngsters' attention.

The children ran off toward the barn, the dogs at their

heels. Callie watched that beautiful sight until they disappeared around the corner. "It's wonderful to see them acting like the carefree children they're supposed to be. Bringing them out here was a good idea."

Jack merely nodded as he moved to help her down. Despite the tension between them, his touch was solicitous. There was protectiveness and assurance to be found there.

But as soon as her feet touched the ground he stepped back and gave her a challenging look, dispelling any notion she might have that his feelings had changed. "So, how much do you know about running a farm?"

His tone dripped skepticism.

She refused to let it throw her. "Your brother and I agreed that, besides caring for Annabeth, I would be responsible for the house and vegetable garden, and he would take care of the rest." She lifted her head. "It was always my intention, however, that with Leland's help I would learn more over time so I could be a proper helpmeet to him."

Jack nodded. "If you plan to live out here, there's definitely a whole lot more you'll need to learn. For one thing, there's the care of the animals. This place has two cows that'll need milking twice a day, a yearling and a young calf, a half dozen laying hens and a rooster, a mule and a horse—not to mention Annabeth's pony, the dog and at least one barn cat."

He tilted his hat back. "Then there's the haying, the constant maintenance, like fence mending and upkeep of the house and yard. And how do you feel about mucking out the barn and cleaning out the chicken coop?" He raised a brow. "Of course, if you had the means, I guess you could always hire someone to help out."

She lifted her chin, quite aware that he was trying to scare her away. Well, she was made of sterner stuff than that, as he'd soon find out. "Or I could just sell the whole place," she said giving him a challenging look of her own, "lock, stock and barrel." She tapped her chin with one finger. "With the proceeds I'm certain I could buy a nice little house in town for me and the children. Something cozier, with no animals and less upkeep."

It had been an idle threat, of course. She had no intention of selling the farm. Quite the contrary. She planned to hold on to this little parcel of solitude for all she was worth.

But to her surprise, he gave an approving nod. "Just what I was thinking. Rather than fight over who has the stronger claim, I think it would be better for all of us if I just bought it from you." He waved a hand. "As you said, lock, stock and barrel. I'm sure we can reach an agreement over a fair price."

Callie frowned. Surely he knew she hadn't been serious.

"Besides," he continued, "this is more than a farm. It's a Tyler family legacy. My granddad and dad built this place with their own hands. I don't intend to stand by and see it fall into some stranger's hands."

Did that include her? "Mr. Tyler, I'm very sorry if I gave you the wrong impression just now. I'm embarrassed to admit that I said what I did in a fit of pique." Which should teach her to guard her tongue more closely. "Selling this place is not an option I'd seriously consider."

She tugged her bonnet forward. "I'll admit I don't know anything about running a farm—*yet*. But I'm not afraid of hard work, and I consider myself very teachable."

He faced her head-on. "You're right. You *don't* know anything about running a place like this." He took hold of both her hands and turned them palms up.

Her pulse jumped. When was the last time anyone, outside of her family, had held her hands so deliberately?

She couldn't remember.

And it certainly hadn't been with hands as large and calloused as these. Hands that seemed to contain a tightly leashed power and an ability to protect.

She gave her head a mental shake, trying to rid herself of the fanciful thoughts. Whatever his intentions, there was no affection in his touch, just a sense of purpose and tried patience.

But for a heartbeat, as her gaze locked on his, she saw his resolve falter, saw his expression shift into something she couldn't read. Had he felt that same off-balance feeling that she had?

Then the moment passed and his expression hardened again. "Look at these hands." His tone said clearly that he didn't approve of what he saw. "Not a callous in sight. These are *not* the hands of a person used to hard work."

Callie snatched her hands back, trying to ignore the unexpected feelings his touch had evoked. "I may not have callouses, Mr. Tyler, but that doesn't mean I'm a stranger to work." She clasped her still-tingling hands tightly in front of her, and drew herself up, both physically and mentally. "I ran my father's household for ten years and I pride myself on the very high standards I maintained in doing so. I have every intention of staying here and making a go of this."

She couldn't bear to face returning to what she'd left behind in Ohio. And moving into a town full of strangers, even a town as small as Sweetgum, didn't sound much more appealing.

No, she'd been looking forward to the freedom the open expanses and relative privacy of farm life could afford her. She wasn't about to trade it away without a very good reason.

He dusted his hat against his leg. "Then it seems this is another topic we're at odds over."

Callie managed to hold her shoulders back, though the temptation to slump was strong. "Mr. Tyler, I truly don't want to fight you over any of this." How could she get through to him? If only he was the kind of man his brother had been—solid, caring, patient. Julia had used those words and more to describe Leland. "There must be some way we can make things work to everyone's benefit."

"You're the one who's been doing all the praying. You get any answers?"

Callie winced at his flippant attitude. "Surely you know that God's timing is not always our own," she said calmly. "His answer will come if we wait on it."

The reappearance of the children forestalled whatever response he might have made.

Annabeth skipped up to them and latched on to Callie's hand. "Cinnamon was very happy to see me."

"I'm sure she's missed you this past week."

"And Clover's new calf has really gotten big. Simon says we should name him Buster."

"That sounds like a fine name for a growing calf." Callie smiled at the bubbly chatter coming from the little girl. "How would you like to show me the inside of your house?"

"Okay." She tugged on Callie's hand. "Just follow me."

"Mind if I tag along?"

Callie noted the determined set to Jack's jaw. Was he afraid she'd try to stake her claim while he wasn't looking?

As the three strolled toward the house, Emma joined them. Simon, however, chose to stay outside and play with the dogs.

Callie felt at home as soon as she stepped across the threshold. Everywhere she looked she saw the stamp of Julia's presence. Everyday things her friend had written about were all around her, as if a favorite storybook had sprung to life.

While the girls continued down the hall, Callie stepped inside the front parlor. She was immediately drawn to the large, leather-bound Bible that sat in a place of honor on a table next to the window. Opening it, she found a listing of the Tyler family tree going back to Jack's great-great-grand-parents. She remembered Julia writing to tell her what a proud moment it had been for her when Leland added her name to the lineage chart as his wife, and later, how special it had been for them to add Annabeth's name together.

Jack peered over her shoulder. "Thinking of adding your name?" he asked dryly.

"No, of course not." The thought hadn't even entered her mind. Her short-lived marriage to Leland would have absolutely no impact on the Tyler lineage. It didn't deserve so much as a footnote.

She turned and realized he was no longer focused on her.

Instead, he studied the open Bible, a tight expression on his face. "I guess I should update the entries on Nell and Lanny."

It took Callie a second to realize he was referring to notating the date of their deaths.

She placed a hand on his arm. "There'll be time enough to take care of that later."

He stared at her hand, then gave a quick nod and turned away. "Come on," he said, his tone once again easy. "The kitchen's this way."

But before Callie had a chance to do more than glance around, Annabeth reappeared at her side and tugged her impatiently from the kitchen to the next room. "This way. I want to show you the new room Daddy built."

Callie smiled as she entered the washroom. "Julia was so proud of this. She wrote to me when they were building it."

"Of course she did."

Callie ignored his dry tone. "She asked me for suggestions, but Lanny pretty much designed and built the whole thing himself. She was very proud of him, and of this." Callie ran a hand along the clothes wringer. "It made life a lot easier on her, especially once she…well, what I mean is, during those last few months."

But Annabeth, as impatient as ever, didn't let them linger long in this room, either. "Let's go see my room."

As soon the child was certain she had their attention, she darted ahead of them up the stairs.

"Here it is." Annabeth opened the door to the first room on the left and made a beeline for her bed. She scrambled up on the mattress and hugged the doll sitting there. "Hello, Tizzy. Did you miss me?"

Callie's smile faded when she saw the way Emma looked at the doll with longing, the way her eyes ran over the other items in the room, pausing to study each of her younger cousin's possessions with an almost bittersweet hunger.

Callie felt as if a hand had reached inside her chest and was squeezing her heart. That Emma and Simon had lost both their parents at once was an unthinkable tragedy. To have also lost every jot and tittle of their former life, including mementos of those dear loved ones—it added a poignancy that absolutely broke one's heart.

All they had left from their old life was each other.

And God's love.

Callie's arms ached to gather Emma up and hug the child for all she was worth. But that would serve no purpose right now, other than drawing attention to the child's heartache.

"Ready to see the rest of the rooms up here?" Jack seemed impatient to move on.

Callie nodded, glad for the distraction.

Keeping a tight hold on her doll, Annabeth skipped ahead of them to the room across the hall.

"This used to be my daddy's room when he was a little

boy," she said as Jack opened the door. "And you, too, Uncle Jack, wasn't it?"

"That's right, Little Bit."

Callie tried to picture Jack as young boy, spending time in here with his older brother. Perhaps this was what had taught Leland that deep patience Julia always spoke of.

Annabeth bounced onto the closest bed. "Daddy was getting it ready for you, Aunt Callie. See the pretty vase and lamp he set here?" She fiddled with her doll's dress, very carefully not looking up. "That's when he thought you were going to be my mommy instead of my aunt."

"He did a very nice job." Callie tried to ignore the heat creeping into her cheeks. Jack had no doubt suspected that the marriage between her and Leland was supposed to be a platonic one. But having this stark evidence blatantly revealed was mortifying. And somehow, having it revealed to Jack himself made it more so.

To his credit, Jack gave no clue that he noticed anything out of the ordinary. And he didn't linger in this room, either. With only a cursory look around, he herded them down the hall.

"This was Mommy's workroom," Annabeth explained before Jack had so much as opened the door.

As soon as Callie stepped inside and saw the nearly finished baby quilt, she stopped in her tracks. It was such a painful, unexpected reminder of her friend's death. Julia had slipped and fallen just one month before the baby was to be born. The ensuing early labor had killed both her and the baby.

"Momma was making this for my new baby brother or sister." Annabeth was standing beside her.

Callie rested a hand on the child's shoulder. "Yes, I know." She stepped forward and fingered the lovely bit of piecework.

"I tell you what, sweetheart. Why don't we take this beautiful quilt and put it somewhere safe? One day, when you're old enough, perhaps you can finish it yourself. Would you like that?"

Annabeth nodded vigorously.

Callie decided the girls—not to mention she herself—needed something more cheerful to focus on. She looked around the room seeking inspiration and found it hanging among the rafters.

Jack drifted toward the window, listening to Callie and the girls chatter. They seemed to be making a game out of identifying all the varieties of flowers and herbs hanging from the ceiling.

Callie was probably trying to lighten the mood a bit. He'd sensed the tension in her earlier. Was it because she was picturing the life she would have had here had Lanny not died? A life that was lost to her now?

Unbidden, the memory of that moment when he'd taken hold of her hands returned. He had felt the pulse jump in her wrist, had suddenly become aware of her as feminine, small and vulnerable, yet full of warmth and a woman's strength. It had taken a full measure of resolve to push that unwelcome awareness aside and move forward with the point he'd wanted to make.

A pair of girlish giggles from across the room broke into his thoughts. Callie's doing, no doubt. Jack rubbed his chin as he stared unseeing out the window.

How was it she always knew the right thing to say and do with the kids? Maybe Lanny hadn't been so crazy after all in choosing her to be Annabeth's stepmother. The woman sure seemed to have a knack for the job.

And apparently that's all Lanny had been looking for—

more of a glorified nanny than a wife. Had sticking her down the hall in the guestroom been her idea or his?

Not that it was any of his business. Or that it even mattered.

Still, he'd give a pretty penny to know whether her embarrassment back there had been due to his finding out about the arrangement or from being faced with the proof of Lanny's expectations.

The muffled sound of Simon's voice caught his attention.

He opened the window, but before he could call out he saw what had caught the boy's notice—a wagon leading a cloud of dust down the road was headed their way.

"Somebody's coming," Jack said.

He heard Callie step up behind him. "Do you think they're coming here?"

"Only one way to find out." He turned to the girls. "Looks like we might have visitors. What say we head outside to see who it is?"

Chapter Nine

The girls clattered down the stairs while he and Callie followed at a more sedate pace. As they stepped onto the porch, Jack sensed her nervousness. For the second time in as many minutes she tugged that ever-present bonnet forward. That telling betrayal of self-consciousness always surprised him. She certainly didn't seem to lack gumption when it came to anything else.

"Who is it?" she asked, interrupting his train of thought.

He shaded his eyes, following her gaze to the approaching wagon. "It looks like Virgil and Ida Lee with their kids. You met Virgil yesterday when the stage arrived. He's been taking care of this place since Lanny died." Jack gave her a meaningful look. "These folks aren't just good friends, they're also the closest neighbors to this place."

"I know."

Now how would she know something like that?

She must have read the question in his expression. "I told you, Julia's letters were like chapters in a book, and the people of Sweetgum were the main characters."

That comment set Jack back on his heels. If Julia had been

so all-fired gabby, what had she written about *him* in those letters over the years? More to the point, did Callie know about that botched proposal?

He pushed that uncomfortable thought aside as the wagon pulled to a stop. "Hi, Virgil, Ida Lee."

Virgil acknowledged the greeting with a nod. "Sorry if we're intruding. As soon as Ida Lee saw your carriage go by she insisted we head out here to welcome you home, proper-like." He gave Jack a just-between-us-men grin. "Not to mention she's been dying to meet our visitor ever since I mentioned her arrival."

Ida Lee didn't seem at all put out by her husband's words. "Just wanted to extend a neighborly welcome," she said calmly.

Four kids scrambled down from the back of the wagon. Ida Lee made shooing motions. "You all go along and play with the other kids. Just stay out of the house."

Jack offered his hand to help Ida Lee down.

"Hi-dee, Jack." Her expression softened. "I'm right sorry about Lanny and Nell. They were good people."

She patted his hand then smiled that broad, toothy smile he remembered from their childhood. "It's been much too long since we saw you. Now that you're back, I hope you plan to stick around for a while."

He accepted her quick hug. "I'm not figuring to go anywhere for the time being."

"Good." She smoothed her skirts and turned to Callie. "And you must be Julia's Callie. It's good to finally meet you. Julia used to go on about what a sweet friend you were. I'm sorry you got such a sorrowful introduction to Sweetgum."

Ida Lee reached for Callie's hand and Jack was hit again with the memory of how Callie's touch had made him feel.

Callie was trying to reconcile the mental image she'd

formed of Ida Lee from Julia's letters with the reality standing here in front of her. She'd never realized before that Julia's descriptions had actually focused more on people's character and manner than their physical attributes.

Which was probably why folks around here didn't know anything about her birthmark.

And which was also why she hadn't realized Ida Lee was such a big-boned, sturdy-looking woman. The kind you could picture handling farm chores with ease.

But Ida Lee's smile, as big and hearty as the woman herself, was infectious.

"Thank you." Callie found it easy to respond to her warmth. "I apologize for not having any refreshments to offer you."

Ida Lee waved a hand, flopping it from the wrist. "Oh, land's sake, girl, we didn't come here to put you to any trouble." She reached under the buggy seat and lifted out a covered basket. "In fact, I brought you one of my maple pecan pies."

"How very kind."

There was nothing dainty about Ida Lee's laugh. "Truth be told, it's a way to repay you for all the prying I'm about to do." She turned to her husband. "You menfolk go off now and take care of the horse and wagon while Callie and I have us a nice little chat."

Jack and Virgil didn't need to be told twice.

Callie nodded toward the house. "Why don't we get out of the sun?"

"Now that sounds like a mighty fine idea." Ida Lee chattered on about the heat until they reached the porch. Then she plopped down on the rocking chair.

Callie took a seat on the swing.

"Imagine that, Julia's friend Callie right here in Sweetgum. And you're Lanny's widow to boot. If that don't beat all." She shook her head in wonder. "The Lord does work in mysterious ways."

"That he does." Callie glanced over to where the children were engaged in a boisterous game of tag.

"Now don't you go worrying about the kids. The big ones'll keep an eye on the little ones. They'll be just fine." She loosened the strings of her bonnet, letting it hang loose against her nape. Then she picked up a leaf-shaped fan and waved it in front of her face. "Goodness, but it's a scorcher today." She gave Callie a friendly smile. "We don't hold much to suffering for the sake of appearances hereabouts. No point sweltering underneath that bonnet of yours now that we're out of the sun."

Callie weighed what she knew about Ida Lee, both from Julia's letters and from her few minutes of personal acquaintance. "How much did Julia tell you about me?" she asked carefully.

Ida Lee paused in her fanning. "Not a whole lot. I mean, we all knew she had a friend she left behind when she moved out this way. 'The sister of my heart,' she used to call you. But she never did go into any specifics."

"So she never mentioned my birthmark?"

"Birthmark?"

Callie loosened her bonnet and let it fall back just as Ida Lee had done. Out of habit she had sat on the woman's left side, so she had to turn her face for Ida Lee to get the full effect.

The woman winced. "Oh, my."

"I'm sorry." Callie reached for her bonnet. "I'll cover it."

Ida Lee resumed her fanning. "Don't be a ninny. It's too hot for that and you sure don't have to hide your face on my account. Just takes some getting used to, is all."

Callie smiled as some of the tension eased from her spine. The woman's words might be less than genteel, but there was no doubting her sincerity. "Thank you."

"Oh, fiddlesticks, girl. No need to thank me for something like that."

In spite of Ida Lee's assurances, Callie tucked her hair back under the bonnet but let the ribbons hang loose. She didn't want to do anything to make the children feel awkward or nervous if they should join them.

To her relief, Ida Lee let the subject drop. Instead, she leaned forward conspiratorially. "So, let's get down to talking. Having you show up in Sweetgum is the most interesting happening since goodness-knows-when. What do you plan to do now?"

Callie wished she had the answer to that question. "I married Mr. Tyler, Mr. *Leland* Tyler, that is—" why did she feel the need to clarify this? Callie hurried on "—because he wanted me to help raise Annabeth. If anything, she needs me even more now."

Ida Lee frowned. "You're not thinking of taking that child back to Ohio with you, now are you?"

"Oh, no. This is her home." Callie raised her chin. "And I plan to make it my home, too. In fact, I'd also like to play a part in Simon and Emma's lives if I can."

Ida Lee nodded. "All children need a mother's touch. Lanny knew that. And I think Nell and Jed would be grateful to you as well."

Callie waved a hand. "Yes, but it's more than just mothering. These children also need someone to look after their spiritual upbringing."

The rocker halted. Ida Lee opened her mouth as if to speak, but said nothing. Finally she set the rocker in motion again. "What does Jack have to say about that?"

Callie shifted in her seat, searching for a diplomatic response. "Mr. Tyler and I are still trying to work out how to deal with the situation."

"He's wanting to take charge of it all, isn't he?"

"His concern is understandable." Callie felt oddly defensive of Jack's stand. "I mean, not only am I a stranger, but I have no knowledge of the workings of a farm." She fiddled with the edge of her bonnet. "Even if I do have a claim to the place."

"Why, that's right," Ida Lee gave a bark of laughter. "I guess this place is rightly yours now. Don't that beat all. I reckon Jack is fit to be tied. He never could abide having to share what he thought was rightfully his." She gave Callie a probing look. "He's fighting you over who gets those three young'uns, isn't he?"

"He is their uncle, after all. It's only natural that he'd want to be a part of their lives."

"No need to mince words around me. Jack Tyler no more knows how to care for three kids on his own than you can run this farm. He's just too ornery and prideful to admit it."

"I think perhaps you're being a bit harsh."

Ida Lee shrugged. "Maybe you're right. Lanny and Nell's deaths must have hit him hard." She leaned forward and patted Callie's knee. "I know he stayed away all this time, but deep down he's a family man. Always has been, even if he won't admit it, even to himself. And right now, those young'uns are the only real family he has left."

The words struck a chord with Callie. She couldn't deny the man his right to be close to his family. But she couldn't abandon those children if God had truly sent her here to minister to them.

There had to be a way to make this work. *Lord, please help me find the path You want me to follow in this matter.*

She looked up to find Ida Lee staring at her. "I wish I knew the answer." She tucked a few more stray hairs under her bonnet. "I've been praying about it ever since I found out about Leland."

Ida Lee nodded approval. "Then you're on the right track. I'll add my own prayers. The right answer will come."

"So, how are you and the widow getting along?"

Jack grimaced. "She's one stubborn woman. I can't believe this is the same gal Julia spoke of with such admiration. The two are nothing alike."

"It's not being alike that makes people friends. Look at me and you."

Jack plucked a stem of grass and slid it between a thumb and forefinger. "She's trying to stake a claim on the farm. Not even willing to let me buy her out."

Virgil gave Jack a puzzled look. "I'm surprised you let that bother you so much. Lanny was always the one with farming in his blood, not you."

One more thing he'd never be as good at as his brother.

Virgil rubbed his chin. "I figured you'd be heading back off to your work with the railroad as soon as you settled matters here."

Not a far cry from the truth. At least that had been the plan when he first headed back to Sweetgum.

"I'll admit the idea of staying put and working a farm isn't something I'm looking forward to. But I'm the last of the Tylers, except for them kids. Taking care of this place and those three young'uns is my responsibility, and it ain't one I intend to shirk."

"You aiming to handle the farm and the kids all on your own?"

Jack heard the doubt in his friend's voice, but refused to

admit he shared it. "Don't see why not. Other men have done it. And Simon's old enough to help."

"Sure, it's been done." Virgil gave him a hard look. "But it ain't easy, even if you've had some practice. Why, even Lanny figured he needed help raising that little girl of his."

Virgil raised a hand before Jack could do more than stiffen. "I know you don't like being compared to Lanny, but I'm just saying it ain't as easy a job as you seem to think."

Jack flicked the blade of grass away. "I didn't say I thought it would be easy. But that's my worry. And I'm sure I'll get the widow to come around. So that'll be one less person for me to look out for."

He rested his arms on the paddock fence and stared off toward the far tree line.

"So, tell me about the fire."

Virgil hesitated, then joined Jack at the fence rail. "Nell hurt her ankle two days before," he said quietly. "Jed naturally insisted she stay in bed and let him run the café on his own. But you know Nell. She wasn't going to stand that for too long."

Jack knew Nell, all right. She'd been the sweetest person he ever knew. But when she'd set her mind to something, there'd been no stopping her.

"Anyway," Virgil continued, "on that Tuesday, she insisted on hobbling downstairs to help Jed cook for their lunch crowd. Lanny showed up after most of the customers had cleared out, and he helped Jed convince Nell that they ought to close up for the afternoon. Mr. Dobson from over at the mercantile stopped in about then to buy one of Nell's pies. According to him, Lanny told Nell he had some big news to share but he wasn't going to tell them anything until she was settled upstairs in her rocking chair."

Big news, huh? Well, that one was easy to figure out. Jack

found his gaze wandering back to where Callie sat chatting with Ida Lee. Nell would have liked her, he was sure of it. In some ways, they were a lot alike.

"They sent Mr. Dobson on his way and closed up," Virgil said. "It was probably thirty minutes later when the fire started."

Virgil cut Jack an apologetic look. "'Fraid we couldn't figure out what started the thing. But best we can tell, it started in the café kitchen downstairs."

Jack clenched his jaw, determined to hear Virgil's story without interrupting.

"They probably didn't realize anything was wrong until it was almost too late." He teased a splinter from the fence rail. "We found Jed and Nell near the foot of the stairs, pinned down by a beam. Jed still had his arm around her." Virgil swallowed hard. "Lanny was there, too. Looked like he was trying to free them before he was overcome himself." Virgil straightened. "I just thank God the young'uns were down at the livery when it happened."

"I can't see as how God deserves much gratitude for any of what happened."

Virgil leaned forward, his brow furrowed. "Look, Jack, I know you're upset, and no one could blame you for that. But you need to keep in mind that they're all in a better place now." He clamped a hand on Jack's shoulder. "None of them would want to hear you talking like that."

Jack pushed away from the fence, ready to change the subject. "Thanks again for keeping this place going for me the last few days. If there's anything I can do—"

Virgil shook his head, still studying Jack with that sober expression. "Ain't no need for thanks. Lanny helped me out many a time and I'm glad I could do something to return the favor, though it's little enough, considering…"

Jack nodded, then forced a smile for Virgil's sake. "While you're still feeling so neighborly, come over to the barn and let me know what you think about this yearling."

Chapter Ten

At supper that evening, the children regaled Mrs. Mayweather with their adventures of the day. Callie was pleased to see they had truly enjoyed themselves. Even Simon seemed more animated.

"And Aunt Callie said I could move back to my house soon," Annabeth said toward the end of the meal. She looked around the table. "Does that mean all of us?"

Callie ignored the look Jack sent her way as she took a sip from her glass.

Mrs. Mayweather shook her head. "If you were including me, I thank you for the kind invitation, but I shall have to decline. I have my own house and I happen to like it very well here."

"But you don't have other houses, do you, Aunt Callie and Uncle Jack?"

Callie set her glass down. "Why, no, but—"

"Good. Then you can come live with us. Like a family."

"They aren't really our parents, you know," Simon said sullenly. Seemed his change of temperament had only been temporary.

"No, we aren't," Jack said calmly. "No one can ever replace your mother and father. But I'm your uncle and I'd like to try to take care of you if you'll let me."

"As would I," Callie chimed in.

"But we *are* going to all live together, aren't we?" Emma's voice was a timid counterpoint to Annabeth's enthusiasm and Simon's anger.

The girl was obviously looking for some kind of reassurance that her life would regain a sense of normalcy. And she wasn't the only one. Annabeth looked from Jack to Callie with troubled eyes.

Callie wanted to give all three of them the reassurance they needed. But what Emma was asking for was impossible. How could she explain that it would be highly improper for both her and Jack to live under the same roof?

Callie glanced Jack's way but found no help there. She took a deep breath. "Your Uncle Jack and I haven't quite worked everything out—"

Mrs. Mayweather stood, interrupting Callie's floundering attempt to answer Emma's question. "It sounds as if you children have had a full day. Why don't you go on and get ready for bed. The grown-ups will take care of the meal clean-up tonight."

"Yes, ma'am." The children excused themselves and scampered out of the room as if afraid she would change her mind.

Callie pushed her chair back, concerned about the impression their discussion had made on the children. "Perhaps I should go with them."

Mrs. Mayweather stopped her with a look. "They'll be fine. You're needed down here." She turned to Jack. "You may help Callista clear the table while I prepare the wash water in the kitchen."

"Yes, ma'am."

Even Jack didn't argue when she used that schoolmarm tone.

As they worked at clearing the table, Emma's last question lay between them like a sleeping bear—something to tiptoe around and avoid poking or prodding at all costs.

As usual, Callie couldn't stand the silence. Hugging a large serving bowl to her chest she managed to catch Jack's gaze. "Perhaps I should help Mrs. Mayweather while you finish in here." He hadn't so much as completed his nod before she fled to the kitchen.

Mrs. Mayweather raised a brow at her precipitous entrance, but merely asked her to fill the kettle and set it on the stove.

Callie studiously kept her gaze focused on the water flowing into the kettle as Jack, his arms loaded with dishes, made a more sedate entrance a few moments later.

"Place those over there with the others." Mrs. Mayweather wiped her hands on her apron as she turned to Callie. "Would you mind washing tonight?"

Callie set the kettle on the stove. "Not at all."

"And Jackson, you may dry."

As the two took their assigned posts, Mrs. Mayweather crossed her arms and watched them with a prim expression. "I want to know what your intentions are."

Callie glanced sideways, watching as Jack quirked a brow, a humorous gleam lighting his eye. "Intentions? Why, Mrs. Mayweather, I had no idea you had such tender feelings for me."

"Don't be impertinent, Jackson."

Was there a hint of a smile lurking in the reprimand?

"I mean," she said sternly, "what do the two of you have in mind for the children's future. They've been hurt quite enough already. I won't allow you to trifle with their feelings while you circle around each other like a pair of dogs fighting over a bone."

Jack's demeanor closed off immediately. "We still haven't worked that out yet."

Mrs. Mayweather nodded. "I take it you both feel you have a claim to Annabeth, and to the family farm."

"As Leland's widow—"

"As a Tyler, I have—"

The school teacher gave an inelegant "Harrumph!" Jack and Callie fell silent. "I understand a great deal has happened to you in a short period of time," Mrs. Mayweather continued, "but you cannot put the children in the middle of this tug-of-war. A few more days like today and those three will be forming attachments and making assumptions. In fact, unless I'm mistaken, they've already started."

Callie knew she was right. It wasn't fair to the children. But no matter how much she prayed and pondered, the solution eluded her.

"I've enjoyed having them spend time with me, but they need a more permanent home, a sense of normalcy and family in their lives again. So let's start with you, Callista."

Callie braced herself and turned.

"I know you already feel something for the children," the schoolteacher began. "I watched you put them to bed last night, sing them lullabies, tuck them in. And I could tell by the way you helped with their prayers that you are a God-fearing woman. That's an important quality for someone who's going to take on the care of young children."

"Thank you." Callie couldn't resist a quick glance Jack's way.

His glower was back and the plate he held was getting an extra vigorous rubbing.

"You talk to them without talking down to them," Mrs.

Mayweather continued. "Children notice and respond to such things. You are a natural mother figure, and those children need a mother figure in their lives."

A tingle of pride warmed Callie. It was nice to have her actions recognized and appreciated.

Then Mrs. Mayweather straightened and the look on her face erased all trace of the smugness Callie had felt a moment earlier.

"On the other hand, besides having no idea how to run a farm, you have no claim on Simon and Emma. This tragedy has formed a bond among those children, a bond that runs deeper than that of most natural-born siblings. It would be a terrible blow to them if you split them up now."

She adjusted her shirtwaist. "Then there is the matter of the markings on your face."

To Callie's surprise, almost before she herself could react, Jack spun around and focused his glower on Mrs. Mayweather.

Jack couldn't believe he'd heard right, especially not from Alberta Mayweather. The woman had never been one to judge others by their appearance.

But he'd barely opened his mouth to protest when she held up a hand.

"Come now, Jackson, we must face facts, even unpleasant ones. While I do not feel Callista's birthmark lessens her suitability, there are more narrow-minded folk who may hold it against her."

"She's right." Callie's tone was flat and matter-of-fact. "Even the children have some reservations about seeing me without my bonnet."

"Only because you took them by surprise," Jack argued. "They'll get used to it."

He caught Callie's startled look and pulled himself up short. She sure didn't need to be reading anything special in his defense of her. He was simply being fair-minded, that's all.

"Then we have you, Jackson," Mrs. Mayweather said as she shifted her focus to him. "I know family is important to you. But more to the point is knowing how important family is to those children, especially right now. You are their uncle, the only tangible connection to their parents they have left, *and* you have a claim of sorts to all three of them. Also, unlike Callista, you are perfectly capable of running the farm yourself."

Jack nodded in agreement. About time somebody saw things his way.

"However, while I know your love for these children will grow, I don't think you are as comfortable in the role of parent as Callista is. Not to mention how awkward it might be for you to try to raise two young girls alone." She gave him a direct look. "I have always believed it is more difficult for a man to raise daughters than it is for a woman to raise sons."

That comment hit home, but Jack refused to admit it. "That's not necessarily true for all men."

She raised a brow, then moved on. "Even so, I don't believe you can manage the farm and properly care for the children on your own."

He didn't plan to. "I'm sure there's someone here in town who'd be willing to take on the job of housekeeper."

Callie stiffened. "Those children need a mother, not a housekeeper."

"That's a matter of opinion."

"Putting that and everything else aside," Mrs. Mayweather said firmly, "we still have the matter of your wanderlust, Jackson. Can you honestly tell me that after a few months back here you won't feel any inclination to leave again?"

Jack resisted the urge to squirm. To be honest, he didn't know how he would handle setting down roots, or even if he could.

No point in announcing it to the world, though. "Despite what I may or may not want, I'll honor my responsibility to Lanny and Nell's children."

"I wouldn't expect anything less. But if your heart is not in it, if your desire is to be somewhere else, the children will sense it. And what they desperately need right now is to be with someone who will make them feel wanted and cherished."

Not liking the turn this was taking, Jack took the offensive. "It sounds like you've given this quite a bit of thought. Do you have a solution to offer?"

She met his gaze head on. "I do."

That set Jack back on his heels. It wasn't the response he'd expected.

"And what might that be?" Jack prompted.

Mrs. Mayweather folded her hands in front of her with a self-satisfied air. "Isn't it obvious? I believe you should consider making the same decision Leland did, Jack. For the good of the children, of course."

Chapter Eleven

It took a moment for the meaning to sink in, but when it did, Jack nearly dropped the dish he was drying.

"What?!"

Callie looked just as stunned as Jack felt. "You can't mean—"

The schoolteacher raised hand to halt their outbursts. "Far be it from me to dictate what you should do."

Hah! That was *exactly* what she was trying to do.

"Only the two of you can decide on the best course of action." She gave them both a stern look. "And by that I mean the best course for the children."

The woman had obviously lost her senses. Jack tried to take back control of the conversation. "What seems best for the children today is not necessarily the right thing to do in the long run. I think this decision requires an objective, analytical perspective."

"I agree."

Before Jack had time to feel any sense of victory, however, she continued. "And if you consider this objectively, I don't see why either of you should have any serious

objections. Marriage to each other seems the ideal solution."

Jack heard what sounded suspiciously like choking coming from Callie's direction, a reaction she tried to cover by clearing her throat.

"Callista, unless he has changed significantly since leaving Sweetgum, Jackson is a hardworking, forthright fellow, every bit as fine a man as his brother. Seeing his determination to do his duty by the children should assure you of that."

Nice of her to give him that small shred of praise. She'd actually put him on even footing with Lanny.

"In fact," Mrs. Mayweather continued, "this proposal is not so different from what you and Leland agreed to."

"I'm sorry, but I believe it is." Callie's voice was respectful but firm.

Not that he didn't agree with her, but why did she have such a problem with this proposition? Did she think he wouldn't be as good a husband as Lanny?

"How so?" Mrs. Mayweather asked the question for him. "If I recall correctly the bargain was struck for the purposes of providing Annabeth with a mother. That need still exists, only in triplicate."

"True." Callie tugged on her bonnet. "But this situation is different in a number of ways. For one, Leland *wanted* to marry me. He wasn't begrudging, much less outright resistant. For another, though we never met, I believe I knew him well and, more importantly, he knew me. We felt we'd get along comfortably together." She paused and glanced at Jack as if uncertain whether or not to continue.

She had a point there. Getting along "comfortably together" was not something he could see the two of them doing.

"Is there something else?" Mrs. Mayweather prompted.

"Please," Jack said dryly, "don't feel the need to spare my feelings."

She tilted her chin up. "Very well. Since we are being frank, my impression of Leland, based on Julia's letters and my own recent correspondence with him, was that he was a deep-rooted family man and one who had a close walk with the Lord. Those are two qualities I believe to be very important."

"And you don't feel the same is true of Jackson?"

Callie shifted uncomfortably. "He admits he's in no hurry to set down roots. As for the other, well, I won't claim to be qualified to judge another's relationship with God. I just don't know."

Jack's jaw clenched. How self-righteous! Did she think that his faith was weak or false just because he didn't spend time praying every day the way Lanny apparently did? So what if he didn't feel the need to bother God every time he needed something?

He believed in God, all right. He just knew better than to count on him to take care of things in his life. He'd made that mistake before and paid for it with outright rejection and shredded pride.

Mrs. Mayweather lifted a brow as she turned to him. "Jackson, do you have anything to say to that?"

What he *wanted* to say was more appropriate for a railroad camp than ladies' ears. But Jack gritted his teeth, tempered his thoughts and chose his words carefully. "The widow is quite right. She's not qualified to judge the depths of my faith or lack thereof. It's a personal matter between me and God, and one not open to debate or discussion."

Her face reddened slightly and she gave him an apologetic look. "You're right, Mr. Tyler. Forgive my presumption." She leaned forward. "It's just that I feel very deeply that it's im-

portant for parents to set the proper example and direction in spiritual matters for their children."

Mrs. Mayweather nodded. "Very true." She turned back to Jack. "Well, what about you? For all your posturing and blustering about being able to take care of everything yourself, you know quite well you are not able to raise those children on your own. And Callista not only has the right qualifications, she's agreed to do this very thing once already."

She paused and gave him a considering look. "Unless… Your affections are not already otherwise engaged, are they?"

Jack cleared his throat. "No, but—"

"We already know Callista was Julia's trusted friend and Leland's choice for his second wife. That gives us a firm basis to believe she'll make a good wife and mother. So surely you don't object to her on those grounds."

"As someone has already pointed out," Jack said, cutting a hard glance Callie's way, "I'm a very different man than my brother, so his choice is not necessarily a good indicator of my own preferences."

Mrs. Mayweather waved away his objection. "Even so, a marriage between you two would solve all of the problems. Callista, you could take care of the children and the house, and Jackson, you could provide for them and take care of the farm. The children would have both a mother and a father to provide the guidance they'll need."

Jack and Callie avoided looking at each other.

"And if you do feel the need to return to your job again, you can do so knowing the children are in good hands, Jackson. Really, this does seem to settle matters nicely for everyone concerned."

Jack's hands balled into tight fists. The woman had definitely overstepped her bounds.

"However, as I said, this is merely a suggestion. You are

free to pursue another course of action if you wish. But you need to decide quickly, for the sake of the children. Now, I'll go check on them while you two discuss your options."

Once she'd left the room, Callie stood there, acutely aware of Jack standing beside her, mechanically handling the dishes, the minutes drawing out between them in brittle silence.

Marry this man! How could Mrs. Mayweather expect her to seriously contemplate such a step? Did the woman think she'd be willing to marry just anyone who seemed in need of a housekeeper and nanny?

Callie remembered her first impression of Jack back on the stagecoach—a ruggedly handsome, dangerous sort of man. Not at all the type of fellow to be comfortable setting down roots and nurturing a family. And not at all the type of fellow who'd be looking for the likes of her in a wife if he did.

His aversion to the whole idea of marrying her, in fact, had been immediately obvious. No, Mrs. Mayweather had been wrong—this wasn't the answer.

Actually, she'd been right about one thing. They couldn't keep going the way they were.

Finally, as she handed him a saucer to dry, Callie broke the silence. "She's right, you know."

His brow raised.

"Not about the marriage thing." Goodness, but this was awkward. She tried to ignore the heat rising in her cheeks and push on. "But about the need for us to reach a decision."

Callie reached for the next dish on the stack. "I agree with her that it's not fair to keep the children in limbo. Annabeth doesn't understand why she can't go back to her own house. And Simon and Emma need a place to set down new roots."

Jack placed the dry saucer in the cupboard and held out his hand for the next one. "So what do you suggest?"

Callie dipped a plate in the rinse water and handed it to him without meeting his gaze. "Perhaps we could divide the responsibilities the way she described—I manage the children, you run the farm—but do it without a marriage. I mean, it is a big house after all."

He gave a grunt of cynical amusement. "Not if you want to be able to show your face in this town." As soon as the words were out of his mouth he gave her a penitent look. "I'm sorry, I meant—"

"That's all right, Mr. Tyler, I know what you meant. Please don't feel like you have to watch your words with me." She wiped her brow with the back of a wet hand. It was almost amusing the way he tried to bend over backwards to make her believe her birthmark wasn't an issue. "I suppose you're right. Conventions can be bothersome at times, but they are there for a reason."

She plopped the last bowl in the dishwater with a splash. "So, do you have an alternative to offer?"

"I'm still not convinced I couldn't handle this on my own. I might have to hire a housekeeper to help out, but otherwise we'd be fine."

The man didn't seem to know the meaning of the word compromise. "That's not a solution."

"Why not?"

He knew very well why not, but she refused to let him goad her into losing her temper. "Well, for one thing it cuts me out of the picture and I refuse to let that happen."

She handed him the bowl then wiped her hands on her apron, maintaining eye contact with him the whole time. "But even if that weren't the case, a housekeeper is not the same as a mother. There's nothing to hold her to the children but a wage. That's one of the reasons Leland discarded that option in favor of marrying again."

She finally turned away and took a seat at the table, her hands twisting in her skirts. This was impossible!

He joined her, taking a seat directly across the table. "Lanny and I didn't necessarily share the same views on everything."

She wondered at his tone, but now was not the time to try to figure out his personal issues. "So you said. Still, you have to agree that it's not what their parents would want for them."

He tilted his chair back, letting it balance on the two back legs. "So what do you suggest?"

Callie stared down at her hands, clasped together on top of the table. *Heavenly Father, if it is truly Your will for me to be a part of these children's lives, You're going to have to help me work this out.*

She finally looked up and met Jack's gaze. "I don't have one yet."

"Then it seems we're back at square one."

Callie wondered again at his tone. Did he object to marriage in general, or just tying himself to her? After all, he wasn't Lanny. He hadn't known of her disfigurement for years, nor had he gotten to know her through her letters and the filter of Julia's love.

Even given his pronouncement that her birthmark didn't bother him, it was a far cry from wanting to tie himself down to her. A man like him would want a woman who was pretty, vibrant, worldly. She was none of those things.

Did he still use Julia as his gold standard for judging women?

Gathering her courage, Callie forced her voice to remain even. "If it's me you object to, I mean, if there's another woman you'd prefer to marry, to help in raising the children—"

"No."

His protest was too quick, too sharp. Perhaps he was trying to spare her feelings. Or maybe he didn't want to admit the truth, even to himself.

He rubbed the back of his neck, something he seemed to do whenever he was uncomfortable. "I mean, if marriage is really the only answer—and that's a big 'if'—then of course it should be between the two of us. We're the ones who share a feeling of responsibility for the children's well-being."

Fine sounding words, but she wasn't buying it.

His face got that closed-off look again. "I'm just not convinced yet that it *is* the only answer."

But what if it was? Could they live with such an arrangement? "If we do this, it would strictly be for the sake of the children." She traced a circle on the table with one finger, avoiding even so much as a glance his way. "I mean, we would naturally agree that it would be in name only."

Jack let the chair fall forward. "Of course."

She forced herself to continue. "And we would need to come to a clear understanding of what we would be agreeing to."

"For instance?"

She finally dragged her gaze up to his. Seeing the intense look on his face almost doused her resolve. Almost. "Do you intend to go back to your old job?"

He folded his arms. "Not right away," he said slowly. "I mean, if we did get married, I'd stay around as long as you and the kids needed me to. But once things settled down, say after a month or so, then I don't see why I wouldn't." He rested his still-crossed arms on the table. "I'm good at my job and I make good money at it, more than I could make off of the farm."

"Money isn't everything, Mr. Tyler. Lanny and Julia, for instance, seemed to do quite well on the farm alone."

A muscle at the corner of his mouth jumped. "Let me put this another way. I'm not Lanny and that's not the life I planned for myself."

Apparently she'd said something to ruffle his feathers again. No, theirs could never be a simple, comfortable relationship.

Even with the bonds of matrimony.

That unbidden thought brought heat to her cheeks. Luckily, Jack didn't seem to notice.

"If you're worried I'm going to abandon you and the kids, though," he continued in that tight voice, "you can put your mind at rest. When I go back to doing demolition work, I'll make a point to come back several times a year."

"I see. In that case, if you're really willing to stay here long enough to teach me how to take care of the place, we could probably make this work."

One eyebrow went up. "Even if I gave you daily lessons for a month, do you really think you could learn to run the farm by yourself?"

His lack of confidence in her abilities stung. "Julia was a city girl like me and learned to do most of the chores as well as any girl born to this life."

"But Julia started her learning at age eleven, not twenty-five."

She refused to back down. "That just means I'll have to work harder, not that I can't learn. And, as Mrs. Mayweather said, we can hire someone to help out a few days a week."

"So you admit you'll need help."

She let out a huff of irritation. "I'm not a ninny, Mr. Tyler. I know my limitations. I will freely admit that I'm not capable of caring for the children and a farm on my own." She studied the back of her hands. "There is one other thing."

"And that is?"

"I intend to raise these children to know and delight in the teachings of the Bible. You profess to be a Christian, just not the 'praying sort.' While I don't understand how this can be, I won't attempt to judge you. Each person must wrestle with his beliefs in his own way." She sat up straighter. "But, while you are here, I ask that you support me in providing the proper encouragement and example to the children. Surely you agree that bringing them up in the Word is important?"

She waited for his nod, then continued. "So you understand that we have a big responsibility before us. As the head of the household, your influence on the children would be strongest. I'd expect you to take part in family Bible readings and to accompany us to Sunday services. And of course we'd say grace at every meal and make certain the children say their prayers when they go to bed at night."

He didn't say anything at first, and Callie held her breath. Surely he wouldn't balk at such a request, would he? "I believe it's what your brother and sister would have wanted for their children."

His jaw clenched, but he finally nodded. "You're right. Such things are important in bringing up children."

Such things were not just for children, but now was not the time to push that issue.

Callie felt a sudden fluttering in her stomach as the import of what they were contemplating sunk in. At some point they had moved from talking about it in abstract terms to figuring out how to make it work.

She gave him a weak smile. "We're really going to do this, aren't we?"

His answering smile held a touch of self-mockery. "It appears so."

"When?"

"No point putting it off. We can talk to the preacher tomorrow and set a date."

Not the most romantic of proposals. Callie kept her hands tightly clasped in her lap, trying to remain anchored in this suddenly shaky reality.

Heavenly Father, is this really what You desire for me? Jack is nothing like his brother. Can he truly be the life partner You prepared for me?

She turned to Jack, trying to picture this new turn her life seemed to be taking, trying to see through the emotionless façade he'd erected, to figure out his true feelings. But it was no use. "So what now?"

A hint of her inner turmoil must have communicated itself to him because his demeanor changed and some of the hardness left his face. She was struck again by his ability to set his own worries aside. Here he was, being pushed into a corner, being forced to give up much of the freedom and footloose independence he obviously craved. But he was ready to do it without further complaint.

All for the sake of the children.

He stood and held out a hand to help her rise. "I guess now we tell Mrs. Mayweather that, once again, she was right."

Chapter Twelve

"We have something to tell you."

Breakfast was over and all three children sat side by side on the parlor settee, looking equal parts apprehensive and curious.

Callie caught her bottom lip between her teeth and risked a quick look Jack's way.

He gave her a barely perceptible nod, but seemed content to let her take the lead for now. Almost as if he were saying this was all her doing so she should handle it.

She turned back to the children, making a point to capture the gaze of each of them in turn. How were they going to react to the news?

Annabeth suddenly sat up straighter, her expression hopeful. "Are we moving back to my house today?"

"Not today," Jack answered, "but very soon."

"Then what's the news?" Simon's surly response indicated he wasn't expecting to like whatever it was.

Callie said a silent prayer for the right words and plunged in. "Your Uncle Jack and I had a long conversation last night. We decided we would like for all five of us to live together as a family. But if we are *truly* going to be a family then we need to start acting like one. So," she took a deep breath, "the two of us are going to get married."

Annabeth wrinkled her brow as if not certain what to make of the news. "You mean, just like a real mommy and daddy."

Simon stiffened. "They're *not* my mom and dad, and no stupid wedding is gonna change that."

Callie leaned forward. "Oh, Simon, we know that no one can ever take the place of your parents in your heart." She looked at the girls, including them in the discussion. "But they're up in heaven now and you all need someone to look out for you until you're grown up enough to take care of yourselves."

She waved a hand in Jack's direction. "And we would dearly love to be those someones."

Simon leaned back, crossing his arms tightly over his chest. He obviously wasn't taken with the idea.

She tried a different approach. "And that also means you need to start thinking of each other as brother and sisters, not just cousins. How does that sound?"

The girls nodded, but Simon remained closed off.

"Simon, this is especially important for you. You'll need to be a big brother to Annabeth as well as Emma, which means looking out for both of them. Do you think you can manage that?" She held up a hand before he could say anything. "It's a very important responsibility. Don't say yes unless you mean it."

"Simon already takes care of us," Annabeth said quickly. "Don't you, Simon?"

Simon nodded. "Don't worry." He thrust his chin out. "I'll look out for them, same as I've been doing since the fire."

"When are you gonna get married?" Emma's quiet question gave no hint as to what she felt.

"We're going to talk to Reverend Hollingsford today." Jack had apparently decided to get involved in the conversation. "If he's agreeable, we'll have the ceremony sometime in the next couple of days."

"*Then* can we move back to my house?" Annabeth seemed to have a one track mind.

"Yes, we can." Jack leaned forward. "But it won't be just your house any more, Little Bit—it'll be a home for all of us together."

There he went again, surprising her by dealing with the children's concerns in a straightforward but sensitive manner.

She gave him a quick smile, then touched Annabeth's hand. "You won't mind that, will you, sweetheart?"

"No." Annabeth twisted one of her ringlets around her finger. "But do I have to share Cinnamon, too?"

"Cinnamon is all yours," Callie said. "But it would be nice if you would let Emma and Simon ride him sometimes."

The child nodded. "I can do that."

Jack stood. "And since we're all going to be living at the farm, your Aunt Callie and I thought it might be a good idea to take another trip out there this afternoon to start getting things ready."

Annabeth bounced up and down with excitement. "Oh, yes! And I can visit with Cinnamon and Taffy and Pepper again."

Seeing the little girl's enthusiasm, some of Callie's uncertainty faded. This might just possibly work.

As Jack escorted Callie through town to Reverend Hollingsford's place, he mused over the turn of events. Now that he'd had a chance to sleep on it, this marriage really did seem to be the ideal solution.

If you looked at it right, it gave him the best of both worlds.

He'd be making sure Lanny and Nell's kids were well taken care of, aided by Lanny's hand-picked candidate, no less. And he'd still be free to leave Sweetgum and return to the life he'd so carefully built for himself for the past eleven years.

It wasn't a love match, but that had never seemed to be in the cards for him anyway. The only thing that stuck in his craw was that he would be marrying Lanny's widow, which felt irritatingly like making do with another of his brother's confounded hand-me-downs. But that wasn't Callie's fault and he was man enough to not blame her for that unpalatable piece of this pie.

He could do a whole lot worse, he supposed. That stubborn streak of hers was offset by an unintimidated mettle that was growing on him. And she *was* good with the kids. Add to that the fact that she was going into this with her eyes open and it seemed to be a can't-miss proposition.

"The children appeared to take the news well," Callie said, interrupting his thoughts.

"No reason why they shouldn't."

"Simon seems a bit sullen, though."

The woman sure did like to talk. "He'll get over it."

They walked on in silence and he hid a grin, wondering how long it would take her to say something.

"How well do you know Reverend Hollingsford?"

Three minutes. "I've known him all my life. He's been the preacher in these parts for nearly forty years. He performed the ceremony at my folks' wedding. And at both their funerals. I guess he'll do the same for me—wedding ceremony, that is."

She tipped her head to one side. "Sounds like you're surprised."

He shrugged. "Guess I just never thought that much about getting hitched." Not in a long time, anyway.

"You mean not since Julia turned you down."

He paused. So she did know.

When he resumed walking, he'd hopefully erased any emotion from his expression. "Julia wrote you about that, did she?" he asked as casually as he could manage.

"Yes." Callie gave him a sympathetic look. "She was worried you wouldn't understand and asked me to add you to my prayers."

"Well, she needn't have worried. I survived." But it had taken a long time to get over the bitter taste her rejection left in his mouth.

"Did you love her?" The question was soft, almost wistful.

Jack thought back to the boy he'd been. It seemed a lifetime ago. "I thought I did at the time." He shrugged. "But I was only seventeen. And as it turns out, she loved Lanny." That was what had stung the most. It had seemed the ultimate betrayal—by both of them.

"Yes, she did. Very much." She bit her lip and cast him a sideways glance.

He resisted the urge to roll his eyes. "Whatever it is, you might as well tell me."

"It's just, well, it was more than the fact that she loved Leland. It was also that she knew he loved her. And she was fairly certain you didn't."

Jack absorbed the words as if they had been a body blow. Julia had thought he didn't love her?

"I'm sorry, maybe I shouldn't have said anything."

She was able to pick up on his moods—he'd have to watch himself around her. "Don't be ridiculous. It was a long time ago. It's not like I've been carrying the torch for her all this time." Not a torch, but maybe some resentment.

"Of course not."

Her tone conveyed doubt, but he refused to dwell on the subject further. "There's Reverend Hollingsford's home. Prepare yourself for a boxcar load of questions."

* * *

That afternoon, when the buggy turned into the drive that led to the farm, Callie looked at the place with fresh eyes. Yesterday it had been Annabeth's house and the place where Julia once lived. Today it was her soon-to-be home, where she would belatedly start her married life.

Strange what a difference one day could make.

Once Jack had taken care of the horse and wagon, and Annabeth had a chance to say hello to her animals, they trooped into the house.

"First thing we need to decide today is where everyone will sleep," she announced.

"I already know where I'm going to sleep," Annabeth said confidently. "In my own room."

"Well, let's just think about that for a minute." Callie gave Annabeth an encouraging smile. "Remember how we said we were all going to have to make some changes in order to help us come together as a real family?"

Annabeth nodded cautiously.

"Since there will be five of us living here now, you'll need to share a room with Emma."

Annabeth shot a quick glance at Emma. "I guess we can put another bed in my room." There was a definite hint of martyrdom in her voice.

"But the room across the hall from yours already has two beds," Callie reasoned, "and it's also bigger than yours. Don't you think it makes more sense for you and Emma to share that one and for Simon to have the smaller one?"

Annabeth's lower lip jutted out. "But why does Simon get a room all to himself?"

Jack finally stepped in. "Because Simon is a boy and he's the oldest," he said firmly.

"But I like my old room," Annabeth said petulantly.

"I know, sweetie. But you want to do your part to make this work, don't you? And you can bring all your things with you to your new room."

Annabeth plopped down on the sofa with a grudging huff. "I guess it'll be okay."

"I don't want a frilly ole girl's room." Simon, arms crossed over his chest, looked ready for battle.

"Don't worry." Callie ignored his churlish attitude. "It won't look like a girl's room once we move Annabeth's things out and put yours in."

"I don't have any stuff."

Callie felt a pang at this reminder of their loss. That was the real root of the boy's rebellious attitude and she needed to make allowances. "You do have a few things. And you'll get more over time." She deliberately lightened her tone. "And this way you'll be able to make it into anything you want it to be."

But Simon didn't return her smile. "I liked living in town. That's where my friends are. And I don't know anything about farm chores."

"Well, you'll have your sisters to play with here, and you can visit with your friends whenever we go to town. And of course you'll see much more of them when school starts."

"But it won't be the same."

She touched his shoulder. "No, it won't. Not for any of us." She withdrew her hand but gave him a smile. "And I don't know anything about farm chores, either. Your Uncle Jack will have to teach both of us."

"What if I don't want to learn?"

Jack stepped forward. "You'll do your share of the work around here, whether you feel like it or not. Just like everyone else." His tone was brook-no-arguments firm.

"And another thing," he continued. "You'll speak with

respect when you're addressing your Aunt Callie, or any adult for that matter. Understand?"

"Yes, sir."

Callie sat back and stared at Jack. He'd done it again— employed a firm hand with the children without being over-bearing. Just the kind of loving discipline they needed. The fatherly skill seemed to come so naturally to him.

How could a man to whom family was so important not have married before now? Had his feelings for Julia been so strong? Had he been holding out for someone like his first love?

Her pleasure in the day dimmed as she realized he was now settling for her.

"My word, Callista dear, you're nervous as a cat who's been tossed in a kennel."

Mrs. Mayweather's prodigious understatement managed to tease a smile from Callie as they sat side by side at the kitchen table, shelling peas.

It had been a long day. Today's visit to the farm hadn't had the playful, exploratory atmosphere that yesterday's had. They'd spent most of the afternoon moving furniture around, scrounging forgotten pieces from the attic and generally re-arranging things, trying their best to satisfy everyone. An impossible task, of course.

In the end, the place likely felt as unfamiliar to Annabeth as it did to the rest of them.

Now supper was over, Jack had returned to the farm, and the children were playing quietly in the parlor.

"It's only natural for a bride to be a bit nervous," Mrs. May-weather continued. "What you need is something to take your mind off of the upcoming nuptials."

"No offense, ma'am," Callie said, attempting to keep her

tone light, "but I don't think there's anything that can distract me from that particular event right now."

She knew all about prenuptial jitters. She'd watched all four of her sisters go through it. This was something entirely different. This was a feeling of wrongness that came from the certain knowledge that she was about to enter into marriage with a man who not only didn't love her, but who felt as if he'd had a gun held to his head to agree to it.

Not the most comforting of feelings for a bride-to-be.

"Come now." Mrs. Mayweather seemed blissfully unaware that anything was amiss. "You've prayed about it and I've prayed about it. It's in God's hands now."

"You're right." Callie grimaced. "And I know it shows a lack of faith on my part, but I can't help but wonder if we're doing the right thing. Marriage is a sacred institution, not to be entered into lightly."

"From where I'm sitting, neither one of you seems to be entering into this lightly."

Callie sensed a touch of dry humor in the woman's tone.

Mrs. Mayweather dropped another handful of peas into the bowl. "You've both given it serious thought. And you're both committed to making it work for the children, are you not?"

"Yes, of course." That was the only thing that had gotten them to this point—the thought that they both had the interests of the children at heart.

"Well, there you go. I'm certain God will see fit to bless what you two are doing."

Callie fervently hoped she was right.

"Oh, by the way."

The very casualness of Mrs. Mayweather's tone set Callie on the alert. "Yes?"

"I've invited some of the local ladies to come by for tea

tomorrow afternoon. I thought it was high time you became acquainted with a few more of your neighbors."

Callie froze. Her heart seemed to pause for a moment before stuttering painfully back to life. *"Tomorrow?"*

"Of course. I sent the invitations out while you and Jackson were talking to Reverend Hollingsford this morning."

"How many?" Callie was too appalled to be embarrassed by the croak in her voice.

Mrs. Mayweather lifted her shoulders in a genteel shrug. "A couple of dozen, more or less."

A couple of dozen! Would Mrs. Mayweather's parlor even hold that many?

"It's a last minute thing, but I expect most everyone to accept." She gave Callie an amused look. "You must know the whole town is abuzz with your remarkable story. Rather gossipy of us I know, but I also know you're charitable enough to overlook and forgive us our curiosity. We don't get much excitement in our little corner of the world."

Callie rallied enough to attempt a protest. "But the wedding is the day after tomorrow. There are things I need to take care of and I need to get the children ready to move." All true statements. "Perhaps now is not—

"Balderdash! Everything for the wedding is taken care of. And sadly, there's not much for the children to pack." She patted Callie's hand. "I thought it best that folks meet you before the wedding so they can see what a fine person you are."

Callie tried again. "Thank you, but—"

"No need to thank me." She settled more squarely in her chair. "Now, let's finish with this little chore and we'll plan out our menu."

Callie added peas to the bowl with hands that weren't quite steady.

This was a disaster in the making. Crowds, especially crowds of strangers, made her nervous. She'd wanted to ease her way into this community, to give folks here a chance to get to know her one or two at a time before she unveiled herself—the way she had with Mrs. Mayweather and Ida Lee.

Of course, it wasn't as if she'd show her birthmark to them tomorrow. That would be a true disaster. They would likely have a negative reaction, and that reaction would affect Jack's perception of her.

She knew theirs wasn't a love match, but she'd at least hoped to build a life with him that was based on mutual respect.

All of those hopes could be summarily dashed if tomorrow did not go well.

Chapter Thirteen

The next day, Callie stood in Mrs. Mayweather's parlor, surrounded by at least twenty-five ladies of varying ages.

The children had escaped to the backyard, where Jack and Virgil had engaged them in a game of horseshoes.

Callie envied them. She couldn't remember ever being in the midst of such a crowded room, much less finding herself the center of attention at such a gathering.

Her family would never have allowed it. One of her sisters would have stood beside her at all times, keeping her company while shielding her from undue attention. Far from serving in that capacity, Mrs. Mayweather was busy circulating amongst her guests.

During a lull in the ever-shifting conversation, Callie stole away to the corner table where a punch bowl sat. Her head spun from all the introductions. How in the world was she going to remember all those names, much less which faces they went with?

But at least she hadn't made any embarrassing missteps yet. Perhaps Mrs. Mayweather's plan hadn't been so dreadful after all. Callie filled one of the delicate crystal cups and took a fortifying sip before turning to face the room again. She found herself nearly toe-to-toe with two of the ladies she'd met earlier.

The women were Alma Collins, president of the Sweetgum Ladies' Auxiliary, and her vice president, Jane Peavey. But Callie couldn't remember which was which.

"Mrs. Mayweather makes the most delicious apple peach cider, don't you agree?" the one in the blue dress asked.

Callie moved aside to allow the women to refill their cups. "Yes, quite delicious."

"We hear you're a friend of Julia's," the one in the yellow dress added.

"Yes." Perhaps she could carry on this conversation without using names. "We lived next door to each other as children and kept in touch after she moved here."

"Well, I must say, I do so admire you. It must have taken so much courage to agree to marry a man you'd never met." Mrs. Blue Dress placed a hand to her heart. "And then to travel all this way by yourself! Why, land's sake, I just don't know if I could have done such a thing."

"Actually, some friends of the family accompanied me on the train ride." Another of her father's precautions. "It was only when I boarded the stage at Parson's Creek that I was without an escort."

"Still, Alma's right, that was mighty brave of you."

Aha! That meant Mrs. Blue Dress was Alma Collins, which made the speaker Jane Peavey.

Callie smiled, glad to have navigated past that conversational pitfall. "It's kind of you to say so, but I'm afraid I truly can't claim to have much in the way of courage. In fact I was quite nervous every step of the way. It was faith that brought me through. I felt God's presence with me all the way here."

"What a wonderful attitude." Mrs. Collins sketched a toast with her cup. "It does you credit, my dear."

"And it's so compassionate of you to take all the children in," Mrs. Peavey added.

"Not at all." Callie resisted the urge to bolt from the room. She could barely stand being the focus of these women's attention. "I'm looking forward to caring for the three of them. I only pray that I'm up to the task."

Mrs. Peavey took a sip of her punch and gave Callie an arch smile. "I must admit, I am surprised you were able to convince Jack to join forces with you. He's always been so footloose. Why, even when we were all running about the schoolyard, Jack would talk about how he wanted to travel the country. And from the looks of things he certainly hasn't let anything tie him down since he left."

Callie's back stiffened, but she kept her smile firmly in place. "People change. And to be honest, Mr. Tyler was quite insistent that he have a hand in raising the children."

Mrs. Peavey raised a delicate brow. "Is that so?"

Callie's discomfort was quickly changing to irritation. "Absolutely. He's going to make an excellent father."

The women shared an arch look that caused Callie's grip to tighten around her cup.

"That's a wonderful sentiment, dear," Mrs. Collins said. "And perhaps you're right. It has been eleven years, after all."

She was spared the need to respond by the appearance of Mrs. Mayweather. "I have something I want to show you."

Callie smiled, grateful for the excuse to change topics.

When Mrs. Mayweather opened the box she was holding, however, all thoughts of the previous conversation fled. Inside, elegantly displayed on a bed of black velvet, was a lustrous strand of pearls with a matching set of earrings. "It's beautiful," Callie breathed.

"My father gave these to my mother on their wedding day." Mrs. Mayweather brushed a finger against the pearls, then met Callie's gaze. "I'd like you to wear them on your wedding day."

"Oh, I couldn't possibly—"

"Nonsense. I know you didn't come prepared for a wedding. And it would make me very happy to see someone put it to such meaningful use again after all these years."

"I don't know what to say, except thank you." She was truly touched by the gesture. Her first wedding had been little more than a formality. No one, not even her sisters or her father, had done anything to try to make it a special day for her.

Of course she hadn't really expected them to. It was a proxy ceremony for a marriage to a man she'd never met. How could she blame her family for not bothering to celebrate her wedding day?

"Why don't you try it on?"

Mrs. Collins's question pulled Callie back to the present. She reached out a hand to touch the heirloom piece. "May I?"

"Of course." Mrs. Mayweather lifted it from the box. "I'm afraid the catch is broken. But don't worry, it's long enough to slide over your head, if you remove your bonnet."

Callie's hand drew back as if scalded.

Remove her bonnet? In front of all these strangers?

Had Mrs. Mayweather forgotten why she wore the less-than-stylish piece in the first place?

"Perhaps I should wait."

Mrs. Mayweather gave her a look that said she knew exactly what Callie was thinking. "I insist." Her voice carried that combination of the compassion and firmness that was peculiar to schoolteachers. "I really do think you should try it on now so everyone can see how lovely it will look."

Callie searched her hostess's face. She hadn't considered

the woman cruel. So why was she attempting to force Callie to unmask so publicly?

But there was no getting around it. Explaining why she'd prefer not to would be almost as awkward as actually doing it. This was her worst nightmare. She thought about Jack, out in the backyard. What would he want her to do? He said her appearance didn't matter, but would he feel the same once all his friends and neighbors knew?

She took a deep breath and sent up a silent prayer for courage and decided to trust Mrs. Mayweather's instincts. "Very well."

Quickly, before she could talk herself out of it, Callie reached for her bonnet strings. Her fingers were trembling. The look of approval Mrs. Mayweather sent her way, however, gave her a much needed boost of support.

"I believe it only fair that I warn you all of something." Callie was surprised at how calm her voice sounded. "I have a rather prominent birthmark on the left side of my face."

With that, she removed the bonnet.

There were several muted "Oh, my"s and a sharp intake of breath or two, but Callie refrained from trying to identify the sources. Such initial reactions were normal, and she had learned long ago that it served no useful purpose to harbor resentment.

Instead, she moved to a mirror hanging in the foyer and gently eased the strand over her head, trying to ignore the sounds of shifting and clearing throats and even one nervous titter that was quickly shushed. Fidgeting with the necklace long enough to give everyone time to compose themselves, she finally turned to Mrs. Mayweather and pasted on a bright smile that hopefully masked her embarrassment. "Thank you for the loan of such a treasure. I promise to take very special care of it."

"You're welcome, my dear. And I think it looks absolutely lovely on you."

Callie removed the necklace and tucked it back in the

box. Then she donned her bonnet once again and gazed around the room.

Suddenly there was a rush of voices, nervously eager to fill the silence. No one, except for Ida Lee and Mrs. Mayweather, met her gaze.

Perhaps Mrs. Mayweather had been right. Painful though it had been, maybe it was best that she got this revelation over with all at once. She just hoped she'd never have to go through such an ordeal again.

The question was, now that everyone knew her secret, how big a difference would it make in their eagerness to welcome her into the community?

And what difference would it make to Jack and the children, and how they felt about her?

Callie's second wedding day dawned clear and beautiful.

She had lain awake long into the night, praying and searching for answers that wouldn't come.

And wondering about the repercussions of her unveiling at Mrs. Mayweather's tea party.

It felt strange, dreamlike. For so much of her life she'd accepted that she would never marry and have a family of her own.

Now, in the space of a few short weeks, she was preparing to say her wedding vows for the second time. And again it was to a man who wanted a mother for his children, not a wife for himself.

The morning dragged on interminably. Callie helped the children pack the few possessions they had with them. That, along with most of her own belongings, were loaded into Mrs. Mayweather's buggy.

Once the ceremony was over, the newly formed family of five would proceed directly to their new home together.

Home.

Callie let out a wistful sigh. Would that farmhouse ever truly feel like the home she'd dreamed of when she'd imagined her life with Leland?

No matter. Just thinking of the alternative strengthened her determination. She didn't want to go back to Ohio, and it made no sense for her to stay here and *not* do her part to help this family. And she so looked forward to the sense of freedom country life promised.

Even if she did have strong reservations about her ability to manage the place on her own once Jack left. Just the thought of taking on such a task twisted her stomach in knots. Perhaps Jack would change his mind, decide to stay and work with her to make this a real family.

Callie squelched that thought before it could take root. He'd been very clear on what he was and was not willing to give up when they'd struck this bargain. Expecting him to do a sudden turnaround now was unrealistic and unfair.

No, better to draw comfort from the knowledge that the good Lord wouldn't have set her feet on this path if He hadn't had a purpose for her.

The question was, did she really have the fortitude to see it through?

Callie barely touched her lunch. Later she couldn't recall what was served.

And suddenly it was time to go to the church. Callie donned her best Sunday dress along with the pearls Mrs. Mayweather had loaned her, clutched the flower bouquet Emma and Annabeth had picked for her, and piled into the carriage with Mrs. Mayweather and the children. Simon proudly handled the reins.

Once they arrived, Mrs. Mayweather escorted the children inside while Ida Lee stood with Callie at the back of the church.

A few moments later the piano signaled it was time, Ida Lee gave her hand a squeeze, and Callie stepped from the foyer into the small auditorium.

For a split second she froze, unable to either move forward or retreat, uncertain which she wanted to do more. Every pew was packed. It looked as if all of Sweetgum wanted to see the town's Prodigal Son and the blotchy-faced widow get hitched.

Callie took a deep breath and tugged her bonnet forward. By now everyone would know about her birthmark, but at least she didn't have to bare it to them.

With a quick prayer, she looked straight ahead and began placing one foot in front of the other. She told herself it was perfectly natural for the bride to be the center of attention on her wedding day. But this felt like something very different.

Her hand itched to reach up and tug her bonnet forward again, but she resisted, hoping to portray a serenity she didn't feel.

When her gaze latched on to Jack, her world shifted once again. He looked so different in that Sunday-go-to-meeting suit, so dashing and distinguished. It hit her again that this was not the kind of man who was used to settling for anything, much less a wife.

Her steps faltered. What had they been thinking? Jack didn't really want this. She should—

He met her gaze and a crooked smile curved his lips.

Then, without quite knowing how, Callie was at his side and they were turning to face Reverend Hollingsford.

As the reverend began the service, Callie couldn't help but compare this wedding with her first.

This time it was a solemn church ceremony instead of a rushed civil one.

This time there was a community of neighbors and friends to witness her big day rather than just a few family members.

And this time, instead of some disinterested stand-in, the actual groom stood beside her, gazing intently into her eyes, vowing to honor, cherish and provide for her, as long as they both should live.

And to her surprise, he had a simple but beautiful gold band to slip on her finger as he said those vows. That gesture alone added a special touch to the ceremony.

It might all be for the sake of the children, with no real affection between the two adults, but for the space of time it took to repeat their vows, Callie felt a shiver of emotion.

What would it be like to have someone truly love and cherish her, not as a matter of convenience, but as a matter of the heart? She yearned for that experience with every fiber of her being.

As they turned back to face Reverend Hollingsford, regret sliced through her as she realized that that one brief, mirage-like moment would likely be her only taste.

Chapter Fourteen

They didn't leave for the farm immediately as Callie had expected. When she and Jack stepped outside, they found several tables set up on the church grounds, most of them laden with food. Ida Lee approached them, her generous smile broadcasting that she was pleased with the surprise she'd had a hand in.

"Well, Mr. and Mrs. Tyler, seeing as how you've had to plan this wedding all quick-like without much time for celebrating, the members of the Sweetgum Ladies' Auxiliary decided to throw you this little shindig. Just our way of letting you know we're tickled pink to have you as part of the fold, so to speak."

At the sound of "Mr. and Mrs. Tyler," Callie felt that shiver. Even after her proxy marriage to Leland, most everyone had continued to address her by her first name rather than as a married woman.

It took her a moment to realize Jack was leaving it up to her to respond. "I—I'm certain Jack shares my appreciation for all of this." She stumbled over the first few words, then saw all the friendly, smiling faces beaming at the two of them.

That made it easier to speak from the heart. "You've made our special day so much brighter with your outpouring of support and kindness. I know now why Julia always wrote of Sweetgum and its people with such affection."

"Well done." Jack spoke so low she was certain no one else heard him. But the compliment added an extra bounce to her step as they descended the church stairs.

They stopped at the bottom and stood there while a parade of townsfolk came by to offer well-wishes. The faces and comments swirled about her like schools of fish.

"Wouldn't be right for the new bride to have to cook her own supper on her wedding day."

"We want to make sure you feel welcome here."

"Just wait until you taste Helen Beaman's peach cobbler."

"It's what Lanny and Nell would have wanted for you."

It was all so overwhelming. First the gathering at Mrs. Mayweather's yesterday, then the wedding itself, and now this. Who would have thought she'd feel more hemmed in and crowded in a small town than she'd ever felt in her big city home?

Callie resisted the urge to fidget, or worse yet to bolt and run. Being on display this way was excruciating, but she didn't want to appear ungrateful when these folks had worked so hard to make her feel welcome.

Finally, the last of the wedding guests shook their hands and she and Jack were free to lose themselves in the crowd. They became separated almost at once, drawn into different groups as they began to mingle.

Callie felt some of her tension ease. Better to be part of a milling crowd than to be the center of attention. But after five minutes, she found an opportunity to slip into the church unobserved. Sitting in one of the pews, she closed her eyes and breathed a sigh of relief.

Thank You, Father, for setting me among such neighborly people. Help me remember that it truly is a blessing. And give me the strength and fortitude to accept with good grace their outpourings of friendship, even when it isn't comfortable to do so.

She sat there for a few more minutes with her eyes closed and her head resting against the back of her pew. Muted sounds of conversation drifted in from an open window, punctuated now and then by the drone of insects. She really should return to the reception before her absence was noted. But it was so nice sitting here unobserved, drinking in the peace.

Callie let the serenity of the small country church refresh her spirit a minute longer, then she straightened. The murmur of conversation was drawing closer. It was time she rejoined the others before she was discovered hiding in here like a coward.

Then one of the conversations sharpened, as if the speaker stood right under the window.

"...sakes. Did you see her face yesterday?"

"That poor thing. I suppose it's understandable why she'd rather hide behind those frumpy bonnets."

Callie froze.

"Bless her heart," the voice continued. "No wonder she came all this way to marry a man she'd never met. I wonder if Lanny even knew about that birthmark when he proposed."

"Well, Jack's the one I feel sorry for. I mean, at least Lanny had his time with Julia. But Jack, well, all I can say is, it's very noble of him to go through with this, for the sake of the kids and all."

Callie's face burned with mortification. This was the sort of thing her family had always warned her about, had tried to shield her from.

And she recognized the voices. How could she face these women now that she knew how they viewed her?

Heavenly Father, I know I should turn the other cheek, but sometimes it's so difficult.

"You know Jack. He might not have been as gentlemanly as Lanny, but—"

"Ladies."

Callie stiffened. That was Jack's voice. And she'd thought this couldn't possibly get any worse.

"Uh, hello, Jack."

Callie heard the caught-in-the-act tone in the woman's voice.

"Have either of you seen my bride in the last few minutes?"

"Why, no."

"I'm quite a lucky man to have found such a fine woman to marry, don't you agree?"

"Yes, of course." There was the sound of a throat clearing. "Why I was just saying what a wonderful thing the two of you are doing for those children."

"I'll tell you ladies a secret. Callie took a bit of convincing. Why, I'm almost embarrassed to admit how much arm-twisting it took to convince her to have me."

"Is that so?"

"Yep. But it was worth it. In fact, I'd be mighty put out if I learned someone said something to make her sorry she decided to stay in Sweetgum."

"I'm sure you have nothing to worry about on that score." The rustling of skirts filled the short pause. "Well, if we see her, we'll let her know you're looking for her."

"Thank you kindly, ladies."

Callie's heart warmed at Jack's defense of her. Whatever else he might be, Jack Tyler was an honorable man with a good heart.

* * *

Jack watched Alma Collins and Jane Peavey hurry away. It had been all he could do to keep his tone pleasant while he dealt with them. If they'd been men…

That pair didn't seem to have changed much from the adolescent babblers he remembered. They thrived on gossip and were always on the lookout for ways to stir things up. Hopefully he'd managed to nip in the bud any further attempts to target Callie.

Thank goodness Callie wasn't that sort of woman. She might have some less than docile qualities that got under his skin, but at least she was forthright and fair-minded.

Just where was she anyway? He glanced around, his gaze honing in on Ben Cooper heading for one of the food tables. Time for a quick detour.

"Hey," he said as he clapped Ben on the shoulder, "I've been meaning to talk to you." Virgil had informed him it was Ben, the town's young undertaker, who'd seen that everything was done all right and proper for the funerals after the fire.

"Well, hi there, Jack. Is there something I can do for you?"

Jack shook his head. "You've already done more than expected. I wanted you to know I appreciate your taking care of the three burials for me. And that I intend to pay you back for every bit of your time and expense. Just let me know how much."

Ben shook his head. "I just did what needed doing. And your wedding day is not the time to be talking business. You can stop by my place one day next week." Ben glanced up past Jack's shoulder. "Right now you have a bride you should be tending to."

Jack followed the direction of Ben's gaze just in time to see Callie step out of the church. So that's where she'd disappeared to. Truth to tell, he didn't much blame her. He could do with a bit of peace and quiet right now himself.

Then he frowned. Something wasn't right, though he couldn't explain how he knew. She wore a serene smile and her stride was unfaltering.

And then it hit him. If Callie had been in the church, she may have heard the conversation between Alma and Jane. And if she had, she'd no doubt be feeling pretty low right now.

"Excuse me, Ben, I do need to speak to Callie for a minute."

Ben gave him a knowing smile. "You go right ahead."

Jack rolled his eyes at the implication. Nothing could be further from the truth.

Could it?

He caught up to Callie before she'd reached the thick of the crowd and took her arm. "Are you okay?"

Her eyes widened in surprise. "Of course." She glanced back at the church. "Sorry for slipping off like that. I hope no one noticed. It's just that I'm not used to crowds and so much attention."

"No need to apologize. I'm pretty sure no one else noticed." He studied her face, or at least the part of it he could see. Had he read her wrong? "Are you sure you're okay? We can leave now if you like."

"I'm fine, really."

That little tug she gave her bonnet said otherwise.

She laid a hand on his arm. "Please don't break this up on my account. Everyone has been so neighborly and they worked hard to put this together." She made a shooing motion. "Now go on back to our guests and I'll do the same."

Jack watched her walk away, more certain than ever that she'd caught at least part of the conversation.

He raked a hand through his hair as he moved toward the

food tables. If she'd heard his defense of her, he sure hoped she wasn't reading anything into it. He'd merely been doing what any decent man would do—taking care of his own.

And like it or not, that included her now.

Callie had mixed emotions later that afternoon as she stood on the porch and watched the day draw to a close. They'd left the reception a little over an hour ago, the buckboard loaded down with not only the luggage from Mrs. Mayweather's, but also with the choicest leftovers from the reception.

Now everything had been taken into the house, at least as far as the front hall, and the sun was just kissing the horizon.

Jack was somewhere inside. Emma and Annabeth sat on the porch swing playing with Annabeth's doll. Simon was out in the yard, throwing sticks for both dogs to retrieve.

Callie wrapped her arms around herself. She'd always liked this pre-dusk moment. It was a restful time of day, one that usually brought her a sense of peace and a renewed appreciation for her many blessings.

But the events of *this* day, and the fact that she'd been on display for most of it, left her drained. Overhearing that bit of conversation hadn't helped much.

But Jack had defended her, and so deliberately. That was almost as disquieting, though in a different sort of way. It turned all her ideas of him upside down.

But most of all, the thought that she was now responsible for these children, and that she not only shared that responsibility, but also this house, with Jack Tyler—a man she was beginning to see in a new light—left her unsettled and jittery.

No, she wasn't in any frame of mind right now to appreciate the quiet majesty of the day's close.

Enough of that kind of thinking. Callie pushed away from the porch rail. There was unpacking to do, and food to sort through and put away. And this being their first night together as a family would mean dealing with everyone getting used to a new routine and new sleeping arrangements.

She turned to the front door, but before she could move further, Jack stepped onto the porch. "I'm going to get the animals settled in for the night."

"Yes, of course." She tugged on her bonnet. "I've some chores to take care of myself."

He paused and gave her a long, considering look. "You've had a busy day," he said gruffly. "Whatever you have to do will likely wait until tomorrow."

His concern surprised her and she smiled. "Thank you, but I'm fine. And I'll sleep better knowing things are in apple-pie order, as my mother used to say." She clasped her hands together. "When you come back inside, we can select a Bible verse to read before we get the children ready for bed."

He merely nodded.

"And you do remember that tomorrow is Sunday?" She didn't want to be a nag, but it was important that they get off on the right foot in this matter from day one.

An annoyed furrow creased his forehead. "I know what day it is. That's all the more reason for me to get as many chores done this evening as possible."

As she watched him cross the yard in ground-eating strides, Callie nibbled at her lower lip. Was she being too pushy? Was there some other approach she should use with him?

It was just so important that they set the proper example for the children. On the other hand, if it was obvious that his heart wasn't in it, that could do more harm than good.

As promised, Jack read from the family Bible that evening. He asked Callie to pick the verse, and she selected Isaiah

43:18-19. A passage about new beginnings seemed appropriate.

His reading voice was pleasant, strong and authoritative. A bit like the man himself. And he didn't stumble over the words once. It showed a familiarity with the scriptures she hadn't expected.

Afterwards, as Jack carried the Bible back to the stand by the window, Callie rose. "Before you children go to bed, I have a surprise for you. Stay where you are and I'll be right back."

Callie returned a short time later with four parcels, her insides fluttering. She hoped she had gauged their interests well. "This is the first day of our life together as a family," she said. "And I thought it would be nice to mark the occasion with something special. So I have a little gift for each of you."

The children sat up straighter, a gleam of anticipation firing their eyes.

Callie, feeling a bit of anticipation herself, handed the parcels out. She caught the flash of surprise in Jack's expression as she handed him his. Did he think she would leave him out?

Annabeth opened hers. "It's a book."

"That's right. It's called *The House That Jack Built* and it has some wonderful pictures in it."

Annabeth giggled. "He has the same name as you, Uncle Jack." She turned the pages, her eyes sparkling in delight at the illustrations. "Will you read it to me?"

"Of course. But let's save it for when I tuck you in tonight."

Callie held her breath as Emma slowly unwrapped her parcel. This was the one she'd most looked forward to.

When Emma lifted the lid off the box, her reaction was everything Callie had hoped for.

Her eyes grew round and her mouth formed a little *O* of surprise. "She's beautiful." The words were breathed more than spoken. Emma lifted the doll gently out of the box, smoothing the dress and golden curls. "What's her name?"

"She doesn't have one yet. She's waiting for you to name her."

Emma squeezed the doll in a fierce hug. "Then I'll call her Dotty, just like my other doll."

"That sounds like a perfectly lovely name."

Annabeth clapped, "Now Tizzy will have a new sister to play with, just like me."

Emma nodded, then turned to her brother. She gave him a nudge with her shoulder. "Your turn."

When he didn't move right away, Annabeth offered her own encouragement. "Don't you want to see what's inside? I know I do."

Simon finally untied the string with a great show of disinterest. Once the paper was removed, he stared at the small wooden box as if uncertain whether or not to open it.

Annabeth prodded him again. "Why do you have to go so slow? Let's see what it is."

Simon slid the lid off the box to reveal a neatly arranged group of tiles, each decorated with a series of dots.

"It's a set of dominos," Callie explained. "They're made with real ivory. Have you ever played the game before?"

Simon frowned. "I've only ever seen old men playing it over at the mercantile."

"Well, it *is* usually played by adults. But I thought, since your Aunt Julia told me what a good student you are, that you might be able to learn it anyway."

She leaned forward. "But if you don't want it…"

He moved back slightly, fingering one of the smooth tiles. "This is really ivory?"

Callie nodded. "I found it in a little shop that specializes in items brought to this country from all around the world. The box is made from sandalwood, a tree that grows in India."

She saw the acceptance in his eyes. Deciding not to press the point, she leaned back. "I'm sure your Uncle Jack has played before. He can teach you how."

Jack nodded. "Anytime you're ready."

Annabeth turned curious eyes toward the last package. "What about you, Uncle Jack? Aren't you going to open your gift?"

Jack stared at the parcel as if it might blow up in his face. He still hadn't touched it. With a smile that seemed a bit forced to Callie, he slowly opened it.

He stared at the pocket watch nestled inside for a long minute, then looked at Callie. A small muscle at the corner of his mouth jumped.

Her pleasure in the gift-giving deflated. Something about the watch had upset him. "I know it's not brand-new. It belonged to my grandfather. If you don't like it—"

"No, it's a fine piece," he said quickly. "Thank you."

"You're welcome." She'd never heard a less convincing expression of gratitude.

Annabeth popped up from her seat and stood in front of Callie, her lips drawn down in a melodramatic frown. "But we didn't get you anything."

Callie forced her thoughts away from Jack's disappointing reaction, and smiled at the little girl. "Of course you did," she said, taking both of her hands.

The child's nose scrunched in confusion. "We did?"

"Most certainly. Don't you remember?" She released Annabeth's hands and gave her tummy a gentle poke. "You and Emma picked that beautiful bouquet of flowers for me to carry during the wedding. And Simon drove the carriage to get me there on time."

She held up her left hand. "And your Uncle Jack gave me this lovely wedding ring. So you see," She smiled, determined to end their first evening on a happy note, "I've had plenty of gifts today."

Only she had hoped the watch would mean as much to Jack as the ring had meant to her.

Apparently she'd failed.

Chapter Fifteen

While Callie herded the reluctant children upstairs, Jack stepped out on the front porch.

He pulled out his pocketknife and hefted a thick chuck of wood he'd pilfered earlier from the woodpile for just this purpose.

Sitting on the top step, he placed the pocket watch she'd given him on the porch floor beside him. Then he shaved a long thin curl of wood from the block.

Whittling was something he enjoyed doing at the end of the day, or anytime he just needed to be quiet and think. Sometimes he ended up with a whistle or a crude animal shape, but more often than not, he just ended up with a pile of shavings to use as kindling for the cook fire. In fact, even his better carving efforts usually ended up tossed in the fire.

What use did he have for such trinkets?

Married.

He sliced off a particularly thick chunk as he thought about the woman tucking the children in upstairs. The woman he'd vowed just a few hours earlier to cherish and protect until death should part them. The woman he knew next to nothing about.

Except that she was stubborn enough to stand up to him.

And that she genuinely cared about the kids.

And that she seemed dead set on cramming religion down his throat.

What she didn't understand was that he and God had an understanding of sorts.

For years he'd prayed for all he was worth that God would give him the chance to come into his own, to be something other than Lanny's not-quite-as-good little brother. He'd prayed even more desperately for Julia to say yes when he'd proposed. None of those prayers had been answered.

And he'd finally realized why. It was because he was so full of jealousy and pride that he wasn't good enough even for God. At least not so far as being worth His special attention.

That's when he'd realized that he was the kind of person the adage "God helps those who help themselves" had been penned for.

And it had worked for him so far. He was well-traveled, independent and respected in his field.

Sure, he had a few regrets—not making things right with Lanny was the biggest of them. But there probably wasn't a man alive who didn't have regrets of one sort or another.

Jack leaned back against the porch post.

Speaking of regrets…

He glanced down at the pocket watch and winced. His lack of enthusiasm had hurt Callie's feelings. But trying to explain that accepting a gift she'd selected for Lanny would leave a sour taste in his mouth would have only made matters worse.

Better for both of them that she just think him ungrateful.

Jack ran a thumb over the surface of the wood. He had to hand it to her—passing out those gifts had meant a lot to the kids, especially Nell's.

Seems his new wife had been quicker than him to see that those kids needed things to call their own, things to help them rebuild their sense of belonging.

Jack planed another long curl from the block of wood. He should have been the one to realize that, to take care of their needs.

Mrs. Mayweather had been right. The kids needed a mother, a mother like Callie.

The question was, was he the right man to play the role of their father?

The door opened behind him.

"The children are all settled in for the night."

And why aren't you? "Good." Kicking himself for not putting away the watch, Jack kept his voice even and his attention focused on whittling.

She took a few steps forward, halting just behind him. "I think today was a really good start."

He glanced over his shoulder and gave her a long, steady look. After a minute, he went back to his whittling. "Today was merely recess. Tomorrow the real work begins."

"I agree. And I'm ready."

"Are you now?"

Her sigh conveyed a sense of sorely tried patience. "Mr. Tyler, I—"

"Jack." He glanced up and saw her confused frown. "We're married. Might as well use first names."

"Very well. Jack, I know you think I'm too green for farm work, but with you to teach me, and God to help me, I'm certain I can learn what I need to."

"Then I suggest you turn in. Your lessons start tomorrow, which means you'll need to be up before sunrise in the morning."

"But tomorrow is Sunday."

"Lesson number one. The animals don't know what day of the week it is. They still need to be fed, the cows milked, the eggs gathered." He pointed his block of wood in her general direction. "And that's in addition to fixing breakfast and getting the kids ready for church service."

"Very well." He heard the swish of skirts as she turned. "I'll see you in the morning."

Twenty minutes later, Jack turned down the bedside lamp in his room and plopped onto the mattress, his fingers laced behind his head. It wasn't exactly the cozy marriage bed a man normally slid into on his wedding night.

Not that he wanted it any other way. This whole marriage thing had happened way too fast. This might have been their only option, but he still felt as if he'd been backed into a corner.

He rolled over on his side and punched his pillow into shape. He'd keep up his end of this bargain.

She'd have to be satisfied with that.

Callie slipped under the covers in the four poster bed that had been Julia and Leland's. She'd heard Jack come upstairs a few moments ago and she felt guilty enjoying the comfort of this large bedchamber while he made do with the smaller bed in the room across the hall.

But he'd insisted on those arrangements, arguing that in a month or so he planned to be gone anyway, and that the spare room accommodations were a step up from what he was used to while on the job.

Much as he would deny it, the man really did have a kind heart beating somewhere under that gruff exterior of his.

Too bad he didn't let it show more often.

His insistence that she would have a difficult time with the farm chores was worrisome. Surely he was being overly-pessimistic. She could make this work. She had to.

After all, wasn't this where God intended her to be?

Jack had been as good as his word when it came to the family bible reading. Though he'd asked her to pick out the verse, he'd done the reading himself and then asked Simon to lead them in prayer afterward.

Her heart warmed at the thought that God might be using her to help Jack find his way back.

Dear Heavenly Father, help me to be the sort of example You desire me to be.

And with that, she snuggled down into her pillow. But thoughts of Jack's insistence that he'd be moving on in a month or so made it hard for her to find the easy slumber she'd hoped for.

Chapter Sixteen

Callie woke to the sound of someone tapping at her door. Glancing toward the window through slitted lids, she saw a glimmering of gray pushing out the black of night. It was dawn, way too early to—

Dawn! Her sluggish brain suddenly flared to life.

Oh no! She'd overslept. Callie popped upright and tried to untangle herself from the covers. "I'm awake," she called out.

"Good." Jack's tone was dry, as if he could see her frantic rush to get out of bed. "Meet me in the barn when you get dressed."

Finally kicking off the covers, Callie quickly made her morning ablutions and dressed. She was still tying the strings to her bonnet as she hurried down the stairs, determined that their first full day together go as smoothly as possible.

As she passed through the kitchen she noted that the stove had already been stoked. Jack must have been up and about for some time.

Her guilt for oversleeping deepened a notch.

She quickened her pace as soon as she stepped outside, and

fought the urge to pause when she stepped off the back porch. Normally she'd take an extra second or two to appreciate God's exquisite handiwork in the first glimmerings of sunrise. But today she'd have to admire it on the run. Already a blush of color seeped past the horizon, reminding her that time was slipping away.

Lifting her skirts, Callie sprinted across the last few dew-dampened yards toward the barn. She arrived breathless and all but stumbled across the threshold.

Jack sat on a stool, already at work milking one of the cows. He spared the briefest of glances over his shoulder, then went back to work.

"I apologize for oversleeping." Though how one could call it oversleeping when you were up before sunrise…

He ignored her apology. "I'm almost finished milking Belle." He nodded toward the other stall. "As soon as I'm done, I'll let you try your hand at milking Clover."

Feeling duly chastised, Callie nodded. Curious, she moved closer so she could watch Jack at work.

It didn't look so hard. He merely squeezed on the cow's teats and the milk squirted into the bucket. The animal stood placidly eating from a waist-high mounted feed trough while Jack worked. The animal didn't even seem to notice what Jack was doing, much less mind.

A few minutes later Jack stood and patted the cow. "Thanks, girl." He carefully set the bucket of frothy white liquid on a wooden table next to the barn door, then returned and untied the cow.

Finally, he turned to Callie. "Ready to give it a try?"

She gave a confident nod.

"All right. First, add a bit of grain to her feed trough." He handed her a large chipped bowl filled with corn and some other type of grain. "Always approach her from the right side.

That's also the side you're going to milk her from." He set the stool in place. "Cows are creatures of habit and you want to approach her the same way every time."

Callie nodded and dutifully poured the grain into the feed trough.

"When you're ready, take a minute to pat her side and talk to her so she knows you're there."

What did one say to a cow? She decided to pretend Clover was just a big dog. "Hi there, girl." She patted the animal's side. "I'm Callie and I hope you're going to take it easy on me this morning."

The cow turned her head, looking at Callie with big, soulful brown eyes as if to reassure her. Callie smiled. So far this didn't seem so difficult.

"All right," Jack said. "Now take these two pails." He handed her an empty pail and one with fresh water and a rag.

"Scoot your stool up next to her, then sit at a right angle." He watched carefully as she complied. "You might want to lean your head or shoulder against her flank, just to keep the two of you anchored to each other."

Callie gave him a startled look. Was he serious? But then she remembered that he'd been sitting that way earlier. She leaned forward, her shoulder touching the cow.

"Now take this bucket," he said, pointing to the one filled with water, "and wash down her udder. That'll make sure you don't get any dirt in the milk."

Callie did as she was told, all the while feeling Jack's assessing eye on her.

"That's good. Take the milk pail and place it directly under the udder. Okay. Now you'll want to use your left hand to hold the pail steady. These two cows seem pretty tame, but you never know when one of them will have a bad day. You don't want them stepping in the pail or kicking it over."

"Kicking?"

He shrugged. "It happens. Hurts like h—" he cleared his throat "—like fire if you get in the way. Just keep your eyes open."

Callie shifted uneasily.

He stooped down beside her. "Watch me, then you try it. What you need to do is take one of the teats into the palm of your hand, like this. Starting at the top, squeeze with your thumb and forefinger. Then squeeze with your next finger, then the next, until your entire hand is curled around it. Then you release and do it all over again."

Sounded simple enough.

He straightened. "Think you have it?"

She nodded.

"Then give it a shot."

Callie took a deep breath, then reached up and positioned her hand as he'd instructed. She mentally reviewed his directions as she squeezed.

Nothing happened.

"Let's go over it again." He repeated the instructions, then crossed his arms and waited for her to follow through.

Feeling slightly less confident, Callie tried again.

Still nothing.

Jack stooped down until his head was level with hers. "One more time."

She did, with the same dismal results.

"I think I see what your problem is. Here, let me show you."

Jack shifted forward until they were shoulder to shoulder. He wrapped his hand around hers, encompassing it in a firm yet not unpleasant hold.

Callie was startled by his nearness, by the solid warmth of his hands on hers. She'd felt it before when he held her hand—that something protective in his touch, strong and gentle at the same time.

It took her a few seconds to realize he was speaking again.

"…need to apply a bit more pressure and make your movements smoother, firmer." He used his fingers to manipulate hers and like magic the milk pinged into the bucket. "Do you feel the difference?"

"Y-yes." She cleared her throat, clearing her head at the same time. "That was very helpful. Thank you."

With a nod he released her hand and glanced up. For a moment their gazes locked and she saw something flicker to life in his eyes. Whatever it was, though, it was gone almost as quickly as it had come.

"Well then," he sat back on his heels and broke eye contact, "let's see you give it a go on your own."

"Of course."

To her immense relief, the milk spurted into the pail with a satisfactory splish.

Jack stood. "Better. Now, you just keep that up until nothing more comes out. Then you move on to the next one. Clover's calf needs to be fed so you'll just milk out two teats. The calf will get the rest."

Callie nodded as she continued to work. There was a rhythm to this and she'd almost found it. It helped if she concentrated on what she was doing rather than on Jack.

It took her nearly twenty minutes to complete the task, but Callie felt an immense sense of satisfaction when she'd finished. She turned to share her accomplishment with Jack, only to find him busy spreading fresh hay in the vacated stalls.

Looking around, she realized he'd turned out Belle and filled the water troughs already. And probably a few other things she wasn't yet trained to notice.

And here she'd been feeling so smug about having milked a cow in that time, and only halfway at that.

She stood, stretching her back and flexing her sore hand muscles.

Jack leaned on the pitchfork, giving her an almost sympathetic smile. "Harder than it looks, isn't it?"

"I imagine it'll get easier with practice." She set her pail on the table next to his. "What's next?"

"You take this milk on up to the house." He cocked his head to one side. "That is, if your hands aren't too sore to handle the pails."

She wasn't going to let him see how cramped her hands and arms felt. "I'm fine."

"Good." He wiped his brow. "Morning's getting on. If we're going to get everyone fed and ready for church, you need to get breakfast started and see to the kids. I'll finish up in here and take care of gathering the eggs."

He took a firmer hold of the pitchfork, then paused again. "And don't forget to strain the milk. There ought to be some cheesecloth in the kitchen or laundry room."

She nodded and grabbed the pails.

"Don't worry," he said cheerfully, "tomorrow you'll get a real taste of what farm life is all about."

Jack rubbed the back of his neck as he watched Callie trudge through the barn door with the pails of milk. What was it about holding hands with this woman? There'd been a moment earlier when—

He tamped that thought down and focused instead on what they'd accomplished this morning.

Callie might have more than her fair share of determination, but now she'd gotten a small taste of what she'd be up against. How would she feel about things after a few more days of this? Would her resolve to stay out here waver? If it did, could he really, in good conscience, leave her and the kids here on their own?

He let the calf out of its pen and it immediately trotted over to its mother and began suckling.

He snatched the cloth-lined wicker basket from the workbench and trudged toward the hen house.

As he methodically reached into each nest and plucked out the still warm eggs, Jack began pondering alternatives. Like it or not, these four were his responsibility and leaving them in the lurch was not an option. But neither was his staying here in Sweetgum. So what could he do to make certain both their interests and his were taken care of? Surely he was resourceful enough to come up with something.

Because he was as determined as ever to return to his former life as soon as possible.

Callie set the milk pails on the kitchen counter and went to the washroom to clean up and fetch the cheesecloth. The day was barely started and already she was sore. And Jack implied he'd gone easy on her! Could she really do this?

Father, give me the strength I'll need to see this through. I desperately want to stay here in this place, but help me to not let my selfish desires blind me to what is best for the family as a whole.

It took more time to prepare breakfast and get the children ready than Callie had expected, but finally they were all dressed in their Sunday best and seated in the buggy. She'd have to do something about Emma and Simon's clothing. With the exception of what they'd been wearing the day of the fire, everything had been destroyed. Mrs. Mayweather had found them a few extra items to wear, but they needed more.

Jack flicked the reins and set the wagon in motion. Callie

faced the road with a smile of satisfaction. She'd made it through the first morning without any notable disasters. And with any luck they would make it into town before the church service started.

The silence drew out. This wouldn't do at all.

Callie turned to face the children. "Have any of you ever played the Endless Story game?"

Three sets of eyes stared at her blankly.

"It's a game my sisters and I used to play for hours at a time," Callie said.

"You have sisters?" Annabeth's eyes were round with surprise.

"Yes, four of them, actually."

"I like stories," Emma offered.

"Then you'll enjoy this."

Annabeth propped her arms and chin against the back of the front seat. "How do you play?"

"Well, one person starts telling a story." Callie waved a hand. "It can be about anything at all. But at the end of two minutes they must stop, even if they are in the middle of a sentence. Then the next person picks up the story where the first person left off, taking it in any direction they want. After two minutes, they stop and the next person starts, and so on."

Annabeth clapped her hands. "Ooh, let's play."

Callie looked at the other two. "How about you? Do you want to give it a try?"

Emma nodded somewhat hesitantly. Simon merely shrugged.

"All right, then, I'll start." She turned to Jack. "Can we borrow your pocket watch?"

He hesitated a fraction of a second, then slowly pulled his watch out of his pocket and handed it to her.

She stared at it. It wasn't the one she'd given him.

She did her best to ignore the stab of rejection. Perhaps this one had some sentimental value to him, had come from someone who mattered.

She swallowed her hurt and gave him a smile. "Thank you."

Then she quickly turned to the children. "Now, let's see. In a land far away, there was a castle situated next to the ocean. And in this castle lived many people, including a girl named Flora and a boy named Hawk. Flora's favorite pastime was working in her garden where flowers of every color and scent grew, and where butterflies and insects added color and nature's own music.

"Hawk, on the other hand, preferred to roam through the forest, exploring caves and gullies, discovering new trails and fishing in the many streams…"

While Callie wove her tale, she kept a close eye on the watch. As the two-minute mark approached, she deliberately stopped in mid-sentence. "While Flora was busy deciding what to do about the wilting flowers, Hawk had discovered—" She halted. "Uh-oh, looks like my time is up. Who wants to go next?"

Annabeth raised her hand. "I do."

"So, tell us what happens next."

"Hawk had discovered…he was lost." The little girl tossed her head, dismissing the hapless Hawk. "Back at the castle, Flora looked under her pink rosebush and found a puppy…"

Annabeth happily chatted on about Flora and the menagerie of pets she discovered hiding in her garden until Callie signaled that her two minutes were up and tapped Emma to take over.

Jack listened to the story unroll from each of his passenger's perspective. Callie even managed to coax shy Emma and surly Simon to participate. How did she do that?

He declined when she asked if he wanted a turn, and without missing a beat, she took her turn again.

Her very lack of reproach over both his refusal to participate in their game and his rejection of the gift she'd given him had him mentally squirming.

Shaking that uncomfortable feeling off, he listened to the story as it was reshaped by each speaker in turn.

Interesting.

Annabeth concentrated on Flora and her interaction with the numerous animals she invented for her to play with.

Emma tied the two characters together as brother and sister. She also set the boundary of the garden right at the edge of the forest so that Flora and Hawk could take time out to visit with each other as they went about their activities.

Simon, of course, focused on Hawk's adventures, setting him off in search of lost treasure.

Whenever it came back to Callie, however, she would deftly weave the threads of the story back together and set it dramatically off on a new course before her two minutes were up.

They were still going strong when the outskirts of town came into view.

As the wagon rolled past the burned out remains of the café, all talk ceased.

Jack cast a quick glance at the three children and saw Simon's clenched jaw, Emma's downcast eyes and Annabeth's quivering lower lip.

He should have come into town by a more roundabout route, he realized with regret. So what if they were a little late?

The kids shouldn't have to face this reminder again.

Another black mark on his parenting record.

Chapter Seventeen

Jack cleared his throat, not quite sure what to say, but knowing the kids needed a distraction.

A quick glance Callie's way confirmed that she shared his concern. She pasted a smile on her face and turned back to the children. "Well, there's the church and it looks like we made it on time. Simon, isn't that your friend Bobby there by the steps?"

As if to reinforce her words, the bells started pealing and the small crowd that had been gathered out front began to make their way inside.

Callie adjusted her bonnet, facing forward again. "Thank you, children. You are amazing storytellers. And thank you," she said turning back to him, "for the loan of your watch."

He accepted his timepiece back, mouthing a quick, "Thank you."

She merely nodded as she smoothed her skirt.

A few other latecomers were still making their way inside when Jack pulled the wagon up to the hitching rail.

"Simon, you help the girls down," Jack instructed as he secured the horse.

He knew what his role was today and he was determined to play it well. If only to prove that Callie wasn't the only one capable of making the best of an uncomfortable situation.

He helped her down, then offered his arm. He placed his hand solicitously over hers as he escorted his new family into the church. The fourth pew on the right, the one the Tyler family had occupied all during his growing up years, was vacant. Apparently the townsfolk still favored their same seats, Sunday after Sunday.

Jack sat through the opening of the service, fighting the urge to leave. The only thing he actually looked forward to was the singing. With his mother serving as church organist, there had always been music in his home, especially hymns. He remembered many an evening spent with her playing their old upright piano while the family sang along.

It looked like one of Mrs. Friarson's daughters played the organ now. Was it Cora or Ruby? They were both several years younger than Jack and he hadn't ever been able to keep them straight, even when he lived here. He reached for one of the hymnals and held it so that he and Callie could share it. But when the Friarson girl struck the first few chords and the congregation launched into song, Jack forgot all about identifying the musician.

Callie's voice was amazing. Strong and clear, it had an almost haunting purity to it. There was beauty there, beauty that went beyond any surface definition. He found himself using the shared hymnal as an excuse to lean closer, brushing shoulders with her as he let that wonderful voice wash over him.

It was only when the music had stopped and he saw the faint blush on her face that he realized how transparent he'd been. Jack adjusted his jacket as he faced forward.

No real harm done. If anyone in the congregation had noticed, they would put it down to the fact that he and Callie were newlyweds. And hopefully Callie would assume that he was just playing his part.

But he'd have to watch himself. That little twitch of attraction had been a mite too real for comfort.

Later, as they exited the church, Reverend Hollingsford shook Jack's hand. "It was good to look out over the congregation this morning and see you seated in your brother's place with your family all around you."

Jack nodded, trying to keep his smile friendly. So, even the pew had become Lanny's rather than the Tyler family's.

As soon as they made it past the reverend, the kids ran off with some of their friends, and Virgil called Jack over to join a discussion with several of the other menfolk.

While he talked, Jack kept a close eye on Callie. Just to make sure she didn't feel abandoned or lost in the crowd, he told himself.

But Mrs. Mayweather and Ida Lee had drawn her into discussion with a circle of friends, and as long as they stayed close, he knew Callie would be all right.

"By the way," Mr. Dobson said, claiming his attention, "Lanny had talked to me about placing an order for a new strain of corn he was thinking about planting next year. We were all pretty interested in watching how it went. You planning to follow through with that?"

"I don't know. Hadn't really given it any thought." Jack wasn't ready to tell these folks he wouldn't be sticking around that long. It somehow didn't feel fair to Callie to announce the day after their wedding that he was planning to leave in a few weeks.

Then again, it was probably better to start dropping a few hints so folks could get used to the idea and not think anything objectionable had happened between the two of them when the time came. "Besides," he said, choosing his words carefully, "I may end up going back to my old job once I get Callie and the kids settled in. I have a family to support now, after all."

Mr. Dobson shrugged. "Well, farming was always more Lanny's strong suit, I suppose."

"That brother of yours was both smart and good with his hands," another of the men added. "Always finding ways to improve his crop yield or make life easier for him and his family."

"I'll bet you've seen some exciting things in your travels," Virgil interjected.

Jack could always count on his friend to try to snuff out any "Ain't Lanny wonderful?" conversations before they got too thick. "I don't know about exciting," Jack drawled, "but yes, I've happened on some sights. I've seen the Rocky Mountains and the Grand Canyon. I've seen the Pacific Ocean and I've seen a tree so big it would take twenty men to circle it."

One of the men let out an appreciative whistle. "That must be some tree." Then he turned to someone else in the group. "That reminds me. Didn't Lanny say he'd planned to put in a peach orchard next spring?"

And as quick as that, the conversation turned to Lanny once again.

Jack let the conversation flow around him. He was well-traveled and experienced. Still, to these folks, he was Lanny's shadow of a brother. Nothing had changed for him here.

Nothing ever would.

A few minutes later, the womenfolk began to signal that it was time to go. As the groups reformed into family clusters and headed toward their wagons or moved to the sidewalk that led into town, Jack saw Annabeth run up and take hold of one of Callie's hands.

Simon left his friends grudgingly to join them, and Jack noticed that the boy's surliness had returned.

"Where's Emma?" Callie looked around the dwindling crowd, a frown on her face.

"I saw her picking flowers back behind the church," Annabeth said. "You want me to go fetch her?"

Jack waved them forward. "Y'all go ahead and get settled in the buggy. I'll fetch her."

He headed toward the side of the church, nodding to friends as he did so. But before he'd covered more than a couple of yards, he spotted his niece leaving the cemetery, traces of tears on her cheeks.

Wishing he'd asked Callie to search Emma out, he stood there as the girl caught sight of him and hurried over.

"I'm sorry," she said as she drew close. "I didn't mean to keep y'all waiting."

"That's okay. We're not in any big hurry." Feeling awkward, Jack put a hand on her shoulder. "Any time you want to come out here and visit, you let me know. Okay?"

Emma nodded and offered him a grateful smile.

Jack felt a flash of relief. Apparently he wasn't completely without the skills needed to handle this parent thing.

Callie sat in the parlor, pen poised over a sheet of paper.

Lunch was over and the kitchen cleaned up. The sound of the children playing with the dogs drifted in through the open window. Jack was upstairs doing heaven only knew what. The man was certainly not one to voluntarily share any personal information.

There was absolutely nothing to keep her from finally writing that letter she'd promised her father.

Yet she'd sat here for ten minutes now, just staring at the blank sheet of paper. How could she possibly explain all that had transpired in the few short days since she'd arrived?

The sound of footsteps descending the stairs provided a welcome distraction. But when Jack came into view, he looked dressed for work.

"Where are you going?"

He paused with his hand on the screen door. "There's a section of fence out behind the barn that needs attention," he said as if she had no business asking. He pushed open the door. "I thought I'd—"

She set her pen down. "It's Sunday."

They stared at each other for a long minute. Finally Jack shrugged and let the door close. "All right." He headed toward the parlor and leaned against the doorjamb, crossing his arms. "So what do you suggest we do with this perfectly good afternoon? I'm not much good at just sitting on my hands."

"Well, we could have a talk." She'd like to learn more about this man she was married to.

"Talk about what?"

He made it sound as if she'd asked him to eat a dung beetle.

She'd better start with something safe. "It's not as if we know each other well," she said. "I'm certain there's lots of information we could share to help us get to know each other better."

"Actually, I figure we know all we need to about each other." He crossed one booted foot over the other. "The less personal we make this whole arrangement, the better it'll be."

The words were like salt on a cut. Why was he so determined to keep that wall up? "Very well, then, we should do something with the children, something to help them feel like we're coming together as a family."

"What do you suggest?"

The man was determined not to make this easy.

Remembering the items still packed in her small trunk, Callie stood, a grin spreading across her face. "Actually, I have just the thing." Why hadn't she thought of this sooner? "You gather the children. I'll meet you out on the porch."

Callie was thrilled. She'd found something they could all enjoy together, something that brought them one step closer to being a true family. Now if she could just do the same for her marriage.

When she stepped outside, four pairs of eyes looked at her with varying degrees of wariness and expectation.

She held up the item she'd retrieved from her room. "This book is called *The Swiss Family Robinson*. I thought I might read a part of it to you this afternoon."

Annabeth's eyes lit up. "Is it like our story about Flora and Hawk?"

"It's a different kind of story." Callie sat on the porch swing, where she was immediately joined by the two girls. "But I think you're going to like it every bit as much."

Simon held back, wrinkling his nose. "I'll bet it's just some sappy fairy tale about princesses and such."

"Actually, it's an adventure story. My father read it to me when I was about Emma's age. And I enjoyed it so much I read it on my own when I got older."

Simon looked far from convinced. "What kind of adventure?"

"It's about a family who's shipwrecked and stranded on a deserted island. They have to find ways to survive all on their own." She turned to Annabeth, tweaking one of her curls. "And along the way, they encounter lots of strange and exotic animals."

Annabeth bounced up and down on her seat. "Ooh, that sounds exciting."

"It is." Callie opened the book. "I tell you what. I'll start reading. If any of you get bored, feel free to return to whatever it was you were doing before."

Turning to the first page, she began reading. "Already the tempest had continued six days; on the seventh its fury…"

Thirty minutes later, she closed the book. "Well, that's enough for one sitting."

She smiled at the clamor of protest. Even Simon had edged closer while she read.

Her glance snagged on Jack's and she felt her grin widen at the look on his face.

He'd enjoyed the story, too, had he?

As soon as he realized she'd noticed, Jack stood and stretched as if bored by the whole thing.

"I'm glad you enjoyed it so much," she said, turning back to the children. "But the book is much too long to finish in one sitting. If you like, we'll plan to read a little every day."

Chapter Eighteen

That evening, Jack sat on the porch again, whittling by the light of the moon.

Callie sure didn't fit into any kind of box he knew of. Hiding behind that bonnet and avoiding the limelight the way she did made her seem timid. And the woman was absolutely out of her element when it came to handling the farm chores.

But then again, she didn't seem to let much stand in her way when she wanted something, at least not for very long. In fact, when she happened on an obstacle, she easily went over or around it.

And she hadn't murmured a word of protest this evening when he'd told her it was time to get the animals in for the night. She just asked what she could do to help.

There was no denying she was good with the children. They'd hung on to her every word as she read that story. And to tell the truth, he'd been almost as taken in by it as they were.

The tale itself was part of it—nothing like a rousing adventure to keep you wanting to find out what happens next. But it was more than that. The way she'd breathed life into the words—the animation in her voice and face—had been just plain entertaining. He could see the whole thing playing out as if it were on a stage.

And her singing in church today. She had an amazing voice, using it as a good musician used his instrument. And he was pretty sure he wasn't the only one who'd noticed. In fact he wouldn't be surprised if the choir didn't try to recruit her next time they showed up for Sunday service.

The door opened behind him and she stepped out on the porch.

"Thank you for going to church with us today."

He ran his thumb over the edge of the wood. Did she think he'd done it just to get her approval? "I keep my promises."

"Yes, of course. I didn't mean to imply otherwise."

Jack changed the subject, moderating his tone as he glanced over his shoulder. "Interesting book."

Some of the stiffness left her spine, and she sat on the bench behind him near the door. "I've always enjoyed it. I probably read that story a half dozen times before I turned twelve."

"Seems an unusual choice for a girl."

"Does it? I've always liked books that could carry me off to exotic destinations."

At least that was something they had in common. He turned just enough to see her without turning his neck. "So, you like to travel."

She laughed. "I'm afraid the only traveling I'd done before coming here *was* through books." She tugged on her bonnet. "My family was always good about keeping me close—you know, sheltering me from strangers and large crowds."

Hmm. Couldn't tell much from her tone, but he got that sense again that something wasn't quite right. Was that so-called sheltering something she'd appreciated or chafed at? Or had there been other motives that drove her family to keep her close?

He leaned back and studied her a moment. "You know, you don't need to wear that bonnet around the house."

The smile she gave him was one part wistfulness and three parts resignation. "I think it's probably best I keep it on until the children get to know me a little better."

"They're all in bed now."

She took her bottom lip between her teeth, studying his face as if not certain of his intention.

He felt a stubborn impulse to push the point. "You insist that this is your home now, that me and the kids are your family. Did you wear that thing constantly when you were just among family?"

"Not growing up. But—"

She halted abruptly.

Now wasn't that interesting? He'd give a pretty penny to know what it was she'd been about to say.

Whatever it was, though, she apparently decided against elaborating.

"Very well." With a small nod, she untied the ribbons under her chin. After only a slight hesitation, she removed the bonnet completely and set it in her lap.

It never ceased to amaze him how different she looked without that shield she hid behind.

Sure, she had that birthmark. But she also had rich green eyes and high cheekbones that gave her profile a classic beauty.

Why had God seen fit to mar such a face with that angry-looking stain? As far as he could tell, she was a good and dutiful member of His flock, not a rebellious scapegrace like himself. Surely she'd earned some measure of mercy.

Realizing he'd been staring, Jack went back to whittling. "So, what do you think about Texas so far?"

She smiled as she fanned herself with the bonnet. "It's certainly a lot hotter than Ohio. But I can see why Julia came to love it so much." She gazed off into the night, her smile turning dreamy. "There's a wild sort of beauty here, an untamed quality, that gets under your skin. God's majesty seems closer, more visible somehow."

"Don't you miss your home just a little bit?" Jack asked.

Her grin had a teasing quality to it. "If you're trying to hint that I should go back, I'm afraid it's too late for that. To answer your question, though, of course I miss my family and former home. But my life has taken a new path now and I'm quite happy with it."

He leaned back, resting his spine against a support post. "Speaking of family, you know a lot about mine, but I don't know anything about yours."

She gave him a look he couldn't quite read. Was she remembering that he'd refused her earlier offer to have this conversation? If so, she chose not to throw it back at him.

"There's not a lot to tell. I have four sisters, two older and two younger. All four are married, two have children. My father is a tailor, one of the best in Hallenton."

He heard the touch of pride in her voice and remembered her saying her father had read to her as a child. Theirs was obviously a close relationship.

"And your mother?" he prodded.

"She died of a fever when I was fourteen." Callie paused, seeming to go inside herself for a minute. "About six months ago, my father married a very sweet, lovely young woman whom he met while on a business trip to Philadelphia. Sylvia, my stepmother, has made him quite happy."

The very neutrality of her normally expressive voice hinted that there was more to the story.

"And how do the two of you get along?"

Her expression closed off further and he wondered for a

minute if she'd tell him to mind his own business. But she leaned back against the wall, putting her face deeper in shadow.

"Sylvia is a gently raised woman with very delicate sensibilities. She's been nothing but kind to me. In fact, she went out of her way to make certain I knew I would always be welcome in my father's home, even though she was now the 'lady of the house.'"

Was that it? Had there been tension between the women over that position of power? Or did it have more to do with her stepmother's "delicate sensibilities"?

Suddenly her earlier half-finished answer—when he'd asked about wearing her bonnet in her old home—made sense. He felt a surge of anger that anyone would make her feel she was a burden or someone to be tolerated.

But before he could press further, she turned the tables on him.

"What about you?" she asked. "I know something about the boy you were, but Julia and Lanny never heard from you after you left Sweetgum. What did you do during those years?"

Her words reminded him again of the advantage she had over him because of Julia's letters. "As you said, not much to tell. I drifted around for a bit, seeing different parts of the country. Went to work for the railroad. Joined up with a demolition team and learned the trade. Eventually formed my own team. I've been blowing things up ever since."

"What an odd way to describe it." She tilted her head slightly. "Don't you sometimes wish you were building something rather than destroying things?"

Her question got his back up. Was she judging him again?

"Actually, I'm proud of the work I do. And I'm d—I'm good at it. I've built up a reputation for precision and safety that few others in the business can match."

He shaved another curl of wood from the block in one quick motion. "And I don't think of it as destroying things. What my team does is clear the way so others can come behind and build new things, important things, like the railroad lines that connect people and places."

"I hadn't thought of it that way." Her brow furrowed thoughtfully. "So you enjoy your work?"

"Yes, I do." Time to change the subject. "By the way, I plan to spend some time in town this week clearing away the debris left from the fire."

Her face lit up with approval. "That's a fine idea. It's not good for the children to face that every time they go to town."

"My thoughts exactly."

"And I'm certain the townsfolk will appreciate it as well." Her smile shifted to concern. "But you're not planning to tackle it alone, are you?"

He shrugged. "Normally I would. But I'd like to get most of it taken care of before we go to town for market day on Friday. I asked Virgil after church service this morning to spread the word that I was looking to hire some help. I'll spend the day around here tomorrow making sure everything's in order, then get started on Tuesday."

"Will that be enough time to get it all done?"

"If I get a couple of hard-working youths to help out it shouldn't be any problem. But even if I have to do it all myself, I'll see that it gets done."

Jack watched from the corner of his eye as she twisted her hands in the folds of her skirt. Something was on her mind.

"I wanted to speak to you about Emma," she finally said.

Emma? Of the three children she seemed to be adjusting the best. Sure, she'd been crying at the cemetery this morning, but there was nothing so unusual in that. The girl had just lost her parents, after all. "What about her?"

"She's just too quiet, too closed in."

Wasn't quiet a good thing? "Mrs. Mayweather did say she's always been on the shy side."

"I know." Callie tucked a strand of hair behind her ear. "But this seems like something more than just shyness."

How could she know that after so short a time? "The kid's been through a lot these past few days. Seems to me it's only natural for her to mourn for a time."

"Maybe you're right." Callie didn't sound entirely convinced.

"I'm sure that's all it is." Jack rested his arm on his knee. "I would have thought you'd be more worried about the way Simon's been acting."

She smiled sadly. "Simon is just angry at the world right now. No chance of him hiding how he's feeling. He'll get it out of his system eventually. He just needs a firm hand until he learns to trust us and feels some sense of security again. And thankfully, a firm hand seems to be your specialty."

Before he could respond, she stood. "I guess I'll turn in."

He nodded. "I think I'll sit out here a spell longer."

Once Callie was inside, Jack continued absently shaving on the block of wood.

So, she thought his parenting methods were something to be thankful for, did she? That was a surprise.

What was even more of a surprise was the warm feeling of pleasure brought on by simply glimpsing the light of approval in her eyes. He'd never had a woman look at him quite that way before.

And, in spite of himself, he found he liked it.

Chapter Nineteen

The next morning, Callie had already kicked off the covers and swung her feet to the floor when she heard Jack's rap on her door. "I'll be out in a minute." At least he hadn't caught her still asleep this time.

"I'll meet you in the barn."

Again, when Callie hurried through the kitchen, she saw the stove had been stoked. Just how early did that man get up, anyway?

She entered the barn to see Jack already seated beside Belle with several inches of milk in his pail.

He glanced up. "Think you remember how this works?"

Callie nodded. So much for morning pleasantries.

"Good. You'll find the grain in that sack over there." He nodded his head toward an empty stall. "Scoop up some for Clover's trough, but keep an eye out for rats."

Callie had her hand halfway in the sack before his warning sunk in and she drew back. "Rats?"

"That's right."

Was that a hint of amusement she heard in his tone? Maybe he was just teasing.

"The barn cats do a fair job of keeping them run off," he elaborated, disabusing her of the notion that rats weren't a real possibility, "but every once in a while they slip in past the cats. The feed sacks draw them like a candy store does a youngster."

She swallowed, trying to work up the courage to stick her hand into the sack.

The rhythmic pinging of milk squirting into the pail stopped. "Just knock on the side a couple of times with the handle of the hoe or pitchfork and wait a couple of seconds. If there's one in there, he'll come scurrying out."

Not an altogether reassuring thought. Callie did as she was told, certain he was laughing at her all the while. When nothing stirred, she gingerly scooped up a generous portion of grain and hurried over to Clover's trough.

Jack nodded approvingly. "Once she starts eating, you can get to work. Don't forget to wash her udder and to save some milk for her calf."

Callie found the correct rhythm quicker this time, getting the milk to squirt into the pail on her second try.

Once the milking was done, she set her pail beside Jack's on the worktable and let Clover's calf out of his pen.

She and Jack worked together until they were finished in the barn, Callie filling the silence with a quiet humming. This work was different from what she was used to, but it wasn't much harder than scrubbing floors or doing piles of laundry, both of which she was intimately familiar with.

Jack finally dusted his hands on his pants and shot her a challenging look. "So, do you want to try your hand at gathering eggs this morning?"

"Of course." That chore *had* to be easier than milking cows.

Callie let him lead the way.

First he scattered grain in the chicken yard. "Just throw this about on the ground and let them scratch for it. Most of them will come out to eat, which makes the egg gathering a lot easier. Of course, a few might stay on the nest."

"And what do you do then?"

"You carefully reach under them and slide the egg out." He handed her the basket. "But before you reach into a nest, whether a hen is there or not, it's a good idea to check for snakes or other critters."

"Snakes!" First rats and now snakes?

"For the most part, any snake you find in the nest will be a chicken snake. It might give you a scare, but it won't hurt you. What it *will* do is swallow your pin money."

"Pin money?"

"They eat the eggs. Not to mention baby chicks, if you're trying to hatch some. Eggs aren't just food for our table. Any extras you have at the end of the week can be taken to town on market day and traded for other things you need."

"So what do you do if a snake is in there?" Poisonous or not, there was absolutely nothing that could convince her to touch a snake.

He must have seen the look on her face. "Don't worry, it doesn't happen often. We'll just cross that bridge when we come to it. So, assuming there's no snake, if the chicken is still sitting on the nest, you're gonna have to reach under her to collect the egg. Sometimes they'll let you do it without much fuss, but other times, they'll take exception."

"How?"

"You'll have to watch out for the sharp beaks—I've gotten my hands pecked more times than I care to remember. Or they might try to fly into your face, so be ready to duck. Just don't drop the eggs."

Callie swallowed hard. She'd accepted that farm work

would be difficult. But she hadn't realized it could also be hazardous.

She sent up a quick prayer for courage. She was determined not to embarrass herself in front of Jack

"Good breakfast." Jack set his fork down and stood. "Girls, you help your Aunt Callie clean up the kitchen. Simon, you can help me take care of some chores outside."

The boy met his glance across the table with a guarded look.

"Have you ever chopped firewood before?" Jack asked.

Simon sat up straighter. "No, sir."

"Ever handled an ax at all?"

Simon shook his head again.

"Then I'd say your education has a few holes in it. It's high time we fixed that."

"Yes, sir." Simon stood and gathered up his dishes. Obviously the idea of wielding an ax sounded better than kitchen chores.

Jack saw the protest forming on Callie's lips and gave her a look that silenced whatever she'd been about to say. Last night she'd said she appreciated his firm hand with the kids. She'd just have to remember that and trust him to know what they could and couldn't handle. These three had to learn to take some responsibility, especially if she was to have any chance of making a go of things here once he left.

She certainly couldn't do it all on her own, and there were lots of things the kids could handle with the right kind of training.

Jack carried his empty plate to the sink. "Why, by the time your Uncle Lanny and I were your age," he told Simon, "we were chopping firewood, milking cows and helping with the plowing."

Callie turned to the girls. "All right, ladies. Annabeth, you finish clearing the table. Emma, you can wash the dishes. I'll dry and put them away." She handed Emma a clean apron, then fetched hers and tied it around her waist.

"It's laundry day," she continued, "so I'm going to the washroom to set the water to boiling while you two get started in here."

Jack raised a brow. How about that—Callie was actually taking his cue on something. Maybe he'd been wrong about her teachability after all?

Jack hefted his sledgehammer as he watched Simon. The boy hit a chunk of wood dead center, splitting it into two nearly equal pieces. They'd been at it for almost thirty minutes now and both of them were sweaty and tired. But Jack finally felt that his nephew was getting the hang of it.

He clapped Simon on the shoulder. "That's probably enough for today. Good job."

Simon added his contribution to the woodpile and wiped his brow. "You're planning to go back to work with the railroad, aren't you?" The boy leaned on the ax handle and gave Jack a dark look.

Jack's temper rose in response, then he remembered what Callie had said last night about the likely cause of Simon's orneriness. "Eventually," he said as matter-of-factly as he could. Then he led the way to the barn.

Simon hefted the ax and marched along behind him. "And you're going to just leave us stuck out here on this hayseed farm."

"I'll be coming back for visits every few months. And it's not such a bad place to be, Simon, if you just give it a chance."

"If you think it's so great, why'd you leave Sweetgum as soon as you could?"

Jack put away the wedge and sledgehammer. *Remember, he's just a confused kid.* "That was different. I was a grown man and your Uncle Lanny and Aunt Julia were moving in here to help my mother after my pa died." He held out a hand for the ax. "It was time for me to strike out on my own."

"Momma said you wanted to get away from here ever since you were a kid."

"True. But I don't regret growing up here or learning all the skills my daddy taught me." At least not now when he looked back on it. "I still use a lot of what I learned back then."

"Well, that's where we're different. My pa taught me town skills 'cause that where my home is."

What in Tom's back forty were town skills? "I'm sorry, son, but it's time for you to accept that that place doesn't exist any more."

Simon's expression darkened. "Don't call me that. I'm not your son." He crossed his arms over his chest. "Besides, the land the café and our house was built on is still there. And it belongs to Emma and me. We can rebuild it."

"Maybe. But then what? You and Emma can't live there by yourselves. And your Aunt Callie and Annabeth will need your help whenever I'm away."

Simon's hands clenched at his sides. "That's not fair."

Jack shrugged. "Maybe not. But that's the way it is."

Simon wasn't giving up. "Then they could live with Emma and me."

Jack folded his arms. His patience was growing thin. "And do what? How would you live? At least here there's fresh milk and eggs. There's a vegetable garden out back and meat in the smokehouse."

"I could get a job." Simon met Jack's gaze head on. "I'll bet Mr. Pearson down at the hotel would hire me to run errands."

The boy didn't know when to cut bait. "It wouldn't be enough to support all of you." He placed a hand on the boy's shoulder, trying a different approach. "Simon, when I'm not here, you're going to be the man of the house. I need to know that I can count on you to take care of the womenfolk and always think about what's best for the family, not just for yourself."

Simon shook off Jack's hand and stepped back. "And is that what you're doing when you think about leaving?"

"That's different." Was he really trying to justify his actions to an eleven-year-old? "Look, I need to return to my old job. It's important work, I'm good at it, and my crew and my customers depend on me. And like I said, I'm not abandoning you. I'll come back to visit on a regular basis and I'll be sending money to help Aunt Callie with the expenses."

"So that makes it all okay?"

"Yes, it does," Jack snapped.

He watched as Simon spun on his heel and stalked away.

Jack raked a hand through his hair. So much for holding on to his temper. But confound it, what was it going to take to make that boy see reason?

Chapter Twenty

Jack sat on the top step of the porch, listening to the familiar night sounds while he mulled over an idea that had been taking shape in his mind for the last few hours. It seemed one good thing had come out of his discussion with Simon this morning after all. The boy's idea about rebuilding on that plot of land in town had given him the backup plan he needed.

He wasn't at all surprised when the door opened behind him. In fact, he'd been waiting for her.

"They're all tucked in."

"Good." He glanced up and frowned at her bonnet, pointing his knife at it.

"Aren't you forgetting something?"

He watched the play of emotion on her face. She obviously thought he was being unreasonable. And maybe he was. But he just didn't like to see her constantly imprisoning herself in those uncomfortable-looking headwraps.

Callie moved closer, leaning against one of the support posts that flanked the steps. The one with his father's carving.

With slow, deliberate movements, she removed the bonnet.

It was strangely mesmerizing to watch her unveil in the silvery moonlight.

When she was done, she raised her face to the stars and shook her head, as if to make the most of her newfound freedom. But he noticed she had positioned herself so that her "good" profile was presented to him.

He decided not to press her on that point. Not tonight.

"I dug out all of Julia and Leland's old clothes this afternoon," she said. "I was wondering if you wanted any of Leland's things. For your own use, I mean."

Just what he *didn't* need—more of Leland's hand-me-downs. He shaved a thick curl of wood from the block in a sharp movement. "No, thank you. I'm sure you can find some other use for them."

"Actually, I already have."

He glanced up, intrigued.

"Emma and Simon's wardrobes are sadly lacking," she said, her voice rushing over the words. "I'd like to take the cloth from these garments and fashion them some new things."

One step above a hand-me-down. Would the kids mind?

"Wouldn't it be a lot easier to just buy some new fabric and start from scratch?"

"Maybe. But that would be so wasteful when this cloth is readily available. And I can fashion the clothes so that they look like new, made for children their age. I told you, my father is a tailor. I learned quite a bit from him."

A practical-minded woman. And once again she'd recognized a need that had slipped right by him.

He rubbed his chin, not sure if he felt admiration, jealousy or some combination of the two.

"Suit yourself," he said, then changed the subject. "Don't forget, I plan to work on clearing out the rubble from the fire tomorrow. I'll probably be gone most of the day."

"I'll make sure I get up earlier."

Did she think he planned to leave without taking care of things here first? "Don't worry. I won't head out until the morning chores are done."

"That wasn't what I meant." She turned to face him fully, possibly forgetting she'd removed her bonnet. "What you're planning to do in town is important. And it'll be hard work. I just don't want to hold you back or add to your work."

"Don't worry, you won't." He rested an elbow on his thigh. Time to mention the new plan. "I'm thinking, once I get the place cleared, I might build something new there."

"Oh?" Her unspoken question hung in the air between them.

"Yes. Simon reminded me earlier that that bit of property is his and Emma's legacy. I was thinking, if I put up a new structure, it would give you and the kids a place to go if you decided life out here was too hard."

She crossed her arms. "That won't happen."

"Maybe not." He didn't want to argue with her over this. He was going to provide a safety net for her and the kids, whether she wanted one or not. Yep, by August he could head back to his old life with a clear conscience and the confidence that he'd done his duty.

But right now he'd soothe her ruffled feathers. "Even if you do decide to stay here, we could always rent the place out and have another source of income."

She relaxed, letting her arms drop to her sides. "That makes sense. But how will Simon and Emma react to having someone else live in what they think of as their place?"

"It might be hard for them to get used to at first, especially Simon. But I'll make sure it doesn't look anything like the old place. And as long as we lease it, it'll still be there for them to do whatever they please with once they get old enough."

She brushed a stray lock of hair off her forehead. "Building a new place will be a lot of work."

"Most things worth doing are."

"I agree. But won't it delay your departure?"

Was she disappointed or glad? He caught himself—the answer to that question was irrelevant. "It might delay things a bit. But I think in the long run this will be better for all of us."

It would give him a clearer conscience when he left, that was certain.

Jack arrived in town the next morning to find three youths lined up in front of what was once his sister's home and workplace. He gave them an assessing look as he set the brake on the wagon. One of them was a big lad, probably seventeen or eighteen, and obviously used to hard work. The second was not quite as big or as old, but he still looked like a worker. The third hopeful was slimmer and not near as muscled. But if the kid was willing to work, he could probably still get some use out—

He frowned, taking a second, closer look as he neared the trio. Unless he was mistaken, the third youth was a girl dressed in boy's overalls.

Now who in tarnation had let their daughter out like that?

He stopped in front of his would-be work crew and folded his arms. "So you all want to earn a bit of money, do you?"

Three heads bobbed in unison. "Yes, sir."

"What're your names?"

The biggest of the three spoke up first. "Calvin Lufkin."

"You Walter Lufkin's boy?"

"Yes, sir."

Walter Lufkin was a farmer with a big place and an even bigger brood of children. The man was as honest as the day was long and knew the meaning of hard work. Chances were, he'd passed those traits on to his son. "You'll do."

He nodded to the second boy. "And you?"

"Albert Hanfield. I'm Charles Hanfield's son," he added before Jack could ask.

Charles Hanfield owned a pig farm just outside of town. Albert likely knew the meaning of hard work as well. "All right, Albert, you're hired."

Next he turned to his third candidate.

"Jessie Mills." She offered the name before he even had a chance to ask.

"And would that be short for Jessica?"

The two boys snickered, but stopped abruptly when she flashed a glare their way.

She turned back to Jack and the tilt of her chin reminded him strongly of Callie. "Actually, it's short for Jessamine."

"Well, Jessie, I'm afraid—"

"You didn't ask about my dad," she said, cutting him off. "He's Joe Mills, and he runs the livery and smithy. I'm used to hard work, just ask anyone here in town."

"I'm sure you are, but knocking these timbers down and carting them off is not only hard work, it can be dirty and dangerous, too."

"I work around a smithy and horses that ain't been broke yet. I don't mind getting dirty and I know how to handle dangerous jobs."

There was something about the girl, an edge of determination beneath her bravado, that kept Jack from refusing her outright. He rubbed his chin. "I tell you what. I'll hire you for just this morning and see how you do. After lunch we'll talk again."

"Yes, sir! I promise you won't be sorry."

Jack wasn't so sure of that—he was already second-guessing his decision. But he'd given her his word and he'd stick by it.

He stepped back and spoke to the group as a whole. "The pay is four bits a day, and I expect you to earn every cent of it. I don't have any use for laggards and lay-abouts. I want to have every bit of this wreck dismantled and the whole lot cleared out by Thursday evening. And I want it done without anyone getting hurt in the process. Understand?"

There was a chorus of "Yes, sir"s.

"Good. Then you'll find tools in my buckboard. Calvin, I want you working with me, knocking down these timbers. Jessie and Albert, while we're working on this end, you get a wheelbarrow and start carting off everything that's just laying about down on that end. And that means shoveling the ashes as well. Make sure you keep your eyes open for jagged bits and shaky timbers."

He grabbed a sledgehammer from the back of the wagon. "Take the bigger timbers and stack them in the middle of the back lot. We'll go through 'em later to see what can be reused and what should be tossed on someone's woodpile." He paused. "If you happen across anything that seems salvage-able—anything at all—set it aside for me to look at."

The three nodded and set to work.

All through the morning, Jack kept an eye on Jessie. He had to admit, the girl definitely knew how to get things done. She was nimble and quick, and she didn't complain about the dirt or the work.

When he called a break at lunchtime she sauntered over with a smug smile. "Do I pass the test?"

He took a bite of the sandwich Callie had packed for him, studying her thoughtfully while he chewed.

After a moment some of her cockiness faded and she jammed her hands in the pockets of her overalls. "Well?"

He swallowed and tilted his hat back. "You'll do."

Relief shone in her eyes. "Thanks, Mr. Tyler. I'll do you a real good job this week, you'll see."

He watched as the girl raced off in the direction of the livery stable, wondering what her story was.

That evening, Jessie held back as the two boys headed home. "Mr. Tyler, I want to thank you for taking a chance on me today."

Jack nodded. "Thank you for not disappointing me."

She watched as he dipped his bandanna in the horse trough and washed his neck. "People say you've traveled all over the country."

Jack laughed. "Not all over, but I've visited my share of places."

"That's what I'm gonna do someday." Her voice lost its hard edge. For the first time he saw something of her feminine side. "And not just this country, either," she continued. "I'm gonna travel to Europe and Africa and all those places Mrs. Mayweather talks about in school."

He remembered having those yearnings to see what existed outside the narrow confines of Sweetgum. "I wish you well."

"That's why I'm working so hard. People make fun of me 'cause I'm not like other girls. I'll do most any old job to earn a few pennies, so long as it's honest labor. But it doesn't matter what they think of me. Once I leave here I can become whoever I want to be."

He heard echoes of his own childhood in her words. His eagerness to leave Sweetgum had been tied up in his desire to be looked at differently, to become someone other than Lanny's little brother.

What was her reason?

Not that it was any of his business. He squeezed the water

from his bandanna and put his hat back on. Then he had another thought. "How would you like to earn some extra money?"

Her eyes lit up. "Just tell me what you need done."

"This job requires someone with keen eyes who doesn't mind getting more than a little dirty."

"Then I'm your girl."

"I told y'all earlier to keep an eye out for anything salvageable. I know it may be a lost cause, but I'm looking for anything that survived the fire that would have some value or meaning to Emma and Simon. It'll mean digging through all the soot and ashes to see what might be buried underneath."

If there was any piece of Emma and Simon's home or belongings that remained intact, he intended to find it.

"I'll be doing some looking myself, of course, but it would be good to have another set of eyes."

"I think that's a mighty fine thing to do. The Carsons were always good to me and I'd be right honored to help you do something nice for their kids."

With a nod, she headed home, whistling off key.

He watched her a moment, then climbed into the wagon, ready to get back to his family.

As the wagon passed out of town, he let the mare have her head. She knew the way home as well as he did.

Jack rolled his shoulders and stretched his neck muscles, trying to work some of the kinks out. Clearing the burned out shell of his sister's café was hard work. Demolition, of course, was his stock and trade. But this was not like his usual jobs.

Making sure he got those scorched walls and timbers down without allowing the whole thing to collapse in on him and his young crew made it much trickier.

Despite that, they'd made a lot of progress today. But they'd have to keep up the pace to meet his deadline.

Jessie, especially, had surprised him. The girl was a hard worker with a lot of grit and determination. She had big dreams and wasn't content to just sit back and *hope* they came true—she was doing everything in her power to *make* them come true.

Had she learned that from her parents—both the dreaming big and the working hard? What would his nieces and nephew learn from him? He wouldn't be around much, but when he was, he'd have to make sure he took his role as father figure seriously.

Of course, they had Callie to look to. And he'd challenge anyone to find a better example for a child to follow, especially when it came to a willingness to dig in and get the job done.

Remembering the way she'd tackled the farm chores these past few days brought a smile to his lips.

But only for a minute.

His shoulders slumped at the thought of tending to evening chores when he got back to the farm. It was like having two jobs at once. But it was only for about five weeks, give or take.

At least he'd have a home-cooked meal waiting for him when he finished up, something that was hit or miss at camp. One thing Callie could do well was cook.

The sun hadn't quite set when the horse turned into the familiar lane and Jack pulled her up short. Surprise washed away his fatigue. Callie and the kids were herding the cows into the barnyard.

Seems he'd underestimated the woman once again.

Chapter Twenty-One

Jack stepped out on the porch and drew his shoulders back, watching the fireflies play hide and seek in the front yard.

Callie was putting the children to bed, but he knew she'd be out to join him soon. It had become routine.

When he'd arrived home this evening, she'd only allowed him to take care of the horse and buggy, insisting that she and the kids could handle the rest of the chores while he went inside and washed all the soot and grime away before supper. There'd even been a kettle of water already warming on the firebox for him in the washroom.

A man could get used to that kind of treatment.

He stopped himself once again. It wouldn't do for him to get *too* used to it. He couldn't afford any ties that would make it harder on him or them when the time came for him to go.

He moved toward his usual seat on the top step, then paused.

Maybe he could repay the favor, even if only in a small way. After all, he didn't like being beholden to anyone.

If Callie was going to join him out here every night…

Acting on impulse, he grabbed the bench from its place by

the door and moved it up against the porch rail. He studied it a moment, then slid it slightly to the left.

There.

She'd have a place to sit if she wanted to, but could still stand at the rail if that was her preference.

He stared at the bench, rubbing the back of his neck. What if Callie read something into the gesture he hadn't intended?

Maybe he should just put things back the way they'd been.

He bent over the bench and then halted, a self-mocking smile curving his lips. For a man who prided himself on being decisive, he was certainly acting like a waffley whelp.

Jack left the bench where he'd placed it and pulled out his pocketknife.

Five minutes later, Callie finally stepped out on the porch.

Jack studiously sliced another curl of wood to add to the pile of shavings at his feet. He felt rather than saw her pause a moment before stepping forward. But she took a seat on the bench without comment.

"How did the work go today?" she asked.

He looked up and attempted to hide his surprise. For once, he hadn't had to prompt her to remove her bonnet.

A good sign.

"Better than expected. Three able-bodied workers showed up to help this morning." He resumed his whittling, watching her from the corner of his eye. "One of them's a girl."

She raised a brow. "How did that come about?"

"Jessie Mills is the blacksmith's daughter. She's got a burning desire to earn enough money to travel around the world."

"So, a soul mate of sorts."

He shrugged. "Let's just say I sympathize with her dreams. But she's earning her pay every bit as much as the two guys."

Callie merely smiled that wise-woman smile of hers.

Jack shaved another long curl of wood from the block. "I think we'll get everything cleared out by Thursday evening."

"You're doing a good thing for the children," Callie said, worry in her voice, "but don't push yourself too hard in the process."

"It's just for a few days—I know what I'm doing." He changed the subject. "So how did your day go?"

"We did all right. Today was ironing day, of course, so that took up a big part of the morning. While I worked on that, I had Simon and the girls drag the rugs out to give them a good beating."

"Sounds like you kept busy." He found himself wondering if they missed having him around at all.

"Oh, it wasn't all work. The girls had a tea party after lunch. And Ida Lee's son Gil came over to deliver some of her peach preserves. He stayed and spent some time with Simon."

"Good. Having a kid around here to spend time with might help Simon lose that chip on his shoulder."

Callie leaned back against the porch rail. Her neck looked longer, leaner without that bonnet.

"I overheard Simon telling him about the story we've been reading. They spent most of the afternoon playing shipwreck." She glanced over at him. "I'm afraid Cookie and Pepper were drafted to play the part of the goats," she said dryly.

He laughed, then pointed the wood at her. "I suppose you went ahead and read the latest chapter without me."

"Sorry, but I'm afraid so."

"An apology won't do it," he said with mock-sternness. "You'll have to fill me in on what I missed."

"Really?"

"Of course. You don't think you can abandon me in the middle of the adventure do you?"

Jack half-listened while she launched into a summary of the latest trials and triumphs of the shipwrecked family.

Yes, if he wasn't careful, a man could definitely get used to treatment like this.

Callie drew the brush through her hair, relishing the soothing, rhythmic movements.

She'd enjoyed reciting the high points of the latest chapter of *Swiss Family Robinson* to Jack tonight. His request meant he was enjoying the story, which in turn meant they did have a shared interest or two after all.

A promising sign.

Even more promising was the fact that he'd gone to the trouble of moving that bench for her this evening. Giving her a place to sit while they chatted was an unexpectedly thoughtful gesture. Was he beginning to enjoy those quiet moments together as much as she?

If only he didn't insist she remove her bonnet every evening. Callie stared at her reflection in the mirror, facing the ugliness head-on, something she rarely did. At least outside in the fading light her birthmark wasn't quite so obvious. Maybe that's why he was insistent about the whole thing. In the twilight it must look like more of a shadow than anything else. So he could at least pretend she looked okay.

Yes, that must be it. Having her sit there without her bonnet in the moonlight while they discussed the day's events probably lent a sense of normalcy to what—to him at least— must be an uncomfortable situation.

She set the brush down and reached back to separate her hair into three thick ropes. But before she could begin braiding, the door opened behind her.

"Aunt Callie?"

She turned to see Annabeth peeking through the doorway. "What is it, sweetheart?"

The little girl stepped inside the room. "I had a dream about Daddy."

Callie held out her arms, which was all the incentive the child needed. Annabeth rushed forward and snuggled into her lap. Callie picked up her brush and drew the bristles through the child's sunny curls. "Was it a good dream?"

"Uh-huh. He was leading me around on Cinnamon like he used to, and telling me how pretty I was, that I looked just like Mommy."

"That sounds very nice."

"It was. But then I woke up and I remembered he wasn't here anymore."

"And that made you sad?"

Annabeth nodded.

"It's okay to be sad, you know. My own mommy died when I was fourteen, and I was very sad, too. But do you want to know a secret?"

Annabeth nodded again.

"I was sad for me because I missed her so much. But I was also very happy for her."

The little girl's eyes widened. "You were?"

"Yes. Because I knew she was in heaven, and heaven is such a wonderful place, more wonderful than we can even imagine. I knew Mother was happy there and that nothing could hurt her or make her cry ever again."

"Oh." Annabeth thought about that a minute. "And that's where my daddy and mommy are, too."

Callie heard the question in her statement. "That's right. They're both there together. And your Aunt Nell and Uncle Jed are with them."

"And your mommy, too?"

"That's right. And you know, they're probably watching us right now."

Annabeth snuggled deeper into her lap. "That's nice."

"So even though it's okay to miss them, we can also be very happy for them."

"Okay." The word ended on a yawn.

"Now, it's time for you to get back to bed, young lady." Callie set the brush down and allowed Annabeth to slide from her lap. "Would you like me to tuck you in again?"

Annabeth nodded and slipped her hand in Callie's.

Callie led her down the hall to her room. The child was already rubbing her eyes as Callie pulled the covers up to her chin. Callie leaned down and kissed her forehead. Before she could rise again, Annabeth lifted a hand and stroked Callie's left cheek. "I don't care what Simon says," she said sleepily. "I like your angel kiss."

Callie stood, feeling both warmed and chilled by the artlessly uttered words.

What had Simon been saying?

Careful not to waken the still-sleeping Emma, Callie glided from the room and quietly closed the door behind her. She turned to find Jack standing at the top of the stairs, staring at her with a strange look in his eyes.

He stepped forward, his expression changing to concern. "Is something wrong with one of the girls?"

He spoke in a stage whisper, his voice oddly husky.

"No." She tucked a strand of hair behind her ear. "Annabeth was troubled by a dream she had, but I think she's okay now."

"Good." He cleared his throat. "Well then, I guess I'll say good-night. Again."

"Good-night." Callie, feeling as nervous as a schoolgirl under his peculiar stare, hurried across the hall and into the sanctuary of her room.

* * *

Jack closed the door to his chamber. Now why had he just reacted so strongly to the unexpected encounter? Even if he and Callie hadn't been married, there'd been nothing the least bit improper or suggestive in her appearance. In fact, that prim, buttoned-to-the-chin wrapper she had on would have looked at home in an elderly spinster's wardrobe.

He supposed it was the sight of those waves of unbound hair. Every other time he'd seen her without her bonnet she'd had her hair up in a tight bun or a braided coronet. He'd had no idea it was so long and fluid. She appeared to be a whole different person with her hair down—softer, more feminine.

But there was something else that had tugged at him just now. He'd seen a hint of pain in her eyes, in the slight droop of her shoulders. He itched to find out what had caused it, to see if there was a demon he could slay for her.

Jack shook his head. Now that was a blamed fool way to be thinking.

He splashed water from the bedside basin onto his face. Of course, it *was* natural for a man to want to protect his family. And Callie was part of his family now, the same way the kids were.

No more, no less.

Chapter Twenty-Two

It was already dark Thursday evening when Callie heard the sound of Jack's return. His work hours seemed to get longer with each passing day.

Twenty minutes later she watched him leave the barn and head toward the house. Despite his apparent weariness there was a jauntiness to the set of his shoulders.

Did that mean he'd finished clearing the lot? She hoped so, and not just for the children's sake. He'd worked so hard to make his deadline, it would be a shame for him to feel he'd failed.

As she set him a place at the table, she heard him step into the washroom, whistling. Where did the man get that kind of energy?

By the time Jack entered the kitchen, hair still damp, she had the meal ready for him.

He inhaled deeply as he took a place at the table. "Smells good. And boy, am I hungry."

"You put in a long day today."

"Yep, but we finished all the clearing out work." He scooped up a forkful of potatoes. "In fact, we did better than that. We set down the plank floor for the new building. Those kids won't even see the scorched earth when they go to town tomorrow."

No wonder he seemed so pleased with himself. "My goodness, you *did* get a lot done."

"It wasn't just me and my crew. Apparently word got around about what I was trying to do and why. Virgil came out today, along with several of Lanny and Nell's friends."

"And you're okay with that?"

He shrugged. "I'd rather have done it myself. But there wasn't time and these folks were doing it for the kids more than for me."

Well, well, Mr. I Don't Need Anybody was finally learning to accept a bit of help from others.

When the buckboard turned onto Main Street the next morning, Callie's gaze immediately locked onto the empty lot where the café used to stand. Instead of ashes and charred timbers, a platform of fresh lumber now marked the spot. In fact, several of the town's children were using the place as a makeshift playground.

It was indeed a remarkable transformation. Callie turned to Jack, touching his arm.

Simon also turned to Jack, disbelief and hope on his face. "You're rebuilding our house."

"Not your house." Jack's tone was firm. "It won't be anything like the building you remember. But yes, I've decided to erect a new structure where the old one stood."

Simon leaned forward, clutching the back of their seat. "But we can move back to town when it's finished, can't we?"

"I didn't say that."

"But—"

"One thing at a time, Simon," Callie said quickly. She didn't want to mar this outing with bickering and sullen pouts.

Especially not today.

Simon's eyes narrowed rebelliously, but he settled back in his seat without another word.

Callie closed Mrs. Mayweather's front gate behind her. Jessie Mills had volunteered to take Annabeth and Emma down to the livery to see Persia, the frisky young colt. Simon had disappeared somewhere with his friends, and Jack was working on his construction project.

So, once the shopping was done, she'd taken advantage of the free time to visit with her friend, as a gift to herself. The schoolteacher had been as warm and welcoming as ever, and had seemed genuinely interested in the progress the newly-formed family was making. They'd had a lovely talk over a tasty snack of tea and cake.

But now it was nearly noon. Time to gather the family and head back to the farm.

Callie found herself humming as she walked along the sidewalk toward the center of town. The day was gorgeous, the family had made it through this first week and God had proven once again what a faithful, loving Father he was.

So what if she were the only one who knew what day today was? She had blessings enough to make her content without any added fanfare.

She approached the hedge-lined border of the Pearsons' front lawn. Unless he'd already joined Jack at the work site, Simon was supposed to be here or at the Thompsons' home.

"You really learned how to milk a cow?"

Callie smiled at the sound of the boyish voice coming from the other side of the tall hedge.

"Sure, nothing to it."

Was there a touch of bragging in Simon's voice? Quite a change from the tone he'd used when she tried to teach him the skill a few days ago.

But the other boy laughed. "Next thing you know you'll be mucking out stalls and pulling stems of hay from your hair."

What a snide thing to say! No wonder Simon was so dissatisfied with life on the farm if his friends felt this way. How could she help him learn to—

"So how is life with Old Miss Splotchy-Face?"

Callie stopped in her tracks, stunned by the unexpectedness of the name-calling.

"Oh, you know, she keeps one of those horse-blinder bonnets on all the time." The sullen tone was back in Simon's voice.

"Bet you don't have problems with varmints on your place." There was an ugly snicker underlining the words. "All she'd have to do is take off that contraption and anything with eyes in its head would run for the hills."

"Yeah. She could scare the sweet out of sugar with that face, all right."

Heaven help her, that was Simon's voice. Was that how he really felt about her?

She heard the sound of spitting. Then Simon spoke again. "I have to keep an eye on things so she doesn't pull that bonnet off and scare the girls. You know what scaredy cats they can be."

There was more laughter and talk of how silly girls were, then one of the other boys spoke up. "So, are you going to be moving back to town when your Uncle Jack gets done with that new building?"

"*She* doesn't want to."

Callie had no doubt the "she" Simon referred to with such venom was herself.

"But I think Uncle Jack will get her to come around once he's done. Hey, why don't we head over to where they're working? I'll bet Uncle Jack would let us help if we asked."

Callie had only a few seconds to compose herself before the boys came racing out through the break in the hedge a few yards ahead of her. But she managed to school her features, determined not to let them know she'd heard anything amiss.

Simon saw her first and halted in his tracks. The look on his face was a hodge-podge of embarrassment, defiance and bravado. And maybe just the merest touch of remorse. Or was that only wishful thinking on her part?

As soon as the other boys saw her they pulled up short as well.

Bobby Pearson kicked at a clod of dirt with the toe of his shoe. Then he dug his hands in his pockets. "I just remembered, my maw wanted me to refill that old birdbath out back."

Abe Thompson looked from Simon to Callie, his eyes as round as saucers and his Adam's apple bobbing visibly. "Uh, yeah, I probably ought to help you with that."

Within seconds it was just Simon and Callie on the sidewalk, facing each other. All through that short exchange, she'd felt Simon's eyes on her, studying her, no doubt trying to decipher what she might or might not have heard.

Well, he'd just have to continue guessing.

She spoke up first. "I'm glad I found you. It's time we headed back to the farm. Do you think you could run down to the livery and fetch the girls?"

Guarded relief flashed across his face. Then, with a quick nod, he turned and ran off in the direction of the livery.

Callie watched him go. She reminded herself of all that the boy had been through, told herself his display was at least partly show for his friends and that he might not actually feel that way, but her rationalizations didn't erase the sting of those hurtful words.

She resumed her walk toward the center of town, but the bounce had gone from her step, and she no longer had the urge to hum.

Callie tromped past the barn, heading toward the tree line just north of the open field.

All of the goods from the market had been put away, lunch was long past, and supper simmered on the stove. Emma was sketching. Annabeth was looking at her picture book. Simon and Jack were playing dominoes.

No one had bothered to do more than glance up and nod when she'd announced she planned to take a walk.

Which was just as well. She needed to find a place where she could be truly alone, where she wouldn't be overheard or interrupted. Because she could feel emotions swirling around inside her, emotions that needed to be let out before they overwhelmed her.

And when she did let loose, it would not be a sight for public viewing.

Callie reached the tree line and easily found the well-worn trail that provided entrance to the wood. Julia had written about a spot back this way where the trees opened up on a small grassy meadow fed by a narrow stream.

Sure enough, several minutes later she discovered the flower-dotted swath of green. The stream was little more than a trickle at the moment, but it was sparkling and clear.

Callie sat near the bank, removed her bonnet and hairpins, and shook her hair free as she raised her face to absorb the warming rays of the sun. Closing her eyes, she deliberately opened her other senses to her surroundings.

Birds, insects and gurgling water provided lyrical background music. The scents of crushed grass, pine needles and wildflowers perfumed the air. The warmth of the sun and the slight kiss of a breeze caressed her, filling her with a lazy comfort.

It was peaceful here, every bit as lovely as Julia had described it, and it was a sweet testament to God's artistry.

She hugged her knees to her chest and rested her chin on the makeshift prop.

And found she couldn't hold back the doubts and dark thoughts any longer.

Simon's hurtful words, Lanny's untimely death, the letter she'd expected from her father that hadn't come—all this and more tumbled round and round in her mind.

What if her presence here had actually made things worse for this family instead of better?

Was she really the mother these children needed or had she stubbornly stood in the way of a more worthy candidate? Had she done them a disservice by making it easy for Jack to eventually leave rather than stay and learn to be a real, day-in-day-out father?

Oh, but she missed Julia so much.

Missed being able to pour her heart out to someone who would understand and not judge. Missed getting those wonderful letters with her pithy responses and uplifting advice.

Missed with a deep-down ache knowing that there was someone in this world who loved her just the way she was.

Father, I know You love me unconditionally. I know You are with me always and that that should be enough to carry me through the hard and lonely times without complaint. But I'm a wretchedly weak creature. I want to be loved by someone who will share my walk here. Not just be deemed useful or acceptable, but be truly and deeply loved.

Did admitting such feelings mean she'd failed God as well?

And then the pent-up sobs came.

Jack covered the trail in fast, long strides. Where was she? He hadn't really been paying attention when she'd mentioned going for a stroll. It was only later, when his game with Simon was finished, that he'd thought about how unaccustomed she was to the hidden dangers in this part of the country.

He wasn't worried about her getting lost. Even the greenest of city girls could find their way out of so small a wood, and Callie had a good head on her shoulders. But other things could happen out here—a trip and fall that resulted in a twisted ankle or worse, an unexpected encounter with a snake or other critter, a tangle with some painfully spiky thorns.

He should have known better than to let her wander off by herself.

Jack stepped into the meadow and paused for a moment as memories intruded of past picnics and games played here with Lanny and Nell. But the sight of Callie seated near the stream quickly brought his thoughts back to the present.

She was hunched over and her shoulders were shaking. Even from this distance he could hear her sobs.

Within seconds he'd crossed the meadow and was kneeling at her side.

Putting a hand at the small of her back, he scanned her form, looking for injuries. "Callie, what's the matter? Are you hurt?"

Her head came up like that of a startled doe. The pain he saw reflected there wasn't physical, but it was real and bone-deep.

She made a visible effort to stop the flow of tears, to compose herself.

As gently as he could, he brushed the hair from her forehead. "It's all right," he whispered. "Let go."

And with a ragged breath, she surrendered her effort, buried her face in his shoulder and let the tears flow.

Chapter Twenty-Three

Jack held her as she cried, feeling the tears dampen his shirt, feeling the sobs well from deep inside her.

Had something happened in town today?

Had he done something to upset her without even realizing it?

Or was she beginning to realize she wasn't cut out for this kind of life?

Whatever it was, it seemed to be tearing her up.

And this gut-wrenching weeping was killing him. He had to do something—anything—to comfort her. He found himself whispering soothing nonsense to her, stroking her hair, rocking her in his arms.

Anything to bring her misery to an end. No one deserved to be this unhappy.

Finally, with one last shuddering gasp, she stilled. He continued to hold her, letting her rest. He liked the feel of her in his arms, the trusting way she clung to him, the way her unbound hair tickled his chin.

Mostly, he liked the feeling that she needed him, felt safe with him.

They stayed that way for another long minute, the beating of their hearts the only sounds besides nature's chorus.

At last she gave a little sigh and gently pulled out of his embrace. "I'm sorry." Her gaze didn't meet his. Instead she raised a not quite steady hand and touched his shoulder where her head had rested. "I've gotten your shirt all wet."

"It'll dry." He titled her chin up with his fingers, forcing her to look at him. "You want to tell me what that was all about?"

"It's nothing."

He leaned back on his heels. "It takes a mighty powerful nothing to have an effect like that."

She waved a hand. "I was just feeling a bit sorry for myself, is all."

"Why?" He stood and pulled a bandanna from his pocket, moving toward the stream, giving her a chance to compose herself.

"I don't know." Her voice was husky from all of that crying. "I suppose, with everything that's happened, I hadn't really taken the time to mourn Lanny's passing."

The little kick of jealousy Jack felt was unexpectedly sharp. But he was sure there was something else eating at her.

He squeezed the water out of the bandanna and returned to her side, stooping down next to her again.

She reached for the bit of cloth but he began to wipe her face himself. "Are you sure that's all it is?" he asked.

The flair of guilt in her face was all the answer he needed.

"I was expecting a letter from my father to arrive today," she added, twisting her hands in her lap.

Homesickness then?

She tried to turn the blemished side of her face away, but he had her chin cupped in his hand and he refused to let her. "You realize you only just sent off your own letter a few days ago," he reasoned. "Give him time. I'm sure he'll respond."

She gave a little half smile then. "It's not a response to my letter I was looking for."

He paused in his ministrations, lifting a brow. "Then what?"

She sighed. "This is going to sound foolish, I know. But today is my birthday."

That set him back. He hadn't marked his own for quite some time, but he knew occasions like that were important to women. "I'm sorry," he said awkwardly. "I didn't—"

She touched a finger to his lips. "Don't be silly. I didn't expect anyone here to even know, much less make a fuss. I just expected the few folks in the world who did know to mark it somehow."

She pulled her hand away and tucked a strand of hair behind her ear. "Actually, it was quite selfish of me to feel that way since my family celebrated the occasion in advance, before I left Ohio." She gave him an overly bright smile. "As I said, I was just feeling sorry for myself."

Jack could still feel the gentle touch of her finger on his lips, could see the vulnerability behind her smile, could hear the wistfulness beneath her sensible tone. Something strong and instinctive welled up inside him.

Almost of its own accord, his thumb stroked her chin, and he bent down to give her a kiss. He had intended it to be a quick gesture of comfort and reassurance, nothing more. But her little gasp of surprise caught him off guard, turning it into something altogether different.

A moment later, he reluctantly pulled back. "Happy birthday," he whispered.

He saw the soft wonder in her expression, the way her eyes searched his, looking for answers.

Answers he suddenly realized he wasn't ready to give, even to himself.

What had he been thinking? He didn't need complications like this in his life.

Handing her the still-damp bandanna, he stood. "We probably should be getting back to the house. The kids'll be wondering where we got off to."

Callie was confused, by both the kiss and his abrupt change of manner afterward.

Her first real kiss.

Her mind was awhirl with the unexpectedness of it, with the still-tumbling sensations. His rush to distance himself only added to her off-balance feelings.

Was he regretting the kiss? Or embarrassed by it?

Had she reacted improperly?

Callie fumbled around for her bonnet and hairpins, trying to gather her thoughts at the same time. She accepted his hand to help her up, but released it as soon as she was upright. She couldn't tell from his expression what he was thinking.

For that matter, she wasn't even certain what *she* was thinking.

Without meeting his gaze, she twisted her hair with a few well-practiced motions and had it pinned into a bun in a matter of seconds.

What a fright she must have looked when he stumbled on her—her hair all loose and tangled, her birthmark on full display and the rest of her face nearly as red and blotchy from her crying. It was a wonder he hadn't turned and left without ever coming near.

But naturally he'd felt sorry for her and had been too much of a gentleman to abandon her to her distress.

She stilled a moment. Is that all that kiss had signified— sympathy?

Of course. How could she have thought, even for a moment, that it had been something more?

"Ready?" His question drew her from her uncomfortable thoughts.

She unfolded and shook out her bonnet. "Yes, of course."

He stopped her before she could place the starched cloth on her head. "There's no need for that."

Callie remembered Simon's conversation with his friends. "Yes, there is." She resolutely pulled the bonnet firmly in place and tied the ribbon under her chin. Just as resolutely, she tamped down the memory of Jack's thumb caressing her there. "You forget, there are the children to consider."

He shook his head as he extended his arm. "I don't think you give them enough credit. They are children, after all. They would adjust to your appearance quite quickly, given the chance."

Callie took his arm, glad she'd let loose all of her feeling on the subject earlier. She could face the matter squarely now, without useless self-pity to cloud her attitude. "Perhaps, when the time is right, we'll give it a try."

Then she straightened her skirt and gave him a serene smile. "Now, as you said, we'd best get back before the children come looking for us."

That evening, Callie closed the door to Simon's room and leaned against it as she let out a tired sigh. Though he grumbled that he'd outgrown the nightly ritual, she still went in to hear his prayers and tuck him in, just as she did with the girls. And every night, his prayers consisted mostly of pleas for God to find a way to help him return to life in town.

Tonight, he'd made his plea more specific, praying that Callie would see Jack's construction efforts as the answer to those prayers and allow them to move "home" when it was done.

After his Amen, the boy had scrambled into bed and turned his back to her, not bothering to so much as acknowledge her when she tucked the coverlet up around his shoulders.

Would she ever be able to get through to him?

Callie pushed away from the door, then hesitated. Should she join Jack for their normal chat tonight?

In spite of her protests this afternoon, Jack had told the children about her birthday and they'd put together a little impromptu celebration. Emma had drawn pictures and Annabeth had picked armloads of wildflowers to decorate the parlor. Jack had dug some cocoa out of the pantry and whipped them each up a cup of cocoa and milk for a treat. Then he'd capped the evening off by insisting that he and the children take care of the kitchen chores while she propped up her feet.

But despite the festivities, there'd been a subtle awkwardness between the two of them ever since that kiss this afternoon. Would being alone together on the moonlit porch ease the tension or intensify it?

Callie squared her shoulders. They'd have to be alone together again sometime.

She loosened her bonnet string. Might as well get it over with sooner rather than later. Besides, if she didn't go downstairs tonight, he'd likely read something into her absence that she'd prefer he not.

And she absolutely refused to acknowledge the little tingle of anticipation that shimmied through her.

Jack straightened when he heard the door open behind him.

He hadn't been sure she'd join him tonight, wasn't even quite sure if he'd wanted her to.

"Thanks for the birthday celebration," she said as she leaned against the rail.

A nice, safe subject. Did she plan to ignore what had happened between them this afternoon then? That's what he'd wanted, but still, he'd give a pretty penny to be able to read her mind at the moment.

"You're welcome," he said carefully. "I'm afraid it wasn't much of a party."

"Actually, it's one of the nicest ones I've had since Julia left Ohio."

She must have seen the surprise in his face, because she quickly added, "Oh, I didn't mean to say my family didn't celebrate with me. But this had more the feel of a child's tea party and it brought back sweet memories."

He grimaced. "A child's tea party, huh?"

"I'm sorry." She grinned, not looking one bit repentant. "Does it bother you to think you had a hand in such an event? I assure you, it was done quite well."

Jack relaxed, comfortable with the bantering tone she'd set. "Just don't let word get back to my demolition team."

She crossed her heart. "You have my word."

Then her expression turned serious. "You know Simon is still set on returning to his old life in town. He sees this building project of yours as God's answer to his prayers."

Jack shifted in his seat. He'd never thought of himself as the answer to anyone's prayers. "By the time I'm done, he'll have had more time to adjust to life here on the farm."

"I don't know that a few weeks, or even months, will make much of a difference in his feelings."

He heard the wistful tinge in her voice. "What about you? Are you so certain this is really the life you want?"

"More so than ever."

Not the answer he'd expected. "Why?"

She raised a brow. "Disappointed? I thought you wanted to make certain the farm stayed in Tyler family hands."

"That's my reason." He pointed a finger at her. "I asked about yours. Running this place is hard work and you're more accustomed to city ways."

"It's true that my former home was in the midst of a good-sized city with lots of modern conveniences that haven't found their way out here yet. But I spent most of my days inside that house so it's not like I'll miss the sights and sounds. As for the conveniences, I get by quite nicely without electric lights or fancy shops or so-called fine entertainment, thank you. Moving to Sweetgum proper wouldn't provide those things anyway."

She turned and stared out over the darkened landscape. "My reason? I like it out here. I like the feel of openness and of making my own way. I like the fact that it's forced me to draw on skills I didn't know I had. And I like experiencing God's handiwork in such an intimate way." She turned back to him and crossed her arms. "It's also the life Leland wanted for Annabeth and I feel I owe it to him to give it to her."

Leland again. It always came back to his brother. "What about Emma and Simon?"

Callie sat on the bench and picked at something on her skirt. "I've been pondering on that. I still worry about Emma. But I think the change in scenery and routine has been good for her. Once we figure out whatever is truly bothering her, I believe she'll be happy here."

So she still thought there was something bothering Emma, something besides her grief. He'd have to keep a closer eye on the girl. He was beginning to appreciate Callie's instincts when it came to the kids.

"As for Simon," she said slowly, "I just don't know. He seems to have his mind made up and I'm beginning to wonder if we'll be able to change it. The thing is…" She paused, then lifted her head confidently. "I believe, whether he thinks so or not, this is the best place for him right now."

Chapter Twenty-Four

Callie set a pie on the window sill to cool and glanced out toward the work shed, wondering what Jack was up to.

He'd come back from town at lunchtime today and spent most of the afternoon working on some project out there. He'd been evasive about whatever he was up to, but he'd worn a self-satisfied smile when he came in an hour ago looking for baking soda, wood polish and silver polish.

She shook her head and moved back to the oven to fetch the second pie. As if her thoughts had conjured him up, Jack stepped through the back door.

"Where are the kids?"

She placed the pie atop the stove. "I believe the girls are in the parlor and Simon is on the front porch. Why?"

"I have something to show them. Would you call them in here?"

So, they were finally going to learn what he'd been up to. Intrigued, Callie did as he asked. When the four of them entered the kitchen, Jack stood beside the table. He'd thrown a cloth over it and there were several interesting looking lumps beneath it.

That seemed a strange choice of words. But before he could question her further, she stood. "I think it's time for me to retire. You enjoy the evening."

Jack continued shaving strips off his block of wood. At least it seemed his impulsive kiss hadn't done any permanent damage to the friendship that had begun to take root between them.

Why, he wondered, didn't that give him a sense of satisfaction?

"Here we are," she said unnecessarily.

Jack nodded and waved them forward. "Simon and Emma, while we were working in town last week, my crew and I found a few things I thought you might want." With a flourish, he pulled away the cloth to reveal an odd assortment of items.

A penknife lay next to a silver-plated hand mirror and a delicate teacup.

A tin box held three polished rocks and an assortment of marbles. Next to the box was a gold locket, without a chain.

Displayed on a flour sack were a collection of knobs, handles, drawer pulls and other assorted hardware.

And behind all of these items were three wooden boxes of different sizes and designs.

Simon touched the penknife as if it were a valuable relic. "This was Dad's. He used it to trim the wicks on the lamps."

Jack put a hand on the boy's shoulder. "It's yours now."

He turned to Emma who was running a fingertip over the mirror, as if afraid it would break if she applied even the slightest pressure.

"I know that was your mother's," he said softly. "She got it for her thirteenth birthday."

Emma nodded, her eyes glistening.

Callie watched the children's reactions to these rescued treasures and swallowed back the lump in her throat. Every one of these items had been scrupulously cleaned so there was not a smudge or hint of char on them. The silver gleamed. The locket glowed with the warmth of well-worn gold.

The man was a fraud. Anyone who would go to so much trouble to salvage these treasures for the children was no cold-hearted loner. But then again, she'd stopped believing that about him quite some time ago.

She cleared her throat and touched the rim of the teacup.

The delicate rose-patterned piece had a soft, pearly luster inside and out. "This is beautiful."

"It's Momma's good china." Emma's voice was hoarse with emotion. "We only used it when company came."

Callie nodded, moving her hand from the cup to Emma's shoulder. "Then it deserves a place of honor. What do you say we clear a spot in the china cabinet for it?"

Emma nodded.

Callie picked up the delicate cup and solemnly carried it over to the china cabinet that stood in the dining room. With great care she shifted a few items around and then set the tea cup where it could be admired with ease.

When they returned to the kitchen, Simon was eagerly examining his rocks and marbles.

Jack pointed to the boxes. "I thought you might like to have something to store your treasures in. These are made from the wooden walls and floors of your house. The hinges and knobs are from the doors and windows."

He looked at Annabeth. "Little Bit, I made one for you, too. I thought you might like to have a memento to remember your Aunt Nell and Uncle Jed by."

Callie met his eyes over the heads of the children and hoped he could read her approval.

Lord, thank You for bringing this man into the children's lives. And mine, as well.

The next few days settled into a routine. Callie rose with the sun to help Jack with the morning chores. Then she woke the children and started breakfast. By the time she had the meal on the table, the children were dressed and in their seats, and Jack was cleaned up and ready to join them. After breakfast, everyone scattered to his or her assigned chores for that day, and Jack headed into town to work on the construction.

As the days passed, though, she and the children saw less and less of Jack. He didn't even bother to come home for the noonday meal. Instead he stuffed a chunk of cheese, a thick slice of bread and an apple or pear in a basket to take along with him.

It was usually late when he returned from town. Once he checked that everything was in order with the animals he washed up and came in for supper.

Even their nightly chats grew shorter. Callie tried to look on the bright side of things. It was probably for the best. After all, this was how things would be when he went back to his old life. She should get used to it now.

But she found very little consolation in that thought.

By the end of the week, however, she was worried about the toll the workload seemed to be taking on Jack himself.

He'd been pushing hard—too hard. Rising before sunup, doing his share of the morning chores, then gulping down breakfast before heading to town. The days had been brutally hot, yet that hadn't slowed him down. By the time he came home in the evenings he looked withered and bone tired.

Callie stood in the kitchen Saturday evening, and glanced at the watch pinned to her bodice for the tenth time. It was nearly dark out and there was still no sign of Jack. She'd long since fed the children and cleaned up their dishes.

What was keeping him? Had he run into problems?

Her head came up at the sound of a wagon.

"Your Uncle Jack is home," she announced. "Emma, would you set him a place at the table, please? Simon, run out and see if you can help him with anything."

Callie nibbled at her bottom lip. This was ridiculous.

It was time she had a talk with him. Tonight. Before the fool man worked himself down to a nub.

* * *

Jack inhaled deeply as Callie set a plate in front of him. Coming home to a meal like this in the evening had become the high point of his day. He was sure going to miss it when he returned to life on the road.

Among other things.

Funny how that kind of thinking occupied his mind of late. Must be because he was so tired. The Texas summer heat certainly took its toll on a man.

But the work was coming along well. If his luck held and he kept up his current pace, he could finish in under a month.

Callie took a seat across from him. "Shall I say grace for you?"

He paused with his fork halfway to his mouth. The kids weren't anywhere in sight. But apparently that wasn't the point.

With a nod, he set his fork down and bowed his head.

"Heavenly Father, thank You for the bounty You have provided. Bless the meal and the one who partakes of it. May it nourish him and provide him strength and sustenance. Amen."

"Amen." Jack picked up his fork again and shoveled the first bite into his mouth. Cooking was definitely one of Callie's gifts.

"You need to slow down."

He gave her a wary look as he swallowed the morsel. "Sorry if my table manners offend you. I'm still not used to eating in mixed company."

She waved a hand. "That's not what I meant. You can't keep up the pace you've set for yourself. Are you in such a hurry to get back to your old life that you're willing to run yourself into the ground to finish faster?"

He shrugged. "I'm used to working long hours to get a project done."

"But no one's set you a deadline for this. Why are you pushing yourself so hard?"

Jack took another bite of food, watching her closely while he chewed and swallowed. "I want to make sure it gets done by the first of August."

Her brow furrowed. "Why that particular date?"

"It's the timeframe I set for heading back to California."

That seemed to set her back a bit and Jack took advantage of her silence to continue eating. With any luck she'd let the subject drop.

"Still, you can't—

He held up a hand. Seems his luck wasn't going to hold after all. "Look, I'm tired and I'm hungry. Can this conversation wait until tomorrow? It'll be Sunday and we'll have all the time in the world for one of these little chats."

"Very well." She stood. "But don't think I'll let this drop."

The thought had never crossed his mind.

The next morning, when Jack came downstairs, he was surprised to find the stove already stoked, a pot of coffee brewing and Callie seated at the table.

"Well, well, you're up mighty early. What's the occasion?"

"You're fired."

Jack blinked. "What?"

Her chin lifted in that familiar stubborn tilt. "I decided I've had enough practice. I'm taking over the morning chores."

He couldn't suppress his grunt of disbelief.

She smiled. "Not by myself. The children have already learned to help with the evening chores. It won't be such a big jump for them to learn to help in the morning as well."

"They might feel differently."

"As you've said before, they'll adjust." She leaned forward. "Starting tomorrow, you can sleep a little later in the morning."

"Look, I know you mean well, but I think I'm the best judge of how much I can and can't handle. If I—"

"I'm certain you're just stubborn enough to continue this pace, even if it wears you plumb out."

Hah! She was one to talk about stubborn.

"But," she continued, "I'd prefer not to have to nurse you back to health when you work yourself to the point of collapse."

He poured a cup of coffee, as much to give himself a moment to think as anything else. When he turned around, she still wore that determined expression.

"All right. I agree it would be good for the children to take on a bit more responsibility for keeping this place running. So if you think you can manage getting them to toe the mark—"

"And there's something else."

Of course there was. "And that would be?"

"You need to spend more time here at the farm."

He set his cup down with enough force to splash a few drops onto the table. "You just said you wanted to take on more responsibility for the place."

She waved a hand impatiently. "I don't mean to help with the chores. You need to spend more time with the children." Her expression softened. "They've hardly seen you these past few days. I want them to be able to spend time with you, to develop a real relationship with you—and you with them—before you go running back off to wherever it is you're heading when you leave here."

Whoa. She hadn't really thought this through. "Actually, I thought it would be better all the way around if they don't get too used—"

She lifted her chin again. "You said you owed it to Leland and Nell to see that their children were well-cared for. And also that it was important for blood kin to be close. That's why we ended up in this marriage, remember?"

"Of course I remember. But—"

"Well, you can't see to any of that if you're never here."

Blast the woman, there she went, trying to twist his words back on him. "And I suppose you have something in mind to make everyone happy."

"I do."

That I've-got-it-all-figured-out tone set his teeth on edge.

"Go to town in the mornings," she elaborated. "It's the coolest part of the day, and the children will be busy with their own chores. But come home for lunch, and stay. There are things you can do here, and I don't mean chores."

"Such as?"

"Such as take Simon fishing. Such as teach Annabeth about the wildlife around here. Such as walk in the woods with Emma to find things she can sketch."

Her passion for the children lit a fire in her eyes that was something to see.

She threw up her hands as if exasperated. "Tell them stories about when you and their parents were children growing up here. Let them know you really care about *them,* not just that you feel responsible for them."

She was pushing this just a little too far. "Look, I'm more of the loner type than the jovial fatherly sort."

Her expression rivaled Mrs. Mayweather's for sternness. "Then just pretend." She planted both elbows on the table and laced her fingers. "Those children need you, maybe more than they need me. And you know as well as I do that it's what Leland and Nell would have wanted."

She just didn't play fair.

He stood up from the table. "I'll think about it."

She rose as well and gave him a meaningful look. "And I'll continue to pray about it."

No, she didn't play fair at all.

Chapter Twenty-Five

Callie pinned the last bit of laundry to the line strung under the rafters in the washroom. The rain had started a little over an hour ago, just about the time she'd run the last of the clothes through the wringer. It certainly was nice to have such a wonderful arrangement inside for rainy days.

She wiped her forehead with the back of her hand, glad to have the Monday morning chore over with. She hoped Jack had had sense enough to find shelter to wait out the rain. But knowing him, he was ignoring the weather and still pounding nails into boards.

She stepped into the kitchen and checked the stew simmering on the stove, then went in search of the children.

She found them on the front porch, staring glumly at the water dripping from the eaves. Gil was visiting this morning, so there were four pairs of eyes that turned to her, ready for a distraction.

They looked like woebegone waifs. This wouldn't do at all.

She crossed her arms. "Surely you can find some way to amuse yourselves even if you can't leave the porch."

"It's been raining *forever*," Annabeth wailed. "When is it going to stop? I want to take Cinnamon for a ride."

"You'll just have to be patient." Callie gave them a bracing smile. "Come on now, what will it be? A game of jackstraws, perhaps? Or maybe charades?"

"You can read us some of the story," Annabeth suggested hopefully.

"But it's not even lunchtime yet."

Gil immediately followed Annabeth's lead. "Oh, yes, please, Mrs. Tyler. Simon's been telling me about the story and it sounds like an exciting tale."

She stared at the four hopeful faces and her resistance crumbled. "Oh, very well. Emma, would you fetch the book, please?"

Callie read for twenty minutes, then finally closed the book. "That's enough for today. It looks like the rain has stopped and I need to check on lunch."

"That's one rip-roaring tree house," Gil said. "Sure is clever the way they turned bits and pieces of wreckage into a bang-up place to live."

"Yeah," Simon agreed. "I wish we had something like that around here."

Callie paused in the act of getting up.

Gil popped up and placed both hands on his hips. "If we did, we could spend our afternoons planning our own adventures."

"And designing special devices to furnish it with." Simon's voice had more energy in it than Callie had heard in a long time.

"Why not?" she asked impulsively.

The children looked at her as if she'd just sprouted antlers.

"Ma'am?" Gil's one word question hung in the air for a second while all four children seemed to hold their breath.

"Why not build a tree house?" she elaborated. "That big oak out back is the perfect place for one. And Simon, you're good at building things."

The boy's eyes lit up. "Do you think we really could?"

Callie felt her heart warm at the eager look on his face. Maybe, just maybe, he could learn to see the appeal of life in the country after all. "Well, we'd have to ask your Uncle Jack, of course. And I don't think we could do anything as elaborate as the one in the book."

"But we could design it ourselves and add whatever features we like." Simon turned to Gil. "I know Uncle Jack has some old crates in the barn we could use, and maybe some kegs, too. How about your dad?"

Annabeth clapped her hands. "A tree house! I want to help."

Simon crossed his arms with a sniff. "You're a girl."

"Girls can build things, too." Annabeth turned indignant eyes toward Callie. "Can't they?"

"Of course they can, sweetheart."

Simon wasn't happy with that answer. "Gil, help me here. Tell them this is men's work."

Callie tried to soothe the boy's ruffled feathers. "Simon, remember in the book, it wasn't just the tree house itself that had to be built. There were furnishings, too. I was thinking the girls could work on some of those things."

"Sounds fair to me," Gil said quickly.

Simon nodded reluctantly. "I guess so. But no frilly stuff."

"No frilly stuff," Callie promised. "And remember, we need to clear this with your Uncle Jack first."

Too late Callie realized she probably shouldn't have gotten their hopes up before she spoke to Jack about it. If he objected to the scheme, she was going to have some very disappointed children on her hands. Because the four would-be adventurers were already putting their heads together, discussing plans for the tree house.

To her relief, once Jack was able to sort out the gist of the idea from the eager babblings of the children, he gave his stamp of approval to the plan. But he had a few stipulations.

"Before I say yes, there are some ground rules we need to set. For one, your chores come first. No work gets done on the tree house until that's taken care of."

Three heads nodded agreement.

"And I'll have to talk to Gil's dad and make sure he's okay with Gil taking part."

"I'm sure Mr. Wilson will be okay with this," Simon offered.

"Still, I want to talk to him first. Now Simon, you and Gil will be in charge of collecting most of the materials. I'll help where I can, but this is going to be your project. You can clean out a corner of the barn to store things in."

"Thanks."

"If you boys want to come to town with me one morning this week, you can dig through the scrap pile and see if there's anything there you can use."

"Yes, sir!"

"Next time Gil comes around we can all sit down and draw up some plans. Then you can start work."

Once the children were down for the night, Callie stepped out on the porch. It felt good to have this little ritual back.

She'd missed their talks, discussing the children and the day's events, making plans for the coming days.

When had she started looking forward to it so much?

"The children are excited about the tree house. I could hardly get them to settle down tonight."

"I understand it was your idea."

She gave a little half-grin, not certain if that was approval in his voice or something else. "They were talking about the tree house in the book and I saw how excited Simon was. It's the first time I've seen him take a real interest in something other than moving to town. I couldn't help myself." She gave him an apologetic look. "I'm sorry if I put you on the spot."

He shook his head. "Actually, I think it's a great idea. The boy has a natural skill when it comes to using tools, and this will give him a sense of responsibility to go along with it."

"I'm glad Gil will be working with him on this. The two have become good friends. Maybe he won't miss his friends in town so much."

"So, are you going to fill me in on the latest chapter of our adventure story?"

Callie smiled and gave him a quick recap.

"Just another couple of days and we'll finish *Swiss Family Robinson*," she added when she'd finished. "I think the children will really be disappointed."

"I admit I'll miss it myself."

Callie smiled. "Don't worry. I have some others you'll all enjoy just as much."

"Do you, now?"

She ticked them off on her fingers. "There's *Around the World in Eighty Days* and *Tom Sawyer*. Then there's a new book about a detective named Sherlock Holmes, and one about an undersea adventure. And at least a half dozen others."

"Quite a collection." He gave her a searching look. "These all come from your personal library?"

She reddened slightly. "Actually, I bought them as a wedding gift for Leland. Julia had mentioned once how much he enjoyed reading adventure stories."

His hands stilled and she couldn't quite read the expression on his face. "I thought your grandfather's pocket watch was your wedding gift for Lanny."

She didn't detect anything other than mild curiosity in his

tone. But she had a feeling there was something stronger behind the question. "Now, why ever would you think such a thing?"

He ignored her question. "If you didn't intend to give it to Lanny, why did you give it to me?"

This time she heard a hint of accusation. "I told you, it was a keepsake from my grandfather. I—I wanted to give you a gift that fit who *you* are."

"Oh."

She tilted her head to one side, trying to read between the lines. "Is that why you didn't like it? Because it wasn't bought specifically for you? I didn't feel right giving you something I'd bought for Lanny. That seemed a bit wrong somehow. But there wasn't time to order anything, and I really wasn't certain what—"

He cut her off. "It's not that I didn't like it."

"Then what?"

He went back to his whittling and she saw a tic at the corner of his mouth.

"I'm sorry. I shouldn't have asked that."

He paused, then leaned back against the rail and gave her a long look. "No. I suppose I owe you an explanation." He raked a hand through his hair. "It was actually because I thought you *did* bring it to give Lanny."

"Oh." She tried to make sense of that but couldn't quite.

He stuck the knife point into the block of wood. "Growing up as Lanny's younger brother meant I wound up with every item he outgrew. Things he no longer needed or wanted or could fit into became mine. Guess I got a little tired of always ending up with my brother's hand-me-downs."

Of course. She should have realized. "And you thought I was giving you a hand-me-down gift."

His grin had a self-deprecating edge. "Yep. I suppose that

was a confoundedly fool reaction, even if it had been true. A grown man shouldn't let something like that get under his skin."

"We can't help how we feel about things." She of all people knew the truth of that. Almost of its own accord, her hand touched his shoulder. "I'm sorry I didn't get you something new, something no one had owned before," she said softly.

He paused a fraction of a second at her touch, then gave her that crooked smile. "Don't go apologizing. It was a fine gift, even more so because it had such value to you."

She removed her hand somewhat awkwardly and he leaned back. "I suppose it's really me who should apologize to you. I didn't even thank you proper."

She wondered what he thought of her touching his shoulder. Had she given away too much? "Why don't we just call it even then?"

"Okay by me."

Callie decided she really liked Jack's smile, especially when it was focused on her.

Twenty minutes later Callie climbed the stairs to the second floor. She and Jack had stayed out chatting later than usual.

She paused as she passed the girls' room. What was that sound?

There it went again.

Just a hiccup.

She started to move on, then stopped again. That was a muffled sob.

Callie quietly opened the door and slipped inside the room. All was quiet now.

Had she imagined it? Or was one of the girls making sounds in her sleep?

Letting her eyes adjust to the dark, she studied the forms of the two girls. Annabeth was sprawled with abandon across her bed.

Emma, however, was lying on her side, body curled and facing away from the door. Callie crossed the room and stood over her.

"Emma, honey," she said softly, "what is it? Are you sick?"

Emma shook her head, still not turning to face Callie.

"Having a bad dream then?"

Again a shake of the head.

Poor dear. She was probably missing her parents. Should she force her to speak about it?

Callie sat down on the bed and gently pushed the hair from the child's damp forehead. "Won't you tell me what's wrong?"

Emma finally looked up and met Callie's gaze. The despair filling those teary eyes was almost more than Callie could bear.

"Oh, Aunt Callie, I've done something awful."

The broken words tore at Callie's heart. "Sweetie, whatever it is, I know it can't be as bad as you're imagining."

"You don't know." Another sob escaped her. "Everyone would hate me if they knew."

Annabeth stirred and rolled over.

Callie stood and pulled the covers from Emma. "Come on," she whispered, "let's go down to the kitchen so we don't wake your sister."

Emma took Callie's outstretched hand and slipped out of bed. She allowed Callie to lead her from the room, much as a doomed prisoner would follow along behind his executioner.

Callie led her to the kitchen and seated her at the table. "Now you sit here while I fix us a little treat." She kept talking, careful to keep her back to Emma, giving the child time to compose herself. "I believe we have a little cocoa left in the pantry and I think this is a good time to bring it out." She retrieved two cups and filled them with warm water from the kettle on the stove. "The secret to a good cup of chocolate is to add a touch of vanilla and a touch of peppermint oil." After she'd mixed the aromatic drinks, she carried them to the table.

"Before you say anything, I want you to understand that there is nothing you could possibly have done that will make me hate you. And no matter what it is, you know that God will forgive you and call you His beloved."

"But you don't know what—"

"Then tell me."

Emma placed her hands around her cup but didn't drink.

Finally she took a deep breath that sounded more like a sob.

"The fire was my fault."

Chapter Twenty-Six

Callie fought to keep her expression serene. What a terrible burden for a child to carry. "What makes you say that, sweetheart?"

"Because it's true." Emma's voice trembled.

"Tell me what happened."

Emma sniffed, then nodded. "Momma had bought some pretty new candles that smelled real nice. They were supposed to be used for special occasions, but I was grumpy about not getting the new colored pencils I saw at Mr. Dobson's store."

She looked up with pleading eyes. "I was really careful about where I placed the candle, I promise. And it did make me feel better. Then Simon came in to say he was taking me and Annabeth over to see the new foal at the livery and I forgot all about the candle."

Callie touched the girl's arm. "Oh, Emma, that's not what set that fire."

The girl refused to be comforted. "You don't know that," she insisted.

"But *I* do."

Callie and Emma both turned as Jack entered the kitchen.

"Sorry to eavesdrop, but I heard y'all talking when I came inside." He knelt down in front of Emma, taking one of her hands between his. "I talked to Mr. Wilson after I got here. They don't know exactly what caused the fire, but they could tell that it started in the kitchen."

Emma's eyes filled with both doubt and hope. "It did?"

"That's right. And you didn't leave your candle in the kitchen, did you?"

She shook her head.

"So that means your candle had nothing to do with the fire."

"Then it really wasn't my fault?" The weight almost visibly lifted from Emma's shoulders. With a sob, she threw her arms around Jack's neck and buried her head against his chest.

Callie wanted to throw her arms around him as well. The gift he'd just given Emma, the cleansing of her guilty conscience, was beyond price.

Instead of joining the embrace, she stood and went to the cupboard. "What do you say I fix your Uncle Jack a cup of cocoa so he won't have to just watch us drink ours?"

By the time Callie returned, Emma had finally released her hold on Jack.

Callie's heart swelled as she saw a peace in the child's expression that hadn't been there before.

Jack accepted the cup she brought him and she studied the way he watched Emma as he drank. The mix of satisfaction and concern in his eyes was so, well, so *parental,* that Callie was tempted all over again to give him a hug. Why had Julia's letters never mentioned this softer aspect of Jack?

Because, of course, Julia had been in love with Leland, and Leland and Jack had been at odds. But Callie didn't have that emotional entanglement to fog her vision of the man, and she saw the tender protector, the concerned family man he could be.

He really did love these children—she could see it not just in his eyes, but in his whole presence. His life was now tied irrevocably to theirs, whether he realized it or not.

If only he felt as deeply about her…

Jack looked up and met her gaze. She lifted her glass, covering her emotion with a silent salute to his accomplishment.

He smiled back, his expression almost sheepish.

The three drank their cocoas in companionable silence. Then, as Callie carried the cups to the sink, Emma let out a jaw-stretching yawn.

Jack bent over and scooped up his niece. "Time to carry you back to bed, young lady."

Without so much as a murmur, Emma wrapped her arms around Jack's neck, rested her head on his shoulder and closed her eyes.

Callie followed close behind as they exited the room, enjoying the picture they made. As they reached the stairs, Emma's eyes opened the merest crack and she reached behind Jack to stroke Callie's cheek.

"Annabeth was right," she said drowsily. "Your angel's kiss is beautiful."

"Looks like you boys are doing a good job."

The hammering paused and Gil's freckled face peered down at Jack from the unfinished platform above. "Hi, Mr. Tyler. Is it lunchtime already?"

"Not for another hour or so. I just decided to come back a little early today. Is Simon up there?"

"He went out to the tool shed to fetch a crowbar."

Jack made a quick survey of their progress. "You having some problems?"

"No, sir. We just decided to move a couple of our bigger boards to a different spot."

"Sounds like you have it under control then. Once I talk to Simon's Aunt Callie I'll come back by and lend a hand."

Gil gave a friendly wave and disappeared back behind the tree house's floor. A moment later the hammering began again with renewed force.

Jack headed toward the back porch. Might as well let Callie know he was home.

He'd spent most of the afternoon yesterday working with Simon and Gil on the initial foundation, setting several stout hickory posts for support and laying some of the cross beams that would provide the base for the floor. They'd also fashioned a sturdy ladder and nailed it securely to the tree.

He'd then given them a stern lecture on safety and teamwork issues. Once he was certain they were clear on the rules, he'd told them they could work on their own whenever they had the time.

He'd spent another hour dealing with Callie's concerns, assuring her that at less than six feet off the ground, the boys would be okay. He'd survived tumbles from greater heights than that when he and Lanny had run free around this place.

Jack stepped inside the house to find lunch simmering on the stove but no sign of Callie. Following the sound of muffled conversation, he moved to the dining room.

He paused in the doorway. Callie and the girls were gathered around the table, intent on something Emma was sketching.

"Oh, that's lovely," Callie said. "What color should we make it?"

"Pink and purple." Annabeth's response was immediate and confident. "Oh, and with lots of lace," she added.

Jack found himself smiling, both at the assurance with

which Annabeth made her pronouncement and at Callie's attempt to hide a smile.

"Those are lovely colors, sweetheart, but perhaps they're not quite right for a tree house."

Annabeth's lips tightened into a pout. "Why not?"

"Well, because this is supposed to be a home built in the middle of nowhere by a shipwrecked family. I don't think they had a lot of pretty things to work with." She put a finger on her chin, as if giving it careful consideration. "I tell you what. We'll wait until we get to town and look at what fabrics are available at the mercantile, and then we'll decide."

"Yes, ma'am."

Jack stepped farther into the room. "Sounds like you ladies have been doing some serious planning."

Callie put a hand on one hip. "You didn't think we'd let you fellows have all the fun, did you?"

"Hi, Uncle Jack." Annabeth jumped down from her chair and ran to greet him. "We're going to make curtains and rugs and some big pillows to sit on and—"

"Don't spoil all the surprises," Callie admonished.

She turned to Jack. "Emma has been sketching out ideas. She's quite the artist. In fact, she's come up with one idea we'd like to get your thoughts on."

"Oh?" Jack turned to his niece. "And what might that be?"

Emma slid one of her drawings out of the stack and passed it to him. The tree and tree house were lightly penciled in with a few strokes that nevertheless conveyed their form perfectly. The main focus of the drawing, however, was a contraption that hung from one of the limbs.

"It's a basket on a rope that we can use to lift and lower things with," Emma explained. "That way we won't have to climb the ladder one-handed."

"That's mighty smart thinking on your part." He sat down

next to Emma. It was amazing how much the child had come out of her shell since the discussion of the fire two nights ago. "I see you have the rope pulled over this tall limb and then tied down on a lower one."

She gave him an uncertain glance. "Don't you think that will work?"

"I think it'll work just fine. I have some rope in the barn that's probably long enough." He studied her drawing closely. "And I even have an old pulley out there. What do you think about me and the boys rigging that up while you ladies find us a sturdy basket to use?"

Emma nodded.

"Aunt Callie's going to teach us how to make braided rugs," Annabeth added.

"That sounds like a good idea, Little Bit." He leaned closer and said in a mock whisper, "Maybe you can sneak a little pink and purple in the mix."

Annabeth put a hand over her mouth to muffle her giggle.

Callie stood. "I'd better check on lunch. Emma, why don't you show your Uncle Jack some more of your ideas."

Jack watched her leave, not at all fooled by the excuse she'd given. This was her way of providing the girls time alone with him.

Callie stirred the pot of stew simmering on the stove.

Why was Jack home early today? Had he really taken her words to heart about spending more time with the children?

He came in a few minutes later and stood behind her. Peering over her shoulder at the food on the stove, he placed his hand on the small of her back as if to anchor himself. It took a concerted effort on her part not to lean back into him.

She cleared her throat. "Things going well in town?" she asked as casually as she could.

"Yep. Why?"

"Just wondering what brought you home before midday."

"Disappointed?"

"Of course not. I only wondered, that's all."

"Actually, I wanted to check on the boys and make sure they remembered my lecture on working safely. I'll go back to my regular schedule tomorrow."

He removed his hand and reached around her to swipe a biscuit from the platter on the back of the stove. Dodging her playful swipe with a dishrag, he headed toward the door. "Think I'll go back out and lend the boys a hand."

"Just a minute."

Jack paused, giving her dishrag a wary glance.

This was more like it. She could handle bantering with him more easily than those intense, confusing emotions.

Callie grabbed a small basket from the counter. "The boys have been working out there most of the morning," she said. "Here's a jar of sweet tea and two slices of last night's gingerbread to tide them over until lunch."

Jack gave her a woebegone look. "Only two slices."

But he wasn't winning any sympathy from her. With an exaggerated sniff, she pointed to the half-eaten biscuit in his hand. "You, sir, chose your treat already."

Jack placed a hand melodramatically over his heart. "Undone by my own greed." Then he gave her a wink. "But for one of your biscuits, it was worth it." Saluting her, he made his exit.

Jack chuckled as he strolled toward the oak. Callie was learning to give as good as she got in the teasing department. He enjoyed these exchanges as much as their evening talks after the kids were in bed.

He was still grinning when he halted next to the tree house ladder. "How's it coming along, boys?"

Two heads popped out above the platform this time.

"Hi, Uncle Jack." Simon gave him a confident smile. "Don't worry, we're laying the boards just the way you showed us yesterday."

"I can see that. Looks like y'all are doing a mighty fine job." He lifted the basket. "Your Aunt Callie thought you two might be ready for a little snack."

"Yes, sir!" Gil's freckled face split in a smile.

Jack handed the basket up. "Go ahead and help yourselves. I'm headed to the barn to look for something the girls need."

"Thanks, Mr. Tyler." Gil already had a sizeable portion of gingerbread in his mouth. "Mmm-mmm."

With a wave, Jack moved on.

"You sure are lucky, Simon."

"What do you mean?"

Jack slowed his steps, then bent down to remove a nonexistent stone from his boot. He was as curious as Simon to hear what Gil had to say.

"I mean I wish I had an aunt like Mrs. Tyler."

"Just cause she sent us out some old gingerbread?" Something in Simon's tone got Jack's back up.

"Hey, this is really good gingerbread." Gil sounded affronted. "But it's not just what a good cook she is. You know what I mean. She can read an adventure story so dramatic-like that you get all caught up in it. And it was her idea for us to build this tree house."

"True." Simon drew the word out as if agreeing in spite of himself.

"Just imagine, a woman doing all that. You wouldn't catch my ma or my Aunt Dora doing anything near as fun, that's for sure."

Simon's response was too muffled for Jack to make out. He straightened and resumed his walk to the barn.

Interesting. Maybe seeing Callie through Gil's eyes would help Simon see her virtues. It sure had Jack mulling over a few of her qualities he hadn't given much thought to before.

As Callie walked along the lane that lead from Mrs. Mayweather's to Main Street Friday morning, her thoughts were on Simon. The boy was helping Jack and his team work on the building today. He'd actually volunteered, offering to help in exchange for some coins to buy a few things he'd had his eye on for the tree house.

They'd all put in a lot of work on that tree house these past three days, but Simon most of all.

Callie had taken this as a hopeful sign. He seemed to be slowly moving toward acceptance of his new lot in life. In fact, he hadn't mentioned moving back to town even once in his prayers last night.

That he'd been willing to forgo visiting with his friends in town so he could earn money of his own was a major shift in attitude for the boy.

In fact, when they'd arrived this morning, Bobby and Abe had tried to talk Simon into joining them in some escapade or other. She'd been quietly impressed with the way he'd stuck by the commitment he'd made to Jack.

Simon might not ever truly feel close to her the way she hoped, but maybe in time he would come to accept that she wasn't his enemy, and that she had a place in his life.

Callie turned the corner onto Main Street and halted in her tracks. There was some kind of commotion going on over at Dobson's Mercantile.

Mr. Dobson himself stood at the mouth of the alley that ran alongside his store, holding a squirming youngster by the collar of his shirt. Passersby were stopping to gawk and others were starting to drift over, too.

Well, she'd just as soon avoid the crowded scene, thank you very much.

She lifted her skirts to cross the street, then halted again as the scene registered more fully.

Wait a minute.

Releasing her skirt, she quickly marched forward, elbowing her way past the other townsfolk who were trying to get a better look at what was happening.

A moment later she stood face-to-face with the shopkeeper and his captive.

"Mr. Dobson, please release Simon this instant."

Chapter Twenty-Seven

At the sound of Callie's voice, Simon went perfectly still. He slowly looked up and met her gaze with the expression of a doomed prisoner.

The look sent a needle-sharp stab to her heart. Did he think she'd be so quick to judge him?

A hush fell over the crowd as they waited to hear what would happen next. Callie forced herself to ignore everyone but Simon and his accuser.

"Mrs. Tyler, I'm glad you're here." Mr. Dobson pushed his spectacles higher up on his nose with his free hand. "This young vandal has been up to some very destructive mischief."

"I'll thank you, sir, not to be calling Simon names. Now, please release him as I requested and explain to me what all this fuss is about."

If anything, Mr. Dobson tightened his hold on Simon's collar. "This boy of yours has made a mess of my store and terrorized my customers."

Simon turned pleading eyes her way. "I didn't, Aunt Callie. I swear it wasn't—"

"Hush, Simon," she said sternly. "You shouldn't be

swearing." Then she gave him a slight nod of encouragement before she turned back to the shopkeeper. "Mr. Dobson, if Simon says he didn't do it, then I believe him."

From the corner of her eye she saw Simon's eyes widen.

Mr. Dobson had a similar reaction, but his expression was accompanied by a stern frown. "That's a fine thing for you to say, madam, but just because you have an affection for the boy, that don't change things. He did it, all right."

"I'm certain you're mistaken. Now, I will ask you one more time to please release my son. Then we can discuss this civilly."

When the man still hesitated, she jutted her chin forward. "I assure you, Simon is an honorable young man and he'll stay right here without coercion until this is straightened out." She stared the man down until he finally released Simon's shirt and adjusted his own cuff with a sharp "Humph!"

Callie placed a hand lightly on Simon's shoulder as she continued to face Mr. Dobson.

"Now, tell me exactly what happened and why you think Simon might be involved so we can settle the matter."

"Perhaps we should get Jack."

His condescending tone set Callie's teeth on edge. While it would be more comfortable to have Jack handle the matter so she could fade into the background, Jack would be heading back to California soon. She had to learn how to handle such situations on her own. "That won't be necessary. Please proceed."

"Very well." His mouth tightened as he tugged at his cuff once more. "A little while ago, this boy and some of his friends set a whole passel of squirrels loose in my store. Those critters took off like Beelzebub himself was after them, scrabbling all over my shelves like furry dust devils, knocking over jars and boxes, and scaring my customers half out of their wits. Why, poor Mrs. Collins had to be revived with smelling salts."

"That's terrible." Callie stifled a grin, chiding herself for the comic image his words conjured in her mind. "But you haven't explained yet why you think Simon had anything to do with this. Did you actually see him release the squirrels?"

"I didn't see any of the culprits' faces, but he was one of them, all right." The man's red face and sharp hand movements highlighted his agitation. "I was busy with customers when I heard the side door open. At first I just figured it was supplies from Erlington. Then I heard whispers and snickering. That's when I went to check things out. Next thing I knew there were squirrels everywhere."

"If you didn't see any of their faces—"

"I'm coming to that." He gave her an officious look. "By the time I made it to the door, the others had run off but Simon was still there." He pointed dramatically to an old burlap sack lying on the sidewalk at their feet. "And he was holding that sack in his hands with a squirrel still trapped inside."

The rumblings from the crowd seemed to support the shopkeeper's story.

Callie ignored them. "Simon, I'm certain you can explain to Mr. Dobson how this came to be."

Simon nodded emphatically, swallowing hard. "Yes, ma'am. I was on my way to Mr. Lawrence's shop to get the sheepskin I wanted. But when I passed by this alley I heard A—" he cleared his throat "—I heard someone running and then I saw this sack on the ground with something moving inside." He raked his fingers through his hair. "I just wanted to see what it was."

There were more murmurings of disbelief. Callie ignored those as well.

But Simon's expression took on a desperate edge. "I give you my word, that's all it was. I didn't let those squirrels loose in Mr. Dobson's store, honest."

"I believe you, Simon." She turned back to Mr. Dobson. "You see, it was all a misunderstanding. I told you Simon is not the sort of person to do such a thing and then lie about it."

The man hooked his thumbs in the armholes of his vest and rocked back on his heels. "Mrs. Tyler, surely you don't believe such a preposterous story."

She drew herself up. "I sincerely hope you are not calling my son a liar."

The man's expression took on a self-righteous edge. "Look, I know the boy has had some hard things to deal with, what with the death of his folks and all, but that's no excuse for—"

Callie felt Simon stiffen, and gave his shoulder a squeeze. "No one is making excuses here, Mr. Dobson. We are simply saying that you are mistaken."

"Mrs. Tyler is correct." Reverend Hollingsford stepped forward from the edge of the crowd. "The boy's telling the truth."

"Reverend?" Mr. Dobson pushed his glasses up again, and shifted his weight. "With all due respect, sir, how can you know that?"

The minister made a slight bow in Callie and Simon's direction. "My apologies for not speaking up sooner. But everything happened so fast, I'm just now sorting things out in my head."

He turned back to the shopkeeper. "To answer your question, I walked into the mercantile right after the hubbub started. But I remember now that just before I stepped inside—and this was after I heard Mrs. Collins's shriek—I saw Simon walk toward the alley, and he was empty-handed."

Callie felt a swell of vindication fill her chest. "If you

won't believe me or Simon, surely you will take the word of the good reverend here. Now, I believe you have something to say to my son."

Mr. Dobson cleared his throat. "Well, I suppose, given what the reverend just said, maybe I was mistaken after all."

He paused, and Callie raised a brow.

The man's face reddened slightly, but he nodded. "Sorry, Simon."

When the boy just stood there with a mutinous expression on his face, Callie gave him a little nudge. "Simon?"

He shot her a quick glance, then swallowed his glower and returned Mr. Dobson's nod. "I accept your apology, sir."

Now that the confrontation was over, Callie was suddenly acutely aware of the crowd gathered around them. The urge to move away from the eye of the storm pressed in on her. "If you will excuse us—"

But Mr. Dobson wasn't quite done. "Just a minute."

She tilted her head. What now?

He frowned down at Simon. "You said you saw someone running out of the alley. Did you see who it was?"

Simon ducked his head and rubbed his palm on the leg of his pants, but not before she saw the quick glance he cut toward the edge of the crowd. Following his gaze, she saw his friends Abe and Bobby watching him carefully.

Simon looked up again. "I never did see their faces."

Was she the only one who noticed he hadn't actually answered the question?

But apparently Mr. Dobson was ready to move on. He turned to the rest of the crowd, quizzing those nearest him to find out what they might have seen.

"Come along, Simon." Callie kept her hand protectively against his back. "Let's find your sisters. It'll be time to head back to the house soon."

Simon didn't wait to be told twice. "Yes, ma'am."

When she turned, Callie spotted Jack standing across the street, looking pleased.

Now why had he just stood there instead of jumping into the fray? Surely he could have handled the situation quicker and with more decisiveness than she had. She couldn't believe Jack had been reticent about facing down Mr. Dobson. So what reason did he have for leaving it in her hands?

Before Simon caught sight of him, Jack turned and headed back to the building site. Following his cue, Callie didn't give any sign she'd spotted him.

Simon was subdued as they moved away from the crowd. He was undoubtedly feeling self-conscious about what had just happened. Thank goodness Reverend Hollingsford had intervened or they might still be at an impasse.

And what hadn't Simon said back there when Mr. Dobson questioned him about who he'd seen? Had the boy actually witnessed his two friends running through the alley, or did he just suspect it had been them?

She felt a strong urge to discuss the whole situation with Jack, to get his take on what they should do next, if anything. But that would have to wait until they were alone.

"Aunt Callie?"

Callie pulled the coverlet up over Simon's chest, trying not to show her surprise. Simon usually rolled over as soon as he crawled into bed, completely ignoring her. "Yes?"

"Why did you stand up for me today?"

She didn't hesitate for a second. "Because I knew you didn't do what Mr. Dobson said you did."

"But *how* did you know I didn't do it?"

"Because you said so."

"Just like that?"

"Just like that." She smiled at him as she smoothed the covers. "Simon, I'm not your mother, but I am a good judge of character. And while I know you might not be above pulling a misguided prank occasionally, I am absolutely certain you are above lying to avoid the consequences."

"Oh."

"Now, time to get some sleep. You've had a long day today."

The boy searched her face a moment longer, then nodded. "Yes, ma'am." With that he rolled over and shut his eyes.

Callie studied him a moment before shutting the door. For the first time she felt some hope that he might let her be the stepmother she longed to be.

She descended the stairs slowly, untying her bonnet as she went. She hadn't had any time alone with Jack since they left town today. Perhaps now she would get some answers.

Jack studied the block of wood, examining the grain and contours. There was a certain flow to it that was suggestive of a deer or maybe a horse. He absently began shaping the wood with his knife, waiting for Callie to join him.

She'd been magnificent today, a lioness protecting her cub. The fact that she was normally uncomfortable being the center of attention hadn't even seemed to come into play.

He'd have to admit, Lanny had chosen well after all. He should never have doubted his brother's instincts.

Except his brother had planned to relegate her to a spare bedroom. Lanny had wanted a nanny, not a wife.

For the first time in his life, Jack considered his brother a fool.

"You did a good thing today," he said as she stepped outside.

She grimaced. "Actually, it was Reverend Hollingsford who saved the day, not me."

"None of that false modesty now. The good reverend might have pushed the plunger, but you planted the charges and strung the fuse."

She grinned. "An interesting way to put it."

"Just don't go selling yourself short." Jack refused to let her minimize the part she'd played. "You stood up for Simon when he needed a champion. That's something he won't soon forget. And neither will I."

He saw the blush darken her cheeks. But then she tilted her head and gave him a puzzled look. "Speaking of which, how long were you standing there and why didn't you step in?"

"I arrived about the time you were telling Dobson to get his hands off Simon." He shook his head. "That was a sight to behold. Just plain stopped me in my tracks." He couldn't believe the transformation in her from shrinking violet to fierce protector.

"But if Reverend Hollingsford hadn't stepped in—"

"You would have found another way to convince the crowd Dobson was wrong." He gave her a straight-on look. "Believe me, if I'd thought you needed help, I would have stepped in. But I never saw the need."

In fact, if he'd had any concerns about her ability to look out for the family in his absence, they'd been erased today.

A not altogether comfortable thought. Because he'd just realized that it meant he wasn't as needed, wouldn't be as missed around here, as he'd imagined.

And that thought didn't sit well with him at all.

Chapter Twenty-Eight

"Uncle Jack."

Jack tested the saw blade he was sharpening. "Hmm?"

"Does Aunt Callie's face bother you?"

Jack paused and looked up. Simon's earnest eyes were focused directly on him and Jack knew his answer was important.

"I suppose you're talking about her birthmark."

"Yes, sir. I mean, my ma and Aunt Julia were both real pretty. Don't you wish she was more like that? Or at least normal looking."

Conscious of the weight of the moment, Jack chose his words carefully. "Your ma was pretty, all right. But did you ever see that scar she had on her arm, all crooked and puckered-looking?"

"Uh-huh. But that was different."

"Why? You can't deny that it was ugly. Even she thought so. It made her look different from everyone else so she always hid it by wearing long-sleeved dresses."

"But that was just a scar."

"You think it's not the same as your Aunt Callie's birthmark, but that's only because Nell was your mother and you loved her."

Jack leaned forward. "You're old enough to realize that it's what's inside a person that matters. And your Aunt Callie is a loving, generous woman with a good heart. Besides, there are all kinds of beauty, and your Aunt Callie has a beauty all her own. So, no, her birthmark doesn't bother me, not even a little bit." In fact, he'd gotten to where he hardly even noticed it anymore. There was so much more about her, things to admire and respect.

Simon scuffed a toe in the dirt. "Not even when other people make fun of her?"

So, someone had said something to him, had they? "Well, for one thing, folks around here know better than to make fun of her, or any member of my family for that matter, in front of me. I'd set 'em straight faster than a hummingbird can flit." He let that soak in a moment, then added, "The same way your Aunt Callie set Mr. Dobson straight yesterday."

Simon reddened. "You heard about that?"

"I witnessed it."

That set Simon back. "Then why didn't *you* step in? Did you think I was guilty?"

"Of course not. By the time I got there, your Aunt Callie had it under control. I figured she was doing just fine without me." He lifted a brow. "Don't you agree?"

Simon nodded, and jammed his hands in his pockets.

Jack set the saw down. "Listen, Simon, this is something that shapes the kind of person you are at the very core. Making fun of people, especially for something they have no control over, is a mean-spirited, cowardly thing to do. Any man worth his salt, a man who considers honor not just a word but an actual way of life—would never indulge in such a thing."

"I suppose." The boy studied the ground as if answers to the secrets of life were inscribed there.

"Let me ask you a question. Forget for a minute that she has that birthmark. If you think over everything you know about your Aunt Callie firsthand—the things you yourself have seen her do or heard her say—what would you think about her?"

Simon shrugged.

Jack tried again. "It's simple. Just decide whether your life would be better or worse if she'd never showed up in Sweetgum." He waited, letting the silence draw out.

"Worse, I guess," Simon finally answered.

Jack wanted to clap the boy on the back for taking that small step, but he maintained his solemn demeanor. "So why should a mark on her face, something that's nothing more than a discolored patch of skin, make any difference in how you think about her?" He picked the saw back up. "You don't have to answer me, just ponder on that a bit."

Jack watched from the corner of his eye as Simon squirmed uncomfortably. He waited until the boy looked at him again and then held his gaze with unblinking firmness. "And I hope if ever anyone *does* say something mean-spirited about your aunt in your presence, you'll have the gumption to do the right thing."

Jack watched Simon walk away, hands jammed in his pockets, shoulders slumped as if weighted down. He certainly hoped he'd gotten through to the boy.

Strange. He wasn't certain exactly when it had happened, but discussing Callie's looks with Simon just now made him realize that he truly *did* think of her as beautiful, and not just on the inside. Her appearance was dearer to him than he would ever have believed possible.

He cherished those moments with her on the front porch

in the evenings, moments when she unveiled, both literally and figuratively, and was totally herself and totally at ease with him. Whether she realized it or not, that trust was a precious gift, one he'd come to value dearly.

And one he was very much afraid he was going to miss keenly when he left.

Chapter Twenty-Nine

Jack lightly buffed the back of the carved horse with a piece of sandpaper, then rubbed a thumb over the spot. The toy horse was taking shape nicely, if he did say so himself. Annabeth's birthday was in a few weeks and he could almost picture the smile on her face when she unwrapped the package to find this inside.

Too bad he wouldn't be here to see it.

He pushed aside the twinge of regret.

One had to make sacrifices to pursue one's dreams. After all, he had to remember that he'd actually be getting the best of both worlds. He could go off and experience the freedom of his former life, and he could come back here three or four times a year to enjoy a taste of hearth and home.

Yep. What more could a self-made, independence-loving man ask for?

Still, he was strangely reluctant to tell Callie that he had almost finished with the house in town.

When had he become so comfortable with the idea of being part of this family?

Jack swatted at a june bug.

Ridiculous thought. As long as he stayed here he would never be anything more than Lanny's little brother. And he couldn't go back to that again—he'd worked too hard to establish himself as an expert in his field, someone to be looked up to.

No, the first of August was around the corner and he'd managed to accomplish what he'd set out to do. He'd settled his debt to his family and saw that the kids were well cared for. He'd even provided a fallback plan for Callie, just in case she was overwhelmed by managing the farm.

Better yet, things had settled down considerably over the past few weeks. Simon had lost that chip on his shoulder and was turning into a hard worker, Emma smiled much more these days, and Callie—well, Callie was pulling the whole lot of them together into a true family.

So there really was nothing left to keep him here.

His thoughts turned to Callie—smiling approval at something one of them had done, sitting on the swing reading to the children, humming while she worked at the stove.

The sweet way she'd looked at him when he'd kissed her at the stream—

Stop it! Jack took a deep breath and deliberately turned his focus back to the wooden toy in his hands. He scrubbed the sandpaper across the horse's neck, smoothing away a rough spot, sweetening the curve.

What if Callie asked him to stay? What if she didn't feel ready to handle the farm and the children on her own yet? He couldn't blame her for that, and he definitely couldn't just leave her in the lurch if she felt she needed him. In fact, he'd be honor bound to stay.

He blew away the sawdust. Far be it from him to shirk his duty.

And what if, unlike everyone else, she saw him as more than a poor imitation of the man Lanny had been?

Did *she* ever think about that kiss they'd shared?

The sound of the screen door opening brought his thoughts back to the present.

"I didn't think I'd ever get them settled down tonight."

He heard the smile in her voice.

She sat on the bench, grasping the edges of the seat with her hands and leaning forward as she faced him. "They're having so much fun with the tree house, now that it's finished. Not that you'd think it was complete to hear them talk. They're already thinking of ways to make it even better." She gave a soft laugh. "I told them to give it a few weeks before they start hammering away again."

He likely wouldn't be here to see that, either.

"Speaking of finished," he paused, eyeing the length of one of the horse's legs, "we'll be ready for those curtains you're working on by the end of the week."

"Oh." She caught her lower lip between her teeth, but other than that showed no emotion. "You're ready to wrap up your work in Sweetgum, then."

"Yep. Just some painting and a few other finishing touches left to go."

"So, you'll be leaving us soon."

Her voice was flat, her tone even. What emotion was she trying to hide? Regret? Relief?

"Unless you need me to stay longer." He hoped that came out matter-of-factly.

But she gave an emphatic shake of the head. "I can't ask that of you. It wouldn't be fair." She stood and gripped the porch rail, staring out over the darkened yard. "Besides, the children and I need to learn to make it on our own eventually. More time won't make that any easier."

She turned her gaze upward, studying the stars. "No, we made a bargain and I intend to stand by it. Ida Lee told me her oldest boy Jonah would be glad to earn some extra money helping out once a week after you leave. We'll be fine."

It appeared she had everything worked out. Didn't sound like he'd even be missed.

"Don't worry," she continued with a half-grin. "The farm will still be standing when you come back at Christmas."

Christmas seemed a long time away.

"How soon will you be leaving us?"

"I'll stay long enough to get the furnishings installed, and make sure we have a tenant for the apartment or the storefront, or both." He pulled out his pocketknife to add more detail to the mane. "I've already got a few feelers out to folks who might be interested in renting the place."

"Another week or two, then."

"More or less."

If she felt any regret, she was certainly doing a good job hiding it.

He felt an unfamiliar tightness in his chest. So much for thinking she might ask him to stay.

Callie pulled the brush through her hair, fighting the urge to cry. It had been so hard this evening to pretend she was okay with his leaving, to not break down and beg him to stay.

Only her pride had saved her.

It would have been absolutely humiliating to have him look at her with pity, if not outright horror, when he found out how she truly felt. Admitting her feelings would only distance him from her, not draw him closer.

She had to keep reminding herself that the friendship that had grown up between them was just that—friendship. He'd made it quite clear from the outset that he didn't want to be tied down to either the farm or her.

She stared at her reflection in the mirror. *Foolish, foolish girl. You knew this time would come, that Jack wouldn't stay here forever. How could you have let your guard down so completely?*

She'd played a dangerous game with her heart, pretending that, given enough time, Jack would begin to feel for her what she'd already begun to feel for him.

She should have known better.

Sure, he was more accepting of her disfigurement than other folks. But that didn't mean he could actually develop tender feelings for her.

She should be grateful for the time she'd had and for the fact that they'd become such good friends despite their rocky start. But, heaven help her, she was selfish. It wasn't enough, not nearly enough.

She wanted what she knew she would never have, should never have allowed herself to hope for.

Hadn't her father and sisters warned her that she should focus on making herself useful, that looking for something more in a relationship would doom her to disappointment?

Why hadn't she remembered that lesson when it counted?

She supposed it was Jack's unique brand of kindness and his hard-won friendship, something she'd never experienced with a man before, that had lulled her into thinking he might stay. And to be fair, he'd certainly stayed in Sweetgum longer than they'd originally planned. But it had just been to make certain everything was in order before he left, not because his feelings for her had changed.

She realized that now.

Callie set the brush down, crawled into bed and pulled the covers up to her chin before she lost the battle with her self-control and the tears started flowing.

"We have our first tenant." Jack stepped into the kitchen the next afternoon and plucked a carrot from the bowl on the counter, feeling mighty pleased with himself. With a little help from Mrs. Mayweather, he'd set a plan in motion today that would be his parting gift to Callie, if it didn't backfire on him.

Callie looked up from the stove. "Tenant?"

She wore a starched apron over her dress with a couple of wildflowers pinned to her bodice, and her face was flushed from the heat of the stove. She was the very picture of domesticity, of the heart and glue of a home-sweet-home.

If only he could talk her into taking that silly bonnet off when they were in the house. If only he'd had more time to try to get through her skewed thinking.

Maybe, after tomorrow…

He realized she was still staring at him. "Ben Cooper wants to lease the building in town to use as a photography studio and business office," he explained.

A puzzled wrinkle appeared above her nose. "The undertaker?"

"Yep. Apparently he's done a little bit of that kind of work for funerals already. Says he wants to start capturing some happier occasions, too."

"Oh, that is good news." She set the spoon down and wiped her hands on the apron. "That was a very clever idea of yours, to build a storefront area within the building, I mean."

He grinned. "Not so clever. I just borrowed the idea from what had been there before." He leaned back against the counter and crossed one booted foot over the other. "I also thought, since Ben is looking to get the word out about his new enterprise, that it might be a good idea to have a family photograph taken before I left."

Her eyes lit up. "Oh, yes, let's do. It'll give the children something to remind them of you while you're away."

And I'll have something of you all to take with me as well.

"I'm glad you agree. Especially since I already told him we'd be there at ten o'clock tomorrow morning."

Her hands fisted on her hips, and her brow furrowed. "That was mighty presumptuous of you, sir." The sweet quirk of her lips, however, spoiled the mock stern expression she'd obviously been going for.

He only hoped she was still smiling when she learned of the other surprise he had in store for her.

Chapter Thirty

When they arrived in town the next morning, Jack noted with approval that Ben had finished getting things ready. There was a large sign that read Cooper's Photography and Business Office hanging out front, and the shades were rolled up on the big glass fronted window facing the sidewalk.

A number of townsfolk were gathered around, talking with interest about the new business venture.

Jack halted the wagon right in front and set the brake. "Simon, help your sisters down, please." He jumped down and strode quickly around to lend Callie a hand.

Once she was safely on the ground, he retrieved a box from under the buggy seat. "I bought you a little something."

She gave him a startled look. "What's the occasion?"

He shrugged. "Call it a late birthday present. Or something to remember me by."

She opened the lid and, to Jack's relief, gave a cry of delight. "Oh, Jack, it's lovely." She lifted the hat out of the box, turning it this way and that to examine every ribbon and flower. "I've never owned anything so beautiful."

"Mrs. Mayweather helped pick it out." Jack fidgeted with

the brim of his own hat. "The green ribbons were my idea though. I thought they matched your eyes."

Her expression softened as she fingered the ribbon. "It's such a thoughtful gift."

He saw the moment the realization hit her. Her eyes lost some of their sparkle and regret mingled with apprehension on her face. "But I can't—"

He wasn't about to let her back down. "It would mean a lot to me if you'd wear it for the picture."

"But—"

Jack touched a finger to her lips and saw her eyes widen in reaction.

"When I look at this picture in the coming weeks," he said, not bothering to lower his voice, "I want to see *you* looking back at me, the woman I had all those late night talks with, not some shrinking violet hiding behind a bonnet."

She hesitated and her gaze darted to the nearby crowd.

More than likely a number of them were eavesdropping. At least he hoped so. He didn't want to leave even a faint impression in anyone's mind that he had a problem with the way she looked.

When her eyes met his again he saw her uncertainty was stronger than ever. But he held her gaze, refusing to give in, and finally she nodded.

Pride surged through him, pride in her mettle and in her spirit. He knew the courage it had taken to make that decision. "Good." He reached for the ribbon tied beneath her chin, acting quickly, before she could change her mind. "Allow me."

With deft movements, he untied the bonnet strings and removed it from her head while she held perfectly still. Her gaze was locked onto his as if to a lifeline.

Handing the old bonnet to Emma without breaking eye

contact, he took the new hat and placed it on her head. "What do you think, girls? Full on or at an angle?"

"Definitely at an angle," Emma said with a smile.

"I agree." He set the hat at a jaunty tilt and tied the bow with a flourish.

He ran the back of his hand softly down her blemished cheek, then took a step back to study the effect. "Yes, much better." He offered her his arm. "Shall we?"

Callie nearly melted inside from the sweetness of his touch.

Was this some sort of show he was putting on for the benefit of the town? Or did he truly not mind what she looked like?

All she knew was, right at this moment, she didn't care. Either way, his motives were grounded in a true nobility of spirit. And thanks to him, she'd never felt lovelier in her life.

Callie's courage held all the way up until the actual sitting. Suddenly she became very conscious of the other folks who'd wandered inside or stood outside at the window, watching what was going on.

When Ben tried to pose the five of them, reality flooded back in. What had she been thinking? Why in the world would she want to preserve this hopelessly flawed image of herself?

Ignoring Ben's directions, she turned so that only her good side was showing.

Jack, however, was having none of that.

"I want everyone looking straight at the camera," he announced in his firmest tone. "Just as if they were looking at me." He met Callie's gaze. "Because that's what I want to see when I look at this picture."

So despite her better judgment, Callie swallowed hard, tried to shut out everyone else, and stared at the camera. She imagined it was Jack, way across the country in California, looking back at her. She even managed a wavery smile.

When the sitting was finally over, they headed for the buggy. Callie held tightly to Jack's arm, wanting to shrink away every time they stopped to talk to someone. She felt all those eyes staring at her, judging her by the mark on her face, and pitying Jack for being tied to her.

When they reached the buggy, she offered Simon her seat up front and climbed into the back with the girls before Jack could protest. She told him to let Simon drive them home, that the boy needed to get more practice in.

But the resigned look on Jack's face told her she hadn't fooled him. And moreover, she'd spoiled his pleasure in the gift.

Why couldn't he understand that she had accepted the burden of who she was? She didn't need nor even want to force everyone else to live with it as well.

As soon as they walked into the house, Callie stopped in front of the mirrored hall tree and untied the ribbons under her chin. "Emma," she called as she removed the lovely bit of millenary, "do you still have my bonnet?"

"I think I left it in the buggy," Emma said. "But you don't really need it right now, do you?"

"Well, yes, I—"

"Doesn't it make you feel all hot and stuffy?" Annabeth asked. "Besides, I hardly ever get to see your angel's kiss."

"I know, sweetie, but—"

"But what?" Simon interrupted. "Other ladies don't wear sunbonnets in the house."

That brought her up short. She thought the sight of her birthmark embarrassed Simon.

"It sounds like you're outvoted to me." Jack stood in the doorway, arms folded across his chest.

Callie stared at the four of them and felt something inside her uncoil softly, like a morning glory unfurling at the first hint of sunlight.

Not even her parents and sisters had looked at her that way. With them, she'd always known they were protecting her, were trying to make her feel normal. She'd always felt the need to make herself not only as invisible as possible, but also as useful as possible to justify her place in the family.

The feeling she was getting right now from Jack and the children was that she *was* normal, she was appreciated for who she was, and they truly didn't understand why she'd want to shut herself off.

"Very well." She heard the huskiness in her voice and made an effort to lighten it. "We shall leave the sunbonnets for when I'm out in the sun."

Callie headed upstairs, needing a few minutes alone to absorb the feelings flooding through her. The mix of joy, gratitude and humble appreciation were almost overwhelming.

Thank you, Father, for placing me in the midst of this wonderful family. When I grow lonely or discouraged in the days to come, let me remember this moment and find joy again.

She couldn't bear to put Jack's gift back in its hatbox. Instead, she set it in a place of honor on the top of her bureau where she could see it whenever she was in the room.

It had been such a deliberately kind, meaningful gesture on Jack's part. How could she ever repay him? There wasn't anything she could give in return that could compare—

Her gaze fell on her bedside table.

Actually, there was one thing.

Callie took a deep breath as she prepared to step out on the porch that evening. Then she pushed open the screen door and, bypassing the bench, took a seat on the step beside him.

Jack halted his whittling and gave her a startled look.

"I want you to take this with you." She held the well-worn Bible out to him.

Jack looked down at the book and then his gaze flew up to meet hers. "This is your personal Bible."

She smiled. "I have the Tyler family Bible now. And you can bring this one back to me when you return."

"Callie, I don't—"

"I know. But humor me." She took his hand, turned it palm up and set the Bible there. She placed her own hand on top. "I *want* you to have this. It'll be like taking a part of me with you." *You already have my heart, but that will be my secret.*

They sat like that for a long moment, gazes locked, the Bible sandwiched between their left hands.

Finally Jack nodded. "I'd be honored to guard this for you until I return." He gave her his crooked smile. "I might even read it from time to time."

She held his gaze a moment longer. "I hope so. Because, whenever we do our evening Bible reading here, I'll be imagining you doing the same. It'll be almost like you're in the room with us."

But almost was not nearly the same as actually.

Why can't I be content with what I have instead of always wanting more?

Chapter Thirty-One

Jack leaned back against the seat of the stage, watching the town of Sweetgum roll past the window, still seeing the faces of the four of them as they waved goodbye from the sidewalk outside the Sweetgum Hotel and Post Office.

The goodbyes had been more difficult than he'd imagined. And not just for those he'd left behind.

Strange how different this departure was from that last one eleven years ago. There'd been no one to see him off then, because he hadn't told anyone ahead of time he was leaving. Just left a note and slipped away.

Back then he'd been eagerly looking ahead to new adventures, confident that once he stepped out of Lanny's shadow he'd finally come into his own. And in a way he had. That pushing-forward drive had become a way of life for him, keeping him always moving, always looking to the next job, the next challenge.

And until he read that earth-shattering telegram, he'd never let himself look back.

This leave-taking today, though, had a whole different feel to it. Instead of that sense of anticipation, there was a pull to look back. He couldn't stop thinking about everything he was leaving behind—the homeplace that seemed more like home now than it ever had before, the kids who looked to him to keep their world safe, and most of all Callie, who was so loving and determined and full of the right kind of grit. So much so, actually, that it seemed she no longer needed him.

He tipped his hat down over his face and shifted to a more comfortable position. This strange mood was probably just fatigue and delayed grieving.

He'd no doubt be back to his old self by the time he reached California.

"You have such a lovely voice, dear."

"Why, thank you, Mrs. Mayweather, what a kind thing to say." Callie stepped from the church into the bright sunshine. Jack had been gone for three days and already she missed him almost more than she could bear. It had been hard on the children as well. Did Jack realize how much they'd all come to care for him, how big a hole his departure had left behind?

But she refused to wear a long face and feel sorry for herself—at least not in public.

"Not kind, honest." Mrs. Mayweather fluttered an elegant ivory and lace fan under her chin. "I wish God had seen fit to bless me with such talent instead of a frog-like croak."

Callie was distracted by the discomfort of her tight-fitting bonnet. "I'm sure your voice is quite nice," she said absently.

She ignored the urge to loosen the ribbon. She still wore the poke bonnets when she came to town, of course. But now that she had dispensed with wearing them at home, she found they no longer felt like the part of her they once had.

"Oh, no." Mrs. Mayweather smiled and patted her hand. "No need to worry about my feelings, Callista, dear. I have learned to live with my limitations." She sighed. "It's just that

I do love to sing and I must constantly remind myself to hold back so that I don't disrupt the service."

Callie shook her head, certain her friend had blown the problem all out of proportion. "I'm certain you're being much too harsh with yourself."

"Not at all. Sometimes I do feel it is such a trial not to be able to just burst out in song. But the voices raised in the worship service should have an angelic quality to them, not a rasping one."

Callie stopped and turned to face her friend fully. There was no reason Mrs. Mayweather should think of herself in such unflattering terms. "I am surprised that you of all people should say such a thing. Why, isn't your voice the one God saw fit to give you? As such it cannot be displeasing to Him. On the contrary, I imagine it would give Him great pleasure to hear you lift it up in praise."

"Perhaps." The schoolteacher gave a wry smile. "But it would hardly be fair to the rest of the congregation."

"Nonsense." Callie waved that objection aside, determined to make her friend see how foolish she was being. "And anyone who thought the less of you for it would not be in the frame of mind they should be in when in God's house. You should be proud of that which God gave you."

The woman nodded thoughtfully. "What an enlightened way of looking at things." She closed her fan with a snap and gave Callie a pointed look. "You know, that was such a lovely hat Jackson gave you before he left." She touched her chin with the folded fan, "I wonder why it is you haven't worn it since?"

The schoolteacher's point hit Callie with the force of physical blow. The heat crawled into her cheeks with a relentless sting.

Mrs. Mayweather smiled, aware that her dart had hit its

mark. "It is so much easier to see how others should handle life's burdens than it is to handle our own, is it not?"

Callie nodded numbly. Was Mrs. Mayweather right? Had she been hiding behind her bonnet all these years, not out of respect for the feelings of others, but out of vanity?

How many times had she lectured others as she had Mrs. Mayweather just now on how they shouldn't be ashamed of whatever talent or burden God had assigned to them.

She'd been so eager to find the mote in others' eyes that she'd ignored the beam in her own.

Oh, Father, I've been such a vain, self-righteous fool. Lend me Your strength to follow through and do what I now know is the right thing to do.

Jack stepped onto the station platform feeling tired and out of sorts. He wasn't even certain what the name of this town was, only that he needed to switch trains here.

A check-in at the depot window brought the unwelcome news that he'd just missed his connection and would have to wait until tomorrow afternoon for the next one.

Hefting his bag, he trudged to the town's only hotel, which he'd been assured served a decent meal and had clean sheets.

Up in his room, Jack pulled Callie's Bible out of his bag. Reading a passage every evening had become a habit. One that, for some reason, he hadn't wanted to break.

He opened the Bible and found himself in the book of Psalms. He read the first verse he came to, but his mind was too distracted by other thoughts to really absorb the words.

Who was reading the verses at home tonight? Callie? Simon?

Would Callie step out on the porch to look at the stars after she put the kids to bed? Did she miss their talks?

Surging to his feet, Jack strode out of the room. Maybe finding something to eat would put him in a better mood.

The next morning, after a restless night, Jack woke to the sound of church bells. Was it Sunday? Still half-asleep, he felt his lips curve in a smile. If Callie were here she'd give him one of those looks that made him feel guilty for even thinking about not attending services.

Well, why not? He came fully awake and scrubbed his hand across his face as he sat up. He was stuck here until afternoon and he had nothing better to do.

Jack shaved and dressed quickly, then walked the short distance to the local church. The service was just starting when he slipped inside, and he took a few seconds to get his bearings. It was a much larger church than the one in Sweetgum. But he spotted an empty seat on a pew near the back and quietly slipped in. He received a friendly smile from the elderly couple seated next to him, then everyone faced forward as the organ began to play.

The first hymn was one he already knew, so he sang along. The choir was good, but he missed the sound of Callie's voice.

As the organ stilled, Jack suddenly felt like a fraud. What in the world was he doing? Why had he come here? Was he such a besotted fool that he'd attend a church service just to feel closer to the family he'd left behind?

Not only was this foolish, it was wrong. This was a place for the worthy to come and find love and fellowship, not for the likes of him.

Jack had half risen from his seat when the preacher stepped up to the pulpit and opened his Bible.

"The passage we're going to study this morning is that of Luke 15, the parable of the lost sheep."

There was something about the man's voice, about his earnest expression, that grabbed hold of Jack, made him sit back down and truly listen.

He sat through the sermon, listening to the preacher

expound on God's deep desire to reclaim the lost, and His joyful celebration over bringing even the lowest of backsliders back into the fold. The longer he listened, the tighter the vice-like grip in his chest squeezed.

After the service, he almost ran from the building. He shut himself inside his hotel room and before he'd even realized what he was doing, the Bible Callie had given him was open on his lap and he was turning to the passage the preacher had read earlier.

And he continued reading, moving from that passage to barely remembered verses that had been so alive for him in his childhood.

Why had he wasted so much of his life trying to escape something that didn't matter one jot? So what if he wasn't the man Lanny had been? So what if no one in Sweetgum ever thought of him as the best at anything?

To God he was special, the stray sheep that was searched for until found, the prodigal son whose return was not only marked but celebrated.

And if God truly valued him, why should the rest matter?

He might not have gotten the answers he wanted to those passionately uttered prayers so long ago, but that didn't mean God hadn't been listening. And God had gifted him in the here and now by putting Callie and the kids in his life. Only he'd blindly thrown it all away.

Was it too late?

God, I've been such a pig-headed fool, trying to impose my will on Yours, to wrest control over my life from You. Not only did I do a lousy job at it in the process, but I blamed You when things didn't turn out the way I wanted. Are You really willing to give me another chance, a chance to do it right this time? I won't promise I'll get it perfect 'cause we both know I'd never pull it off, but I will promise I'll try with everything I've got.

Chapter Thirty-Two

Jack stepped out of the stagecoach and hefted his bag. He suddenly felt as nervous as a young buck asking to walk out with the town's sweetheart.

It had been ten days. Would Callie be glad to see him? Or just wonder what had gotten into him?

Well, he wouldn't find out by standing here.

Turning toward the livery, he marched quickly down the street, barely pausing to return greetings from the startled townsfolk he passed. He didn't plan to explain his return to anyone until he'd talked to Callie.

He stepped inside the stable to find Jessie combing one of the horses.

"Mr. Tyler!" She patted the horse and stepped out of the stall. "Good to see you back so soon, but I hope that don't mean something's wrong."

"Nope, everything is fine as far as I know." Jack set his bag down. "I want to rent one of your horses to ride out to the farm. I'll get it back to you tomorrow."

"But…" Jessie's brow drew down in a look of confusion.

Jack rubbed the side of his face impatiently. "You do have a mount available for rent, don't you?"

She nodded. "Sure, we have a couple of real fine horses. But, well, if you're looking for Mrs. Tyler and the kids, they're here in town."

"Are you sure?" It was Wednesday so it wasn't market day. Why would they have made the trip to town in the middle of the week?

"Saw 'em myself not more'n thirty minutes ago. Simon and the girls come by to see Persia." She nodded toward the corral that adjoined the stable. "If I remember right, one of them mentioned meeting Mrs. Tyler over at Mrs. Mayweather's place."

"Thanks." Jack half turned, then paused. "Mind if I leave my bag here?"

"Nope. I'll keep an eye on it for you."

Jack headed back through town, holding himself in check, resisting the urge to break into a run.

As soon as Mrs. Mayweather's house came into sight though, he felt his resolve falter.

This wasn't exactly how he'd planned this meeting. He'd much rather speak to Callie in the privacy of their own home. But he was done second-guessing circumstances. If this was how it had to be, then this was how it had to be.

He pushed open the front gate, marched up the walk and climbed the porch steps.

Mrs. Mayweather answered his knock and smiled. "Why, Jackson, how good to see you back so soon."

It certainly didn't feel like "so soon." "Thank you, ma'am. I understand Callie and the kids are here visiting."

"Sorry, you just missed them. They left not five minutes ago."

Jack tightened his jaw in frustration. Another delay.

No, this wasn't the way he'd imagined his return at all. But if this was some kind of test, he didn't aim to fail it.

"So they're headed back to the farm then?"

"Actually, I believe they planned to stop by the cemetery first."

The cemetery? Not exactly the most cheerful spot for their talk. But so be it. It only mattered that he find Callie quickly.

He tipped his hat. "Thanks."

"Jackson."

Jack had already turned to leave, but he reined in his impatience and turned back. "Yes, ma'am?"

Her smile was warm and knowing. "Welcome back."

Jack gave her a sheepish grin. "Thanks."

This time he took the shortcut through Tom Bacon's cow pasture. And he pitied any bull that tried to get in his way.

He finally rounded the corner of the church house and drank in the sight of the four figures standing in the cemetery.

At last!

But as he drew closer, he frowned. They were all standing around Lanny's grave, even Simon and Emma, and he noticed a large bouquet of fresh flowers had been placed next to the grave marker.

Was Callie still mourning the man she had come here to partner with, the man he would never be?

His steps slowed, then stopped, as all the old insecurities flooded back.

Perhaps returning here had been a mistake.

Then Callie looked up and the unguarded joy that flooded her face reassured him, setting his feet in motion again.

It took a second for the change in her to register. She wasn't wearing one of her stuffy poke bonnets. Here in town, in full view of even the most casual of passersby, she had chosen to wear a pert little hat that sat high on her head and completely revealed her face.

So, the caterpillar had finally shed the last of her cocoon. And what a sweetly special butterfly she made.

The kids finally noticed his presence, and with whoops, ran to greet him. Callie followed at a slower pace, her gaze never breaking contact with his.

Only when Annabeth grabbed him around the knees did he look down.

"Uncle Jack!" Annabeth's voice was nearly a squeal. "I missed you."

"I missed you, too, Little Bit." He put a hand on Annabeth's shoulder and pulled Emma into the hug as well. He smiled at Simon, including him in the greeting. "All of you."

"Did you come here for daddy's birthday, too?"

Of course. It was Lanny's birthday.

And Callie, being Callie, would make a special event of it, for Annabeth's sake.

"Actually, I came here to find all of you," he said, "but it being your daddy's birthday just makes it all the more special."

"Welcome back," Callie said, smiling.

"Thanks." His arms ached to reach for her, but he managed to refrain. "I like the hat."

She raised a hand to touch the saucy concoction. "Why, thank you kindly, sir. It was one of Julia's. I find I share her taste, in hats, at least."

"Are you here for a long visit?" Emma's voice held a hopeful note.

Jack glanced down at his niece. "I'm not sure yet." He looked back at Callie. "It depends."

He pulled a couple of coins from his pocket. "Simon, why don't you take the girls down to the mercantile and the three of you can pick out some penny candy. Your Aunt Callie and I will meet you at the buggy later."

Simon looked from Jack to Callie, then nodded. "Yes, sir. Take your time. I'll watch the girls 'til you two get there."

Callie couldn't stop looking at him. She still couldn't believe it. He'd come back!

He said he'd missed them. Was that all it was? Dare she hope there was something much deeper going on here?

He offered his arm and she placed her hand there, feeling suddenly tongue-tied.

"Let's have a seat, shall we?" He swept an arm toward the bench beneath the cottonwood. "We have some things to discuss."

Not trusting herself to speak, she nodded and let him lead the way.

A moment later, he seated her on the bench, then sat beside her. "I missed you."

She tried not to read too much into that statement. One could miss good friends. "I missed you, too. The porch feels much too empty in the evenings since you've been gone."

He smiled, then ran a hand through his hair.

"Callie, there's something I need to tell you, a confession of sorts." He took a deep breath. "All my life I've known I was second-best to Lanny, never quite good enough to meet the standard he set. It's the real reason I left Sweetgum eleven years ago. I even think it's why I proposed to Julia. A part of me knew she loved Lanny and I wanted to claim her for myself."

Why was he telling her this? What did it have to do with his reason for coming back? But if it was reassurances he wanted…

"You're not—"

He put a finger to her lips. "Hush and let me finish. I was so jealous of Lanny that I let it eat at me until I lashed out at him. The last words I said to him were said in anger. I'll have to live with that for the rest of my days."

She touched his arm in sympathy, aching to ease his pain, but remained quiet, as he'd requested.

"I had a hunger to find someplace where I could be the best at something, could be respected for myself, the way Lanny was here. I knew it was vain and wrong, and that it was unchristian. So I quit praying, closed myself off to God, and hardened my conscience." His jaw tightened. "And I thought I found what I'd been seeking when I formed my own company and gained the respect of my peers. But I was wrong. You, sweet, dear Callie, helped me to see that."

This was torture. Couldn't he see she wanted something much deeper than his gratitude?

"Over the past few days I've been doing a lot of thinking and a lot of praying."

Callie's pulse jumped. Praying! "Oh, Jack." She breathed more than said the words, giving his hand a squeeze. Suddenly her own desires seemed selfish and insignificant.

He smiled. "Yes, I've finally come to my senses. Thankfully our God is a God of patience and forgiveness, because it took a long time to get the truth of His Word through this thick head of mine. It's not Lanny's standards I need to measure up to, I understand that now. God has given us each our own unique talents and gifts, and we should focus on using them in ways that best serve Him."

"Jack, I'm so happy for you." It was ironic how they'd both had similar revelations that had come to them only after they'd been apart.

He sat there in silence a long time, his gaze distant, his mind seemingly miles away.

Finally, she couldn't stand it any longer. "Jack, I'm very happy you shared this wonderful news with me. But I have to know, was that the only reason you came back?"

He gave a crooked grin. "I can always count on you to fill

the silences." Then he sobered and took her hand. "I came back because I couldn't stay away. Not from this place. Not from those kids." He touched her cheek. "Not from you."

She wanted to lean into his hand, but dared not. She didn't want to do anything to spoil the moment.

"Here is where I belong. Because I realized something else while I was away." He squeezed her hand. "Callie, I love you. I think a part of me has loved you since you sat right here that first day, looking so brave and noble with your chin lifted high, letting me stare my fill at your face."

Her heart hitched in her chest and she found it suddenly hard to breathe. He didn't mean it. He couldn't mean it. Yes, she'd finally come to accept who she was, but no man—

"I know I'm not the man you came to Sweetgum looking for, but I'm hoping you can see past that. Because when I'm with you, I feel anchored—not in a hold-me-back way, but in a here's-where-I-belong way."

"No."

She saw surprise and then hurt in his eyes.

He released her hand and shifted his weight away from her. "I see. Well—"

"I mean, no, I won't let you do this. It's not love you feel for me, except perhaps the love of one friend for another. It's very sweet of you, but it won't do either of us any good for you to pretend otherwise."

"Look at me, Callie." He put a finger under her chin and lifted it. "Really look at me. Tell me what you see in my eyes. Is it friendship, or is it the very real love I feel for you from the depth of who I am?"

His jaw worked. "If you don't return that love, if what you feel is mere friendship, then just say so and we won't speak of this again. But don't dare tell me I don't love you. Because if you'll have me, I want to live up to those wedding vows we made—to love and cherish and protect you, until death us do part."

She studied his face, not daring to let herself believe what she saw there. It couldn't be.

Her hand reached up of its own accord and rested against his chest. She could feel the strong beat of his heart, a heart that he was offering to her for the taking.

That crooked smile of his appeared again. "I'm sorry," he said softly. "I shouldn't be pressuring you like this. We can step back for a moment, or as much time as you need, and pray for guidance."

Those words finally released the last of her fears. This is what God had been leading her toward, had been preparing her for. And she had almost been too timid, too wrapped up in her own insecurities to reach out and take hold of it.

"Oh, Jack," she said with a laugh of pure joy. "Your faith puts mine to shame."

She gazed deep into his eyes. "You're not Leland. You are Jackson Garret Tyler, and don't you ever dare apologize to me for that again. Because Jackson Garret Tyler is the man I love." She touched his lips the way he had touched hers earlier. "I love your sense of honor, that heart of gold that you try so hard to hide, and the affection you have for the children. I love the way you look at me when we're talking, as if you truly care about what I'm saying. And I love all the small things you do without any sort of fanfare to make the children and me feel secure and loved."

She moved her hand to his cheek. "And I will love you always, for the wonderful person you are, until death us do part."

With a smile as big as the Texas sky, Jack gently folded her into his arms, bringing her home at last.

Epilogue

Eleven months later

"There," Ida Lee said, adding one more pillow behind Callie's back, "that should make you more comfortable." She gave a little chuckle. "Now, I'd better go tell Jack he can come on up before he wears a hole through the kitchen floorboards and rubs the skin plumb off the back of his neck."

Callie merely smiled, unable to take her eyes from the miraculous bundle cradled in her arms.

A little boy. And he was absolutely beautiful. She gently stroked his cheek, marveling at the softness of his skin, praising God for this wondrous gift.

The object of her attention gave a huge yawn and peeked up at her, as if annoyed by the interruption, before closing his eyes again. Her smile widened. Those were Jack's eyes— jaybird blue and oh-so expressive.

She looked up as the door swooshed open and saw Jack crossing the room, his gaze locked on her, his face reflecting a mix of cautious concern and ready-to-burst joy.

He gently brushed the hair from her forehead and placed

a light kiss where the strands had been. "How are you feeling?"

"Tremendously blessed." She loosened their newborn's swaddling cloth. "Meet your son."

"He's so small." Jack eased himself down to sit on the bed beside her, his eyes drinking in the infant with the rapt attention of an explorer who had uncovered an immense treasure. Then he tentatively reached down to touch a tiny hand and the baby reflexively curled his fingers around one of Jack's own.

Callie watched powerful emotions playing over Jack's face, and felt her cup of joy and contentment overflow.

Thank You, Father, for this wonderful family You've made me a part of.

Jack looked up and stroked her cheek with his free hand. "He's beautiful. Just like his mother."

She leaned into his touch, drawing strength and comfort, as always, from his warmth. "But he has his father's spirit."

The baby released Jack's finger and Jack drew Callie's head against his shoulder. "Mrs. Tyler, are you calling our son a troublemaker?"

She chuckled. "Not at all. I'm just saying I can tell he will be very self-assured." She studied the baby again. "We need to give him a name."

"I've been thinking about that. What do you think of the name Leland?"

She straightened slightly so she could study his face. Had his suggestion come from some sense of guilt or dutiful penitence?

Jack met her gaze without flinching. "If it makes you uncomfortable, we'll pick something else. It's just that, well—" he rubbed the back of his neck, the merest hint of ruddiness tinting his cheeks "—I know I didn't act much like it these past several years, but I always loved and respected my big brother. I'd like to do this for him. And I can't think of a better role model for our son."

Callie's eyes welled. "Oh, but I can," she said softly. Then she leaned her head back against Jack's chest. "However, I believe one Jack in this family is quite enough. I think Leland is a wonderful name. And Matthew for a middle name, perhaps? It means 'Gift from God.'"

Jack nodded, but anything he might have said was forestalled by the clattering of footsteps on the stairs.

"The children have been champing at the bit to come up here ever since Doc Haynie left." Jack grinned. "You should have heard Simon's cheer when Doc said it was a boy."

Callie laughed at the thought.

"Selfish man that I am, I told Ida Lee to hold them off a for a bit so I could have a few moments alone with you."

Callie sat upright again, but didn't leave the circle of Jack's arm. It was her favorite place to be.

She gently stroked the baby's head.

"Leland Matthew Tyler, prepare to meet the rest of your family."

* * * * *

Dear Reader,

I've always enjoyed both reading and writing marriage-of-convenience stories. There's so much built-in conflict and room for growth when two people are forced together to know each other and work through their differences after they are joined in marriage rather than before.

This particular story started with a few "what if" questions on my part. What if a woman who felt physically unattractive found a chance to have a family through an arranged marriage with a man who understood her shortcomings? And then what if this woman arrived at her new home to find her husband had died hours after their proxy wedding, so that she had become a widow without ever meeting her husband?

Callie and Jack's story is born from this one little kernel. And oh, how they surprised me as I captured it on paper. Their story brought me joy and tears and laughter as it unfolded. I hope you, too, will find something to celebrate in their story.

Wishing you love and blessings in your life,

Winnie Griggs

QUESTIONS FOR DISCUSSION

1. During the ride in the stagecoach at the opening, Callie spins stories in her mind about the other passenger. What impression did this leave you with about her personality? Do you ever find yourself making up stories about passing strangers you encounter?

2. What do you think about Jack's decision to take Callie to the cemetery to break the news about Lanny's death rather than telling her immediately?

3. Jack seemed to have conflicting emotions about becoming guardian to the children. He was terrified of the prospect, yet he refused to take the out when Callie offered to take on the responsibility herself. What does this say about him? Do you ever find yourself of two minds when faced with making a key decision?

4. Callie hides her disfigurement beneath her bonnet even when she is alone with her family and close friends. Do you think this was done more out of concern for the feelings of others or as a coping mechanism of her own? How did this affect the people around her?

5. Was Jack's resentment of growing up in his brother's shadow and being the recipient of his brother's hand-me-downs believable? How did it color the man he became?

6. Mrs. Mayweather gave advice to both Callie and Jack. Do you think she was something of a busybody or more of a wise mentor? If she had not stepped in and suggested

the two marry, what do you think might have been the outcome of their tug-of-war over the children?

7. Jack made an early admission that he "was not the praying kind." Do you think one can be a true Christian and not spend time in prayer?

8. How realistic do you feel Callie's adaptation to life on a farm and the chores that go with it was? Did you feel this transition was adequately portrayed?

9. Emma carried a tremendous load of guilt over the death of her parents. It was only when she discussed it with Jack and Callie that she began to heal. Do you find this to be true in real life? Have you experienced this yourself?

10. The evening discussions between Jack and Callie on the front porch became a ritual of sorts. How important do you feel this was in drawing them closer together? How important do you feel it is in general for a husband and wife to have some time when they sit down alone together and just talk?

11. Simon exhibited his feelings of loss with anger and resentment directed toward Callie and toward having to live on the farm. Do you feel like his actions were understandable for a boy his age in this situation? Did Callie and Jack respond to his actions appropriately? Should they have done anything differently?

12. What purpose did the building of the tree house serve in bringing healing to this family?

13. The whittling that Jack did changed over the course of the book. What, if anything, did that signify to you?

14. Simon was surprised by Callie's defense of him in the incident with the squirrel. How did this affect their relationship? How did it affect Callie and Jack's relationship?

15. Did you believe the change that occurred in Jack as a result of his renewed understanding of God's grace? Did his subsequent actions ring true based on this experience?